Rites of
Revenge
A Father Flenn Adventure

By Scott Arnold

Rites of Revenge

Rites of Revenge

Copyright © **2019 Scott Arnold**

All rights reserved.

Farne Press

ISBN: 978-1-7337524-1-1

Arnold, Scott.

Rites of Revenge: A Father Flenn Adventure — 1st edition

   1. Fiction-Thrillers-Espionage. 2. Fiction-Crime

United States of America

Cover Photography: Warren Design

Interior Design: Jim Brown

Editor: Margaret Shaw

Dedicated to

Diane
The love of my life

And in our sleep, pain that cannot forget, falls drop by drop upon the heart, and in our own despair, against our will, comes wisdom to us by the awful grace of God.

—*Aeschylus*

Sarah Coverdale spoke slowly and distinctly into the phone. A life hung in the balance. "How much do you know about Predator drones?"

"I've been trained in the basics," answered Zack Matteson. "Why?"

Coverdale ignored the question. "Good. How familiar are you with Hellfire missiles?"

The CIA operative had seen the aftermath from the Assassins of the Sky many times. "They have a kill radius of fifteen meters," he answered, "and a wounding of twenty. Again, ma'am, may I ask why?"

The director for the Measures of Effectiveness Office for the Central Intelligence Agency skirted the question a second time.

"Zack, there won't be any time to waste. I would have called you earlier, but I just had it confirmed. Eric Scudder is definitely out of prison and going to strike tomorrow, March third! He probably thinks of it as poetic justice; it's the anniversary of his arrest."

Zack Matteson took a breath. "So, it'll be on three-three? Then, I'm guessing, at 3 p.m.?"

She hesitated. "I hadn't thought of that. Zack, you've got to get to Honduras before then!"

"Yes ma'am, but, let me ask again... what have Hellfire missiles got to do with all this?"

Zack thought he heard a slight tremor in the director's voice, "Because I just found out Eric Scudder and has four of them and intends to use them to kill Scott Flenn!"

CHAPTER **ONE**

Children's laughter filled the air as the tall priest with wavy brown hair jumped for the soccer ball. Kids scrambled like puppies after a stick as Father Scott Flenn kicked the ball a good 30 feet across the churchyard. The ball sailed past the community fire pit toward the only road which led down the mountain to San Pedro Sula, the second largest city in Honduras.

The children were accustomed to foreigners; missionaries came once or twice a year from Mexico or the United States, often bearing gifts. Dour evangelicals usually brought Bibles, along with words of hellfire and judgment. The children shied away from them. They did like the other visitors though—especially those who had helped maintain the chapel at San Jose de la Montaña (Saint Joseph's of the Mountain). Those missionaries always brought medicine—and toys!

Their parents had told them stories about how the chapel was built two decades ago, when Americans from someplace place called Alabama had worked alongside workers from San Pedro Sula. A large Honduran man wearing a purple shirt and a white priest's collar had come nearly every day to oversee the project. The man in purple had been Juan Almeda, who was still the bishop of the Episcopal Diocese of Honduras.

Teams from Alabama had visited every year at first, but then they just stopped coming. No one in the village knew why. Surprisingly, last year, a priest from Birmingham showed up, along with an interpreter from Bishop Almeda's office. He had played with the children during the day, and at night met with their parents and grandparents. The villagers had showed the priest where repairs were needed in the chapel. The padre had left the village the next morning only to come back two days later with a team of carpenters. Many still spoke about how the priest had rolled up his sleeves that week and joined in the restoration. Within a few days, the chapel had looked better than ever.

Each evening, after all the work was done, Padre Flenn had sat in the small market across the road and chatted with the villagers through his interpreter. He had asked them about their hopes and dreams and what they considered to be their biggest needs. No one had ever asked them that before; the missionaries usually deciding for themselves what the villagers needed.

The residents had told Padre Flenn that they had more than their share of Bibles and religious tracts; what they needed most was a water purification system. (The owner of the market had asked for a new electric generator, but he'd been outvoted.) Waterborne illnesses had plagued the community for decades, and a purification system, they had told Flenn, would dramatically improve the health of their village. It wasn't six weeks before the priest had returned with a skilled team from the United States and a state-of-the-art water purification system—as well as a new generator for the storeowner.

Three days ago, they'd welcomed the priest back with cheers and hugs. His Spanish had improved since last year but he still relied on an interpreter from Bishop Almeda's office.

The priest had news! He told them that the bishop of Alabama had sent him here to assess their ongoing needs. The village was still buzzing with excitement. Flenn didn't tell them that he'd been the one who'd approached Bishop Morrison, or that the money was coming out of his own pockets.

The church had been packed last night, but the meeting with Padre Flenn and his interpreter hadn't taken long. It had been unanimous. What the villagers said they needed most was a school. Flenn was met with thunderous applause when he told them he thought there was a good chance that his bishop would sign off on the project. In truth, he knew Tom Morrison would approve it since Father Flenn would be the one paying for it. Not only was Flenn a former operative for the CIA, he was also from one of the wealthiest families in New England. Flenn Industries had been worth billions when his father, David, had passed away and left it to Scott Flenn and his brother. David Jr. ran things now, but Flenn had managed to tuck away a fortune to prevent the CIA from ever seizing his assets and trying to force him into some unknown future assignment.

When Flenn had left the CIA, he'd told his supervisors it was for good. It was a tough argument at first, but Flenn had been determined. In the end, the one who'd had the hardest time with his leaving had been his former partner, Zack Matteson. Zack could no more fathom walking away from the CIA than a bee could leaving its own hive. Scott Flenn, however, had no interest in the CIA, or the family business. Instead, he had found contentment as an Episcopal priest.

Saint Ann's parish in Birmingham, as small as it was, managed to keep him plenty busy. Unfortunately, Zack had a habit of popping in and out of Father Flenn's life—usually at the worst possible times. (Just last Christmas, Zack had solicited his help to stop Iran and two psychopaths from hijacking the upcoming presidential election.)

Apart from the occasional chaos caused by Zack Matteson, Father Flenn enjoyed a simple life in which he chose to spend his time, and his wealth, on charitable causes—which was why he had travelled to the village of San Jose de la Montaña; although calling this tiny hamlet a village was an overstatement. Less than a hundred of the poorest of the poor lived here. The only permanent structures were the church and a small open-air market, which sold beer, sodas, and limited sundries. Lean-to shanties, made of sticks and pieces of tin, surrounded the church and market. Families slept under the stars or, when it rained, under scrap metal and bits of corrugated plastic. Most of the men and older boys hired themselves out as day laborers down in the city, but seldom earned more than four hundred lempira a week, about $15 in American money. The women spent their days cooking, sweeping the dirt around their meager huts, and having babies. Children gathered fruit and brought water from a nearby stream to help their mothers.

Today, however, their mothers had released them to go play with the tall priest.

Flenn pretended to miss a kick and came down with a thud. About a dozen giggling boys and girls pulled him back to his feet. "Padre!" they shouted. "Juega con nosotros!" Flenn's Spanish was spotty, having spent his days in the CIA studying Korean, Farsi, and Arabic, but the children didn't care as they continued to babble on about a new game they wanted to play. They took him into the middle of the village and instructed him to observe. Grasping one another's hands and forming a tight circle they began to chant a song in which they called out a child's name, followed by a command to dance.

"Diana, Chippy, Chippy!" they sang out, and the first little girl stepped into the circle and began to do an impromptu jig. Everyone laughed, especially as the next child, a lanky boy with no sense of rhythm, jumped up and down and then did a handstand. Somewhere, off in the distance, Flenn thought he heard a small engine making its way up the mountain.

After Diana and the boy finished their dances, the children began to chant yet another girl's name, and that child jumped into the circle and came up with a silly routine. Flenn laughed heartily until two seven-year-olds grabbed his hands and brought *him* into the middle of the circle.

"Padre, como su nombre?" one of the children asked. The sound of the engine grew louder.

"Me llama es Scott," he replied. The children exchanged puzzled looks, so he said it again. They tried pronouncing his name, but it was difficult to form the word, which to them seemed harsh and abrasive. One child's eyes brightened as he came up with a substitute. "Escota!" he cried.

Flenn knew escota meant *sheet*, and it pained him to know that a sheet was only a word they had heard, never experienced. None of these children even had a bed.

"Escota, Chippy Chippy!"

What is a chippy, anyway? No time to ask—only dance; so, with great fanfare, the tall, handsome priest with green eyes and an infectious smile, bowed ceremoniously and broke into his best imitation of a Michael Jackson moonwalk. The children held their sides as they howled with laughter, as did some of the adults watching from the shade of the market across the road.

The sound of the engine grew louder by the second, competing now with the children's song. Flenn watched as a motorcycle rapidly made its way up the dirt road. A pale-skinned cyclist, with a backpack strapped behind him, was heading straight for the village. *Odd*, thought Flenn, *another white man coming here?* The children stopped singing and eyed the stranger as he suddenly leaped from his motorbike, without even turning the engine off. The man was running straight toward them!

Flenn quickly shooed the children behind him and spread his legs apart, ready to knock the stranger on his backside if it came to that. Some of the adults in the market started toward them. The crazed man was within 10 yards when Flenn recognized him.

No, it can't be.

Not him! Not here!

Zack Matteson!

Flenn signaled to the adults and the children that everything was okay. Zack had spotted Flenn—not hard to do in this crowd—but instead of slowing down, Zack reached out and grabbed Flenn by the arm and pulled him along as he continued running. "Come with me, now!" Zack shouted.

Twelve years of placing his life in this man's hands kicked in and, without thinking, Flenn found himself half running and half being pulled behind his old friend toward the jungle.

"Zack, what the hell… "

He'd no more than gotten the words out when they were both thrown violently to the ground. An instant later, he heard the explosion; a second after that, his left shoulder felt as if it were on fire.

Reeling from the blast, Flenn managed to right himself and look toward the village. The spot where he and the children had been playing was nothing more than a huge crater! Dust and debris were falling from whatever had just pounded the village. Torn bits of clothing and tiny bodies littered the landscape.

"OH, MY GOD, THE CHILDREN!" Flenn screamed as he struggled to his feet.

"Flenn, no!" Zack grabbed him by the shirt and pulled him deeper into the jungle just as another blast hit the ground nearby. Dazed, Flenn fell to his knees, then tried to get up, only to fall again. He felt his shoulder, which was covered in something thick and wet. "The children! I must get to the children!"

"Stay where you are!" Zack shouted. You're wounded!" Zack pulled a tee shirt from his backpack and pressed it hard against Flenn's left shoulder. "We need to get out of here, now!"

The pain was excruciating, still the priest tried to pull away. "I've got to save those kids!"

"You can't save them!" Zack was doing his best to hold the makeshift bandage steady while keeping his friend from breaking away. "We've got to go, Flenn! It's *you* he is after. If you go out there he'll see you, and he's got two more of those damned things!"

"Who will see me? What things?"

"Hellfire missiles!"

What in God's name was going on? Flenn tried to stand but his knees buckled, and he found himself falling again, only this time into a blinding light. He heard a voice calling his name over and over, but he was unable to respond. The voice became fainter and the light brighter as Flenn slipped into unconsciousness.

CHAPTER *TWO*

Seoul Korea; twenty years ago...

Scott Flenn stepped onto the tarmac at South Korea's Incheon International to find his former professor, Sarah Coverdale, waiting for him at the top of the stairs to the terminal.

"How was your flight?" she asked.

"Boring," Flenn replied, his eyes barely open.

Sarah turned and they started walking down a long corridor. "Get used to it. That pretty much describes Korea right now."

"Oh great." Flenn swung his backpack over his shoulder as he followed her to get his luggage. She'd already cleared him through customs—one of the advantages of being the temporary bureau attaché for the CIA. "If it's boring in the South, what's it like in North Korea?"

"Trust me, you don't want to know," she said. They followed directional signs with English subscript. While Flenn had learned to speak Korean well enough to get by, he'd never learned how to read its complicated characters. "How long has it been, Flenn? A year?"

"Nearly two," he said, as they rounded a corridor filled with scores of hurried travelers. His plane had arrived at the busiest time of day, whatever day this was... Thursday, maybe? Five hours from D.C. to Los Angeles, then another 13 to Seoul—right now, he desperately needed a Scotch and twelve hours of sleep.

Sarah smiled. "You know, I specifically requested you for this assignment. You were at the top of my class that year." She sighed. "Which is why I need you now."

"So, this is what I get for all that brownnosing," Flenn quipped as the arrows pointed them down yet another corner.

Sarah laughed. "Yeah, looks like all that sucking up paid off, huh? I'm guessing this is your first overseas assignment?"

"Nope. Been chasing some bad guys after that thing in Ireland. Followed them to London, then to Syria and finally to Kuwait."

"Kuwait. I didn't hear anything about that."

Flenn shrugged. "Nobody did. The problem was eliminated."

Sarah understood.

Flenn noticed there were security cameras everywhere. "I take it we're being watched?"

It was Sarah's turn to shrug. "I'm sure half of the National Intelligence Service is zeroed in on you right now. I mean, you're kinda hard to miss. Young, good looking, green eyes, wavy brown hair, and... just how tall are you anyway?"

"From the looks of things," he said, "about twice as tall as anyone around here."

They walked to the escalator and down to baggage

claim where Flenn grabbed a luggage carrier, waving off a skycap. He retrieved three Samsonite bags from the belt and placed them on the carrier. She shook her head. "I guess you didn't take the class on traveling light?"

Flenn yawned. "They told me I'm going to be here awhile. That's about all they said, except that you'd fill me in when I got here." He glanced at his former teacher but it was becoming increasingly hard for him to focus. He yawned. "So, just what are we going to be doing?"

Sarah laughed. "You never could stand to waste time, could you?" Flenn followed her to a white Renault in the parking lot. She helped him with the bags, then got behind the wheel and started the engine.

"You'll be briefed tomorrow by the military, and then by the agent you're replacing," she said. "Personally, I'll be glad when he's gone; the guy's a real jerk. I was assigned to assist him a few months ago after I requested a leave from the classroom for a semester or two. We've been working primarily with General Larry Westinghouse and Colonel Akiko Kasai on the base, mostly basic stuff."

In his exhausted state, that sounded amusing to Flenn. "Base and basic," he repeated, then started to laugh.

She looked over at him. "God Flenn, you *are* tired, aren't you? Didn't you sleep on the plane?"

"Can't," he answered. "Never could."

Sarah shook her head. "Let me get you to your quarters before you turn into a basket case. I'll come by around noon tomorrow. Your briefing isn't until three. You're just across the street from me," she explained. "It makes things simpler. Eric Scudder—the jackass you're replacing—he's across the hall from you."

Sarah glanced at Flenn, who was nearly asleep. "Seriously, do watch what you say. Your apartment may be bugged. I think mine is—Korean intelligence, the NIS. I don't know why they bother; we share almost everything with them. It is all pretty cut and dried down here. Not much cloak and dagger. I know you were trained for deep-cover work, but with your looks and your height you'd never be able to blend in here anyway."

"What do you mean, 'almost everything'?"

She looked at Flenn. "Ah well, that's why you're here." She shook her head. "It's a theory of mine; but in your state, it can keep." Flenn didn't argue.

Sarah pulled up to the curb. "Ah, and here we are."

CHAPTER *THREE*

A little girl, not more than five, stood crying in front of Scott Flenn. He reached down to pick her up, but the child backed away.

"Déjà que te ayude... Let me help you," he cried. She shook her head. "Por favor," Flenn pleaded. He reached out for her hand, but the girl had no arms. He managed to scoop the child up and hold her tightly against his chest, only to find that now she had no legs. Flenn looked up to the heavens as crying and bleeding children suddenly began to encircle him, pressing upon him, pleading for help—help he was unable to give!

Flenn woke up screaming.

Zack assumed it was from the shoulder wound, which he'd stitched the best he could after carrying Flenn deeper into the jungle. Flenn weighed right at 200 pounds, Zack had carried heavier men farther, but the Honduran jungle was full of roots, stones and vegetation. He'd avoided tripping, but just barely, as he managed to carry Flenn not quite a mile before utter exhaustion crippled him.

Flenn had remained unconscious for hours, even as Zack had cleaned his wound and sewn a dozen stiches using the medical kit he'd thrown into his backpack—along with a dozen protein bars, a couple of tee shirts, bug spray, and a satellite phone. Zack had been given little time to plan or pack; no time at all, really. Once Sarah Coverdale informed him of Scudder's plan, he'd grabbed his backpack, rushed to the airport, and caught the first flight to Atlanta, where he'd called Bishop Tom Morrison, one of the few people who knew about Flenn's former life in the CIA.

Although Zack hadn't told the bishop of Alabama why Flenn needed help, he'd managed to impress upon the cleric that this was a matter of utmost importance, and that he needed to find Father Flenn right away. Bishop Morrison gave Zack the name of the village where Flenn was staying—a tiny hamlet up the mountain from San Pedro Sula.

Zack brought along his satellite phone to stay in touch with Sarah Coverdale, but it was of no use trying to call Flenn. As Sarah had already figured out, Flenn's phone was out of range of any cellular towers—if he'd even bothered to carry one with him. The only way to save Flenn was to get there before Eric Scudder's drone took him out!

Zack had managed to find San Jose de la Montaña on a map of Honduras he'd bought at the Atlanta airport. He'd studied the route while on the flight to San Pedro Sula. There was only one way into the village, up a winding road to the top of the mountain. He had memorized the directions but threw the map into his backpack just in case. There'd be no time to waste once he landed, particularly if his hunch about 3 o'clock was correct. He hadn't counted on it taking so long to rent a working motorbike and had only just made it, leaving no time to clear the village before the strike.

"Flenn, I'm right here. You're safe." Zack sat next to him now, checking the bandage. It was dark and stained, but at least the bleeding had stopped. Flenn's eyes darted left and right, trying to make sense of where he was, of the nightmare he'd just experienced, and why in hell Zack Matteson was kneeling over him.

"It's okay, buddy." Zack said. "You took some shrapnel, but I got it out." Flenn didn't understand. He tried to push past Zack and stand up, but his limbs weren't responding. Suddenly a wave of panic came over him as he recalled the child from the nightmare. *Had he lost his arms and legs, too?*

What in God's name was going on, and why was Zack here? He looked into his friend's eyes, trying to make sense of it all.

Flenn felt a tiny prick in his arm.

"It's okay buddy, you're going to be just fine." Flenn wanted to respond, to ask Zack what the hell was going on, what had happened earlier, where they were—but the words wouldn't come. He searched Zack's face for answers, but couldn't find any. Zack's face began fading into the distance, and then, a moment later... gone. In its place the little girl stood in front of him, begging for help.

CHAPTER **FOUR**

One month earlier...

Eric Scudder blinked several times, unaccustomed to being in the sun. His two South Korean guards pushed him forward... toward a man standing beside a long, black car. The chauffeur was holding the door of the limousine open for him. Although Scudder had never met the man waiting for him in the back seat, he knew who'd sent him.

The guards, not hesitating to show their disdain for their former prisoner, stopped at the end of the gravel sidewalk. They were both young, unlike most of the prison staff. *They had been nothing more than babies when he'd been arrested 20 years ago and thrown in that hellhole the Koreans called a prison.* He'd lost 60 pounds during those years, but somehow still managed to remain fat.

"Thank you, children, but I think I can take it from here," Scudder said in perfect Korean. He shielded his eyes as he sauntered up to the chauffeur, walking more like a man out for a leisurely stroll than someone who'd spent the last two decades in prison.

Scudder climbed in beside a pencil-thin, blonde man almost as pale as he was. "I'm Gerald Rudolph," the man offered.

Scudder closed the car door behind him. "No offense, but I don't care who you are. I just want to get the hell out of here. You don't need to explain. Everything was spelled out to me when your boss came to see me two weeks ago." Rudolph gestured to the driver, who started the engine. "I'm assuming everything I asked for in return is still a go?" Scudder said.

Rudolph nodded, "You mean Operation Clean Slate?"

"Clean slate?" Scudder shook his head. "So, that's what you're calling it?" He thought for a moment and then laughed. "Sure, why not. I guess that's better than what I'd thought of naming it." He lowered his window as the car began to pull away from the prison. "Freedom... and revenge," he said quietly, as if to himself. "It's about damn time." He stuck his hand out the window and gave the two guards the finger.

****

Seoul, twenty years ago...

"So, *this* is my replacement?" An obese, 30-something man with greasy black hair, and an even greasier mustache, sat on a vinyl sofa munching a powdered doughnut. It was the dorm lobby at Camp Hovey, only 15 miles from the demilitarized zone. Colonel Kasai of Japan, and Captains David Hollingsworth and Marion Webb were on their way here to brief the new guy.

Flenn felt almost human after a good night's sleep and eating the breakfast Sarah had brought. He offered his hand to the man on the vinyl couch. "I'm Scott Flenn," he said warmly. Eric Scudder just glared at him over the top of his glasses. "but everyone just calls me Flenn."

"Don't bother," answered the fat man. "I'm outta' here in three days; thank God."

"Then I guess you and I need to get together soon."

"What for?" White powder sprayed from Eric Scudder's lips.

"So that you can fill me in on the gaps the military is going to leave out," Flenn said.

"Scott, let me tell you something. The military down here think they own the place. They'll never admit to any gaps."

"All the more reason for us to get together. How about dinner tonight?"

Scudder looked across at Sarah. "You coming?"

Sarah didn't treasure the idea of being with Scudder any more than she had to, but wasn't willing to throw Flenn to the wolves. "I suppose."

"Great, I know just the place." Scudder winked at Sarah. "So do you."

"Damn it, Scudder! It didn't work last time, and it sure as hell isn't gonna work now."

Flenn raised an eyebrow. "What didn't work?"

"He tried to get me drunk on Soju and seduce me."

Scudder popped the rest of the donut in his mouth. "Could've worked," he said, dropping powder all over his shirt, "if you'd had a couple more drinks."

She rolled her eyes. "There's not enough alcohol in the world."

From the front lobby an attractive Asian woman in

uniform was heading toward them accompanied by two Army captains.

Scudder finally stood. "Ah, now that one in the middle would be a good ride, huh son?" Scudder jabbed Flenn in the ribcage with his elbow. "Maybe you'll have better luck than I did. If not, well, then there's always Covertail here. Oh, but don't waste your time on Captain Webb; she's a lesbian."

"Shut up, Scudder," Sarah said as the trio of officers approached. "Colonel Kasai, so good to see you again. This is the man I told you about—Scott Flenn."

"Scott, so nice to meet you." The colonel offered her hand, then to Sarah, but not to Scudder.

"Please, just call me Flenn. Everyone else does."

"Your surname?"

"Flenn nodded. My father did the same thing. Everybody called him Flenn; I just followed suit. Not sure how it all started, really, but I prefer it. Hardly anyone calls me by my first name."

"Well then, Flenn, this is Captain Hollingsworth and Captain Webb."

Flenn exchanged handshakes with each. "Good to meet you. I'm looking forward to what you have to tell me about why I'm here."

Scudder rolled his eyes. "Suck-up," he whispered. "Morning, Akiko." He looked directly at Captain Marion Webb, "and you two… *gentlemen*… as well." Webb glared back at Scudder. "Sorry fellas, but I've gotta take off. *Scott*," he said, as if he hadn't heard Flenn's request to the

Colonel, "see you and Covertail at seven. She knows the place. I'll start a tab in your name."

As they watched him leave, Col. Kasai shook her head. "I will not miss that man."

****

"So, what you are telling me is that you brought me here to catch a thief?" Flenn had assumed the reason Sarah had sent for him had been something more than simple detective work.

"I suppose," Capt. Hollingsworth scoffed, "if you want to condense everything we've told you in the past hour down to just one sentence, then that would pretty much be it."

Colonel Kasai was more diplomatic. "We don't want you to *catch* anyone, Mr. Flenn. However, we would appreciate any help that you can give us in finding the guilty party or parties. We will then pass that information on to the local authorities. Understandably, the government of South Korea wants to know what's happened to their collection of ancient relics. Incense burners may not sound very exotic, but these are solid gold and nearly three thousand years old.

"I'm afraid Mr. Scudder didn't have much luck with his investigation, even after Ms. Coverdale here joined him." Flenn glanced at Sarah, who stared down at the floor. "We're hopeful that you'll have some fresh insight. We'll get the files sent over to you after you have had a chance to settle in; how about Monday?"

"No time like the present, Colonel," Flenn answered.

"Why don't you have them sent to me this afternoon; then I can get a heads up over the weekend."

"Very well." Colonel Kasai nodded approvingly. "Captain Webb, can you see that he has everything he needs?"

"Yes ma'am, will do." Webb made a note as the colonel continued.

"Mr. Flenn, as I said, these artifacts went missing a little over a year ago. Local law enforcement came up empty-handed. They assumed it was an inside job from someone working at the museum, but there was no evidence. Unlike in Japan, not everything in Korea is under video surveillance yet."

"The airport sure was," Flenn quipped. "Too bad there wasn't a camera filming the exhibit; it would have solved their mystery for them. Sometimes lock and key just aren't enough."

"Exactly," Col. Kasai nodded, "but the only camera was inside the front entrance of the museum where the artifacts were on loan—part of a program to share some of the country's treasures with people in the more rural communities."

"Other entrances?"

"One; in the back," she said, "but it was locked and the only two keys are with the curator and the janitor. This is a particularly small museum, with few visitors. There was no guard, only the night janitor; after he finished his work, he sat in the foyer and watched television all night. The lobby video shows him falling asleep in front of the TV at 3 a.m. No one entered through the front door."

Flenn scratched his head. "Hardly what someone would do if they'd just stolen priceless artifacts."

Sarah saw no need to rehash everything they'd already gone over. She signaled to Flenn, then stood. "I think that covers it, Colonel. Thank you for meeting us."

Kasai raised an eyebrow but stood as well, as did the two captains. "It is good to meet you, Mr. Flenn. I trust that you'll make more progress than your colleagues."

Sarah let the insult go. "Speaking of colleagues," she said, grabbing Flenn's shirtsleeve. "I need to show you your new digs before we meet Prince Charming for dinner." Flenn shook hands with the three officers as Capt. Webb promised to deliver the case notes to Flenn later in the day.

As they walked across the base to where the CIA maintained an office, Flenn said, "I take it from the tone of that meeting that there's no love lost between us and the military."

Sarah grunted. "Same as everywhere these days, I suppose. Welcome to the Twenty-First Century."

"We've still got a year to go," Flenn said. "I sure hope the next one is better than this one." They stepped over a pothole. "So, just how did the CIA get involved with this case?"

"The Koreans were doing us a favor at the time, and from what I gather it was a big one, saving a certain bureaucrat from an embarrassment that wouldn't have played well at the White House. I'm not at liberty to say more."

"White House?" Flenn interrupted. "Don't they have enough embarrassments?"

"Apparently they couldn't afford another. Anyway, we owed the Koreans a favor, so Washington asked General Westmoreland for help finding these incense things. The military didn't get anywhere, so they turned it over to Scudder, who was basically sitting around twiddling his thumbs at the time. Scudder got nowhere, so I was assigned to assist. Neither one of us have had much luck, which the good colonel likes to bring up as often as she can."

"Ah, the old Adam and Eve ploy."

Sarah looked at him. "Adam and Eve?"

"Sorry, something my mom used to say every time my brother and I tried to pass the buck. Adam blamed Eve for giving him the apple, and Eve blamed the serpent. Something like that."

They stepped over another large pot hole filled with rainwater. "Not sure anyone is doing any blaming here," Sarah said.

"They will if those artifacts aren't found. The Koreans will accuse the military of dropping the ball, and the military will blame the CIA, and the CIA will blame you and me. Probably why Scudder's getting out."

"All the more reason to find out what happened to them," Sarah said.

Flenn rubbed his temples. He needed caffeine. "And just how did you get involved in this mess?"

"My request for field placement came at the right time." She smiled. "Or wrong time... so here I am." She looked at Flenn. "Scudder is, as you may have figured out, a complete ass. How he got this assignment from Schmitt I'll never know."

"Jeremy Schmitt? The guy in command of Asian intelligence?"

"That's the one," she said. A Jeep honked at them as they crossed a narrow drive on the way to a group of small Quonset huts. Sarah led him toward the one in the middle. "Before his promotion, Schmitt oversaw training new recruits for Asia. Word is that Scudder became one of his favorite students. How that jackass could be anybody's favorite anything is totally beyond me."

"How long's Scudder been in Korea?"

"Not too long before this case came up," Sarah said. "Scudder was in Japan before. Pretty cushy job; don't know why he got assigned here. I know he doesn't look like it, but the man does have half a brain. He even had some insight into how the job might have been done and by whom."

"What happened?"

Sarah shrugged. "Didn't pan out. The guy Scudder pegged was the son of the janitor; he would've had easy access to his father's keys. We checked him out. Nothing."

"He still around?"

"The son?" Sarah shook her head. "He liked to parasail on the weekends. On his last jump, his equipment failed. Scudder and I went through the man's apartment with a fine-toothed comb... nothing ever came of it. After that, Scudder requested to go back stateside. I don't think he likes failure."

"That makes two of us," added Flenn.

"I guess even jerks can get discouraged," Sarah said. "Eric Scudder's the kind of person who likes to do things in a big way. He had this theory worked out about the janitor's son. He was sure he was onto something; I even heard him bragging on the phone about it to Schmitt... but nothing came of it."

They walked up several concrete steps underneath a low-hanging portico. Flenn had to duck to get through the door. Inside was a tiny reception area, with a young Korean man sitting behind the front desk. All smiles, Lee Qwon was 5-foot-nothing and looked as if he would barely tip the scales at 100 pounds.

"Lee's a great receptionist," Sarah said, "and makes the best coffee in Korea."

Lee smiled.

"But, don't tell him anything you don't want the NIS to know. He works for them."

Lee frowned. "Miss Coverdale, I tell you many time, I no work for anyone but United States government."

"Yeah, yeah... and Mickey Mouse and Donald Duck are actually lovers." She smiled at Flenn. Don't believe a word this guy says. Just drink his coffee; it's amazing." Lee buzzed them through to a hallway and a suite of offices. "The one at the end is yours."

"Is that really true, what you said back there?" Flenn said.

Sarah unlocked the door to what had been Scudder's office. "What, about Lee working for Korean intelligence? Yeah, probably."

Flenn held out his hand for the key. "No, about Mickey and Donald. I never knew!" Sarah laughed as they entered the 10-by-12′ room furnished with a simple wooden desk, two computers, a desk phone, and an old photograph of President Clinton hanging askew. Flenn walked over and removed it. "Let me guess, Scudder liked this guy?"

Sarah watched him toss the picture into the trash can. "They were made for each other. I'll requisition you a picture of the new guy right away." She pointed to the two IBM machines on the desk. "Both computers are up to date. The one on the right has access to the base network; the one on the left is completely ours."

Flenn tried out the chair, which was too short for his frame. "Skip the picture; a new chair's more important." He flipped on both computers and waited a full minute for them to boot up. I assume Scudder's left me something to work with on one of these things. What's the password?"

"You'll have to ask him in few hours when we have dinner with the scuzzball." Flenn tried unsuccessfully to log onto the computers. "Same old Flenn," she said, standing in the doorway, "you can't stand not to be busy." She studied him for a moment. "Let me guess, you still don't have anyone in your life?"

Flenn didn't look up. "How much time we got before meeting with Scudder?"

"Thought so. You know what they say: 'All work and no play makes Jack a dull boy.'"

"Jack *is* a dull boy," Flenn said. "Now, you and I have

work to do. Sit down for a bit and tell me everything else you know about this case, from the moment you arrived. And I'll need some pictures of the stolen artifacts."

Sarah turned to leave. "Slow down, we've got time. Everything will be in that file tomorrow."

"No, not everything." He looked at her. "I want to know what *your* theory is."

She looked away. "My theory's absurd. Believe me, you need to read the file first."

Flenn grunted. "Okay, but after that I want to hear this *absurd* theory of yours."

"We'll see. My office is the second on the left toward the reception area. Bathroom's across the hall from you. It's just the two of us... plus the poisoned dwarf out there."

"Ah, come on. He seems nice."

"He likes Scudder. That's reason enough for me not to trust him. I've got some work to do. We'll leave for the restaurant in an hour. Can't wait to see how you and Scudder get along." She left Flenn to fiddle with the computers. After several minutes of getting nowhere without a password, he stepped out into the hallway: eight rooms—six offices, a toilet, and a conference room, which was simply a table, nine chairs, a coat rack, an American flag... and a coffee pot! He poured himself a large cup then checked out the other offices, all empty. Everything here screamed transition. He doubted anyone stayed longer than six months, a year at best. Flenn wandered into the reception area and started up a conversation with Lee. He couldn't see what Sarah held against the man.

Lee Qwon was genuinely friendly, a likable kind of guy. By the time Sarah came out of her office Flenn had discovered that Lee had three brothers, two sisters, a deceased father who'd worked in government, a mother who was an absolute saint, and a girlfriend three years older than Lee. He'd also found out which busses were the best to take around town, where the best night clubs were, and he even got a good recipe for barbecued pork.

"Spilled any state secrets yet?" Sarah asked.

"I keep telling you, Miss Sarah," Lee protested, "I am not a spy for my government."

"Of course you are, darling, but I wasn't asking Flenn, I was asking you! Flenn here is a master at getting to the truth… at least he was in my classroom scenarios."

Looking at Flenn and pointing to the door she added, "So, shall we go see how well you do in the real world?"

CHAPTER *FIVE*

Flenn awoke to utter darkness. Bizarre images of fire and smoke flashed through his mind as he tried to remember where he was. A village of children, a loud noise, a blinding light... and Zack Matteson! *Was he blind; or was this hell?*

Something stirred to his left. "You awake, buddy?"

Things must be bad. Zack only called him 'buddy' when he was injured. Flenn took stock of himself. He felt his head and torso. He moved his feet then his legs—everything seemed to be in working order. There *was* a dull ache in his left shoulder. He ran his right hand across it and found a large bandage.

"Zack?"

"I'm right here." The voice sounded like it was a hundred feet away.

"Where are we?"

"In the jungle."

Flenn tried to sit but was too groggy. Finally, he gave up. "Jungle? Why are we in the jungle?" Flenn was surprised how weak his own voice sounded.

"I wanted to catch a toucan."

Flenn scratched his head. "What?"

"I thought some colorful feathers would look good with your robes on Sunday morning." Zack knew that the morphine hadn't worn off. There was no need to go into any detail just yet.

"Sunday? What's today?"

"Wednesday… no, Thursday. To tell you the truth I'm not really sure."

Flenn closed his eyes. "Is it Easter yet?"

"Not yet, buddy. Don't worry, you haven't missed it."

"That's good." Flenn was silent for a moment; Zack thought he'd gone back to sleep until his eyes suddenly popped open. "Oh, did I tell you what I gave up for Lent?"

Zack leaned back against the kapok tree where he'd been sleeping; the backpack his only pillow. "No. I haven't seen you since right before Christmas, remember?"

"Christmas?" Flenn repeated.

"Yep, that's when you helped me stop Daniel Romero and Benjamin Rye from starting World War Three."

"Rye's a jerk." Flenn was lost somewhere between the present and past.

"*Was* a jerk. We took care of that… remember?"

Flenn couldn't.

Zack had one more dose of morphine in his backpack. His first-aid kit was CIA standard issue, not the department store red bags full of little adhesive bandages and tweezers. His plan was for them to rest here until the morphine wore off, then see if Flenn could walk. Assuming he could, they'd make their way down the mountain into San Pedro Sula, avoiding the main road—*if what he had driven up yesterday could be called a road.*

"Doesn't matter," Zack said. "It'll all come back to you in the morning. Just go back to sleep."

"Sleep?"

"Yeah, sleep." Zack closed his eyes and listened to the curious sounds of the jungle. He was too tired to be worried about what might be out there. *Right now, if something wanted to eat him, he might just let it.*

"So," Zack asked, "what *did* you give up for Lent?"

"Huh?"

"You asked me if I wanted to know what you gave up for Lent."

"Oh, yeah."

Zack shook his head. He'd never seen his friend high before. "So… what did you give up?"

Flenn closed his eyes, and with a faint hint of a smile said, "You."

****

Seoul, Twenty Years Ago...

Scott Flenn set his fork down, uncomfortably full from the beef bulgogi. Eric Scudder eyed Flenn's plate covetously. "Come on, skinny, didn't your mom ever tell you it's impolite not to eat everything you're served?"

Sarah Coverdale rolled her eyes.

"Something about starving children in China," Scudder added, stuffing another dumpling in his mouth. "You know," he added, "there are starving kids much closer than China. I've seen 'em. The North's full of them."

Flenn glanced over at Sarah, then leaned back in his

chair. "So, Eric, you going to miss it here?" Flenn wore a well-practiced smile, pretending not to notice the stray crumbs on Scudder's chin.

Scudder shot a look toward Sarah. "You wanna' tell him, or shall I?" Flenn raised an inquisitive eyebrow. Sarah shook her head as Scudder swallowed his last bite. "Korea's a land of polite little pipsqueaks, who resent our being here but see it as a necessary evil. They fear Americans, but they fear their relatives in the North even more." Sarah groaned. She'd been subjected to Scudder's rants before. "You've met Lee, right? He's a classic case. Buddy-buddy on the outside, but probably sticking pins in his new Scott Flenn doll right about now."

Sarah rolled her eyes. "Koreans don't do voodoo, Eric."

He took a swig of beer. "Sure, they do. Maybe they call it something else but, mark my words, somewhere there's a little Korean dude tonight holding a new doll with an extra-long pin." Scudder waved his hand at the waiter and pointed to his beer bottle—his way of asking for another.

"You and Lee have always seemed to get along," Sarah said. "I guess there's not a Scudder doll?"

"Not any more at least." Scudder squirmed in his seat a bit, as if suddenly uncomfortable. "So, kid, the answer to your question is, no, I won't miss it. Too bad, since I had to take all those crappy Asian-sensitivity classes. Not a total waste, though. I can order Korean food anywhere I go now." He finally wiped his chin... on the back of his sleeve. "I have to admit, I love this stuff."

A tray of baked pears swimming in cinnamon honey

arrived for desert. "Thank you, but I don't know where I'd put it," Flenn told the waiter.

"Where do you put *anything*?" Scudder said. "You look like a poster-child for hunger relief. You need to live it up, kid; you're on the government dime now." Scudder sneered. "Oh, I forgot, you're the son of Daddy Warbucks ... must be nice."

Flenn's expression didn't change. "It has its advantages." He tried a bite of pear, which he had to admit, was delicious. Sarah managed to finish half of hers, and Scudder ordered another helping for himself.

"Might as well live it up. Only two more nights, you know."

"About that," Flenn said, "I'd really like to pick your brain about those missing incense burners. I was hoping we might get started tonight, after dinner."

"Tonight?" Scudder looked over at Sarah. "You weren't kidding, were you?" Then to Flenn, "Not a chance buddy-boy. I've got a date tonight!"

Sarah looked shocked. "With whom... or should I say with what?" Scudder's grin made her skin crawl.

"Don't know yet, but I've got a few hundred bucks in my pocket. Should be able to find someone for a few hours." He winked at her. "Unless of course you've finally come to your senses and changed your mind, sweetheart?"

"Not if you were the last man on earth, Scudder."

Eric Scudder tossed his unused napkin on the table. "Well, that being the case, I'll just leave you two to your evening together. I have a new girlfriend to make." They watched him walk by the waiter and out the door.

Sarah shook her head. "He did it again!"

"Did what?" Flenn asked.

"Stiffed me with the bill!"

"I thought he said Uncle Sam was buying."

Sarah sighed. "Are you kidding? Our per-diem isn't *this* good."

Flenn pulled out his wallet. "Then let me. As your friend said, I am the son of Daddy Warbucks."

"Thanks," she said, "but just to be clear, Scudder's not my friend." She leaned back in her chair and reached for her wine glass. "Do you mind if I ask you a really personal question?"

"Go ahead."

"Why *are* you an agent? I mean, Scudder's right, you come from money. You could be anything you want."

He smiled. "Simple... so I can travel the world." Flenn caught the attention of the waiter and politely asked for a cup of coffee.

Sarah shook her head. "No, really."

"I was Air Force intelligence. It's not such a big leap."

"That's all you're going to tell me?"

Flenn smiled. "Not much else to tell."

Sarah studied his face. "Why is it I can never read you? It's like something's going on inside you, something, I don't know... different."

Flenn shrugged. "Well, if there is, it's something I'm unaware of, Sarah. "

She smiled. "Yeah, I know. That's what makes you so interesting."

CHAPTER *SIX*

Zack awoke the next morning and checked his watch. It was 7 a.m. back in Washington. He had no idea what time it was here, but he'd at least been able to figure out what day it was. He checked on Flenn, who was still asleep.

The jungle seemed especially lush this morning, with luminous rays of light dripping through the trees like honey from a comb. The smell, however, was anything but sweet. The forest reeked of mold and rotting vegetation. The contrast was not altogether unlike Zack and Flenn.

Zack was a spy—fiercely loyal to his country. Resigning from the CIA, as Flenn had 10 years ago, just wasn't in Zack Matteson's DNA. He would die an agent. Zack had traveled around the world for the past twenty-some-odd-years, carrying out whatever missions had been assigned him. Flenn had once been no different, but not anymore. Now he was an Episcopal priest shepherding a small parish in Birmingham, Alabama. These days Flenn's life was spent trying to serve a different power, one that Zack wasn't quite sure existed.

Ever since Flenn's experience on their last official assignment together, Flenn had been a changed man. He'd told Zack that he'd witnessed something in Edinburgh… *something impossible*. Flenn had been under an enormous amount of stress at the time; yet, whatever had happened, it had changed his friend forever. He had left the CIA right after that and gone home to New Hampshire. Less than a year later, Flenn had headed off to a remote mountain in Tennessee to study for the priesthood. At the time, Zack thought his friend had completely lost his marbles, but Flenn had done well in seminary and genuinely seemed happy these days.

Zack had been on assignment in Istanbul when he'd heard that Flenn had landed a position in a tiny mission church in the suburbs of Birmingham. He'd looked it up on the internet at the time. Saint Ann's was a poor church, barely able to keep its doors open, so Flenn's arrival must have seemed something like a miracle to the congregation. Flenn certainly didn't need a salary; his family's wealth afforded him all he could ever need, and more. With Flenn's brother, David Jr., at the helm, Flenn Industries had continued to pursue lucrative interests across the globe. Scott Flenn hadn't been interested in following his father's footsteps the way his brother had. Instead, Flenn had enlisted in the Air Force straight out of college. Someone there recognized his abilities early on and recruited him for military intelligence. From there, it had just been a short hop into covert operations for the CIA.

Zack and Flenn had trained together at Langley. Their relationship had always been… *unique*—so unique their mentors had recommended they be paired together on assignment whenever possible. That rapport had developed into a deep friendship over the years, one which

Zack had been unable to replicate. Zack worked alone these days; he was what the CIA referred to as a "cowboy." Zack liked it this way; plus, no one seemed to be able tolerate him the way Flenn had. As for his former partner... Zack didn't claim to understand the new Flenn, the one that had become a priest after a strange occurrence on assignment in Edinburgh, but he knew that if he ever truly needed someone, Flenn would be there for him.

"I gotta pee."

Zack looked over at Flenn, who was sitting up. His eyes were glazed but Flenn had at least managed to right himself.

"Hang on, buddy. I'll help you." Zack carefully lifted Flenn until he could stand and unzip himself.

"How's Donna?" Flenn asked.

"You're holding your thing and thinking about my ex-wife? God, Flenn!"

"Did you ever call her?"

Flenn had hounded Zack about calling his ex and kids the last time they'd been together, back in December.

"Yeah, I called."

"And?"

"It was rough at first, but Donna said she'd let me see the girls."

"And have you?"

"No."

Flenn managed to fasten his trousers on his own and took a few weak steps before having to lean against a mango tree. "Zack, you need to go see your... " It hit him—the children!

The image of the little ones in the village burned like coal through his brain. "Oh my God! The kids! Those poor kids!" Flenn tried to walk again. "We've got to go back..." Zack grabbed Flenn's arm. "We're not going anywhere, not until the morphine has worn off. You took some shrapnel back there. I managed to get it out, but you've lost a good bit of blood." He fished a protein bar and some water out of his bag. "Here, you need these."

"What in God's name happened? And what the hell are you doing in Honduras?"

"First things first. Drink that water. I'll fill you in as you eat."

"I don't want to eat." Flenn said, too weak to stand any longer. "What the hell happened back there?"

Zack shook his head. "You drink and eat, or I don't tell you anything."

Flenn's eyes narrowed. "Zack!"

"Drink!"

Flenn obliged, albeit begrudgingly, and discovered he was thirstier than he'd thought. He finished the bottle and tore open the protein bar. "Okay, I'm eating. Now, tell me what you know."

Zack sat down across from him. A brownish-gray rodent ran past them. Something large swooped down from the trees and snatched it. The bird must have been watching its prey for some time. Zack looked up at the sky. *No telling what might be watching the two of them.*

"I got a call from an old friend of yours a couple of days ago. To make a long story short, she told me you were in danger. I found out you were here. Then, I... "

Flenn interrupted, "Please tell me you didn't go to my parish!"

"No, calm down. I obeyed your rule about my never coming to Saint Ann's. I called your bishop."

"Oh, great."

"Hey, weren't you the one who told me he knew about your past?"

"Yeah, but I also told you that you that my parish and diocese were off-limits."

"I know. That's why we always meet an hour away in that little town, Cullman. But you were in trouble, and I only had so much time to get you out."

"You could have just looked at our church website. My mission trip has been posted on it for several weeks."

Zack shot him a look. "I did look, *your blessedness*, but the only thing on there was some recipe for something called Heavenly Peach Cobbler."

"Heavenly Peach…? Damn that Delores Dilwicky! The minute I go away, she takes over the website."

"Looked pretty good to me." Zack had never been to a church pot-luck, but he did have quite a sweet tooth. He was craving his favorite, a bag of jellybeans. Right now, he'd even settle for the licorice ones.

"So, you called Bishop Morrison. Go on."

"He told me you were here, so I caught the first flight to Atlanta and then flew Taco Air down here."

Flenn frowned. "Leave out the humor."

"Who's being funny? That's exactly what that rinky-dink airline is like."

Flenn was getting angry. "The kids, Zack, tell me about the kids!"

"Okay, right. After I landed in San Pedro Sula, I rented a motorcycle. I already had directions to the village, which is where your bishop said I'd find you. I came, grabbed you, and hightailed it for the jungle." He looked around at the forest surrounding them. "And as soon as you're well enough, we'll get the hell out of here."

Flenn tried again to climb to his feet. "I've got to get back to those kids' families. They need me!"

"I suspect you're the last person they want to see right now." The priest raised an eyebrow. "I mean, think about it," Flenn. You're standing there with their kids one moment, then some maniac drags you off into the jungle just as a missile takes out half the village. I don't think they'd respond very kindly to you right now, no matter how good your intentions are."

Flenn was silent for a moment before asking: "Why… what…" Flenn shook his head, struggling for the right words. "*How* did you know exactly when the strike would be?"

"There's an informant with Scudder. He got word that you were going to be blown up by a Hellfire."

"Who the hell owns Hellfire missiles down here?" Flenn's shoulder was starting to ache.

"Ah… yeah, about that," Zack looked up at the sky. Even through the dense forestation, he could see the sun climbing in the sky.

"Who?" Flenn asked again.

"We do."

CHAPTER *SEVEN*

Seoul; twenty years ago...

Flenn was naked except for a shower towel wrapped around his waist. He hadn't expected to find Eric Scudder sitting in his living room.

"So, um, Scott... " Scudder had been making a point of not calling Flenn by his last name, "...how about you put some clothes on?"

"You're early," Flenn said. "I wasn't expecting you for another hour."

"Obviously." Scudder said, dragging himself off the sofa. "Tell you what, you get dressed, while I see what you've got in the kitchen. I take it Sarah stocked it for you before you arrived?"

Flenn gestured for the round man to raid his kitchen, not that Scudder was waiting for permission. "She did, as a matter of fact. Is that something you guys do for fellow agents down here?"

"Not me," Scudder scoffed. "I didn't know what Sarah liked before she got here."

And didn't much care either, thought Flenn.

"The guy who was here before me was a vegetarian." Scudder whistled approvingly as he opened the refrigerator door. "How can anyone not eat meat?" Flenn thought Scudder should give it a try.

"I'll get dressed," he said. "There's coffee made. Help yourself." Scudder already had.

When he returned, Flenn was shaved and wearing khakis with a blue, button-down shirt. Scudder was sprawled on the sofa gnawing on a chicken leg. Flenn poured himself a mug full of black coffee then sat in a chair across from Scudder. "I take it you struck out last night."

Scudder glared at him. "What makes you say that?"

"Well, for one thing, you're up early and you've changed clothes since yesterday. You're obviously well rested, but you still have a pent-up look of anxiety about you." Flenn raised an eyebrow. "So, am I right?"

Scudder peered into his coffee. "None of your business, Sherlock. What about you and Covertail?"

Flenn rolled his eyes. "We're friends, Eric, nothing more. And why must you call her that?"

Scudder grinned. "'Cause she hates it.

Flenn shook his head.

"Okay," Scudder said, looking at his watch, "you've got an hour."

"That's all?"

"I'm going stateside in a couple of days, remember? I've got things to do. Besides, Sarah knows as much as I do." Flenn scratched his head. He doubted Scudder often said that about anyone. "Plus, you've got somewhere to be; I hear you and Lee have a date this afternoon."

"Word gets around fast down here," said Flenn. "But, yeah, I've asked Lee to take me somewhere."

Scudder scowled. "Those tombs aren't all that special, you know."

Flenn frowned. "Apparently, Lee keeps you well-informed."

"Only when I ask." Scudder stretched out on the sofa and closed his eyes. "So, here I am; you've got an hour, Junior. Whadda' ya' wanna know?"

"Well, you can start by telling me the passwords to your computers."

"That's easy. The one on the left is Frick."

"Don't tell me, the other one is Frack, right?"

"You're good," Scudder mocked. "I can see why you became a spy."

Flenn was irritated. "Look, Eric, you and I don't have to be friends, but remember, we are working on the same team."

"We are?"

"We sure as hell better be." Flenn understood why Sarah didn't like this guy. "I get it, Eric, you've struck out, but don't blame me for that. *You* get to go home, while I get to take over where you left off. If it's credit you want, don't worry, I'll see that you get some of it... once I've solved this thing."

Scudder's eyes popped open. "Oh, so you're going to solve it, huh? Give me a break; what are you, like twelve?"

"I'm twenty-five."

"Geez. I've got underwear older than you."

Flenn had the perfect retort to that but kept it to himself.

Scudder pulled off his glasses and wiped them on his shirt. "Okay, kid, I'll give you what I've got. It won't take long." He grabbed on the back of the sofa and pulled himself upright. "We never got anywhere on this thing. The museum in Seoul lent the collection to that rinky-dink place in Yeoju." He shook his head. "They should rename that town Hicksville. Security there was a joke."

Scudder drained the last sip from the mug he'd placed on the coffee table... *next* to the coaster. "The artifacts weren't getting much attention from the locals, so the exhibit was on its way to Wonju when the bowls turned up missing. Like I said, security was lax, to say the least. Basically, it amounted to the curator locking the doors at night."

"Who had keys to the place?"

"Just the curator and a night janitor, that's all."

"That's what Colonel Kasai said." Flenn thought for a minute. "Tell me about the curator."

Scudder shrugged. "The man went nuts after the artifacts disappeared. His wife had to check him into a hospital. I interviewed him. He was distraught—you know, all that Asian crap about honor and responsibility. They had to keep him sedated most of the time; suicidal for a while, or so they said."

"What about his wife?"

"Don't get me wrong, she has quite a personality..." Scudder grinned... "in both of them! A real looker."

Flenn ignored the crude remark, something he was having to do quite a lot since meeting Eric Scudder.

"The woman is an absolute nitwit. Stays home and

takes care of their twins all day; couldn't think her way out of a paper bag."

Flenn reached over to move Scudder's mug to the coaster. There was a white, pasty circle on the table beneath. "You said the janitor had keys?"

"Yeah, but everyone I interviewed says the man is above reproach—a devout Christian. I didn't know they even had those in Korea. He' an elder in his church, highly regarded."

"Christians can steal, too," Flenn said.

Scudder reached up and cleaned his ear with his pinky finger. "I suppose. Why, are you one?"

"My mother is. So, tell me more about the janitor."

Scudder looked at his watch. "It is all in the file, Scott." Flenn responded by glaring at him. At last, Scudder sighed. "Okay. The man is in his late fifties, doesn't drink, doesn't smoke, doesn't do anything except clean floors and toilets. I didn't get the impression he cares about art, but he does take a lot of pride in shiny floors. I'm not kidding, the idiot really likes his job."

"Married?"

"Widowed, two grown kids, a daughter who's married and a 20-year-old son who still lived with him. The son died in a para-sailing accident." Flenn got up for more coffee; when he came back Scudder was rifling through Flenn's notes. Scudder looked up. "You haven't been here three days and you already have a dozen pages here?"

Flenn snatched the folder away. "I came to do a job."

Scudder rolled his eyes. "Well, good luck with that."

Flenn set his mug on the coaster next to the notebook. "So, all you've been able to come up with is basically that anyone could have done this?"

"Any halfway decent burglar with some skills, but, yeah, it could have been anyone."

Scott Flenn scratched the back of his head. "Which leaves us nowhere."

Scudder got up to leave. "No, kid. *You* are nowhere. *I'm* on my way home."

CHAPTER *EIGHT*

"You're telling me that my own government fired on me?" Flenn couldn't believe what he was hearing.

"Sort of," said Zack. It's complicated."

"It always is," said Flenn. "Now, before I go back to the village, tell me what this is all about!" Flenn rubbed his wounded shoulder.

"You're not going back."

"The hell I'm not. Now tell me!"

Zack finished half a protein bar and then offered the rest to Flenn, who refused. "Suit yourself," he said, sitting down next to his friend. "Sarah Coverdale contacted me, and said… "

"Wait a minute… Sarah Coverdale? Why would Sarah contact you?"

Zack shrugged. "You're going to have to take that up with her when you get home."

Flenn shot him a 'get-on-with-it' look.

"She knows how close we were, doofus. Who else would she call? Anyway, I'm just minding my own business, when out of nowhere I get a call from Sarah that you're in trouble." Zack winked. "I guess she knows how much you adore me. Of course, anyone could see why, what with my ineffable charm and good looks… "

Flenn's brow furrowed. "Knock it off, would you? Just tell me."

"So, Sarah calls me out of the blue and tells she has been following someone who just happens to want you dead."

"Who could possibly want me dead?"

"Someone with a long memory. Someone you and Sarah used to know quite well."

Flenn was running out of patience.

Zack sighed. "Okay; Eric Scudder."

Flenn stopped rubbing his shoulder and shook his head in disbelief. That was a name he hadn't heard in nearly 20 years. "Scudder's in prison… "

"The Koreans let him out. According to Sarah, she stumbled onto some sort of secret deal negotiated by Jeremy Schmitt."

"Who's he?"

"You don't remember Schmitt? Man, you *have* been out of action a long time. How could you forget him? He's been with the agency forever; he's the director of resources now. His father was Senator Tyson Schmitt, the oil tycoon from Oklahoma."

"Okay, so Schmitt is rich and carries a lot of political clout… what does he want with Scudder?"

Zack shrugged. "Don't know. Sarah's trying to figure it out. There wasn't time to go into all that. She's supposed to call me next time she hears from her informant. I'm hoping Scudder thinks he was successful getting rid of you."

"Wait a minute, wasn't Schmitt the guy in charge of Asia years ago?"

Zack nodded. "Morphine must be wearing off, huh?"

Flenn rubbed his temples. "Okay, so just how did you show up right at the moment the missile was fired?"

"You tell me. Divine providence, maybe?"

Zack was right; the morphine was wearing off, because every nerve in Flenn's shoulder was beginning to scream at him. "Come on Zack, *how*?"

"Okay. Think about it. March third, three o'clock... can you recall anything that happened on that day, say 20 years ago?"

Flenn couldn't.

"According to Sarah, that was the day Eric Scudder was arrested. She's only just put all this together, but it makes sense. Three, three, three. Scudder must think this is some sort of poetic justice; kill you on the anniversary of the day he was arrested."

Flenn scratched his head. "But you got there right at the *exact* moment... how?"

Zack took a swig from the water bottle. "You're the one who works for the big guy upstairs. I'm just glad I made it. After I rented the motorcycle, I only stopped to grab some water and bug spray at the airport shop. I wouldn't have even done that had I known how steep that mountain road was. It took me longer to..."

"Wait, wasn't there a *second* blast?"

Zack nodded. "Scudder has a drone from an airbase down here; Schmitt set it all up. Scudder's probably been watching you from twenty-thousand feet ever since you got here."

Flenn was struggling to put the pieces together. "So, he saw you grab me and run into the jungle... "

Zack finished the sentence, "...and aimed a second missile right where we had run for cover."

"But how did you know he... "

"That drone only carries two Hellfires at a time. He would have blown up the whole damn mountain if he could've. Which is why we can't go back. Scudder has had plenty of time to reload. He knows that if you're alive, that's the first place you'd go."

Flenn's shoulder was on fire, but he didn't want any more morphine. Right now he just needed to concentrate on what Zack was telling him. "Okay, so you dragged me into the jungle... "

Zack grinned, "And saved both our butts!"

Flenn didn't return the smile. "But not the children."

Zack turned his gaze to the ground. "Look... Flenn...I didn't know there would be kids. I was just trying to get to you. I would have gone back for them if I could. There just wasn't time. I'm sorry."

"*He* knew!" Flenn's eyes narrowed. No longer glassy from the morphine, they now sparked a burgeoning rage that Zack had not seen since Edinburgh. "*He* knew about the kids!"

Flenn felt his anger rising faster than the heat from the Honduran sun. "Scudder knew; he just didn't care! He could have fired those missiles a dozen times when no one else was around... I can't believe it! He killed those kids just to get at me—out of what, some sick sense of... what did you call it? Poetic justice?"

Zack didn't answer. *Flenn was right. Eric Scudder could have killed Flenn a hundred different ways. Instead, he had chosen to do it here, away from everything, where it was least likely to ever be investigated, in the middle of a mountain village full of innocent people.* Zack was no shrink, but he wondered if Scudder wasn't just striking at Flenn, but at everything Flenn held dear. The priest had never married, had no immediate family, other than a brother, and no romantic interests—at least, not since Edinburgh. Maybe killing off children whom Flenn cared about was simply fuel for Scudder's sick need for revenge. *Sure,* Zack thought, *Scudder could have gotten the same result by doing something like bombing Flenn's parish back in Birmingham, but Jeremy Schmitt would never have allowed that. Schmitt had likely authorized this mission only because it was on Honduran soil, probably certain it could never be traced back to him.*

Zack didn't know how Sarah Coverdale had uncovered the truth at the last minute, but he was thankful that she had.

"That baseborn, contemptible weasel!" Flenn's rage was no longer containable as he struggled to his feet. "They were just *kids*, Zack!" He hadn't noticed Zack reach into the med kit. "Just little kids…" Flenn barely felt the prick in his arm but knew immediately what Zack had done. "No, damn it! I want to get out of here!"

"Tomorrow, my friend… tomorrow. Right now, you need more rest."

Flenn struggled to stay awake. He looked at Zack with angry yet pleading eyes. "Please, Zack. We've got to find him!"

"That's exactly what we're going to do; but I need you

well enough to help me—which means you need to rest one more day."

As much as Flenn didn't want to comply, in the end he had no choice. His last conscious thought was one of revenge.

CHAPTER *NINE*

Seoul; twenty years ago…

With a population nearing 10 million, Seoul seemed to Flenn to go on forever.

Korea had gained its independence from Japan in 1945, which had been part of the reason for the Korean War in the first place. Competing factions desiring to rule the peninsula had pitched themselves against one another, with Seoul falling to the North early on. The city had been nearly destroyed in the United Nations' efforts to recapture it.

Flenn stared out the window of the limousine and watched speedboats pass sampans along the Han River. His destination today had nothing to do with the investigation; it was more personal than that. Before his mother had died last summer, she'd told him that if he ever had the chance he should visit three places in the world, and think about her. The truth was that he thought about her wherever he went… but he had promised her he would visit all three. The first was Canterbury Cathedral. His mother had been a devout Episcopalian all her life and had taught him much of the history of the Anglican Church when he was a boy. Flenn had pretended to be interested at the time for her sake. He was planning to go to England next year with his father. They'd be sure to see Canterbury.

There hadn't been much time for recreation or vacations since graduating Yale. He'd joined the Air Force straight out of college, instead of going to work for his dad the way his brother had done. David Sr. and Jr. were making quite the team back home; Flenn would have only been in the way.

Flenn's goal of learning to fly had been undermined when his commanding officer had seen Flenn's aptitude tests and recruited him for a special operations unit. Flenn had been intrigued by the idea of signing up with such an elite group and had happily served for two years with the Intelligence Corp. It wasn't long before the CIA had come knocking at his door.

He was now one of the youngest operatives in the agency, excelling at everything they'd thrown at him. When the time came to pull an agent off an investigation overseas and insert some young blood, they'd sent Flenn. He'd jumped at the opportunity, in part because the second place his mother had wanted him to visit had been the Royal Tombs of the Joseon Dynasty. His mom had accompanied her husband to Seoul often. Flenn Industries' Asian office was located here. She had told her son, in her native South Carolinian drawl, how "positively enchanting" the tombs were.

He could see why his mother would want him to visit Canterbury. Even the third place, Edinburgh, he could understand... but a cemetery? How a graveyard could

possibly be "enchanting" mystified Flenn; maybe he'd
find out once they arrived.

Flenn gazed out the car window. Seoul was a city of
progress and prosperity. It was hard to fathom that just 35
miles away, people lived in abject poverty and state-
sponsored paranoia. North Koreans existed for only one
purpose, and that was to serve the needs of their corrupt
leaders. Concentration camps spotted the North, rivaling
the worst of the Nazi workcamps decades before. So-called
"enemies of the regime" were either beaten or worked to
death in those North Korean camps. Flenn shuddered to
think what life was like on the other side of the border.

"So, Mr. Flenn, what do you think of Seoul thus far?"
asked Lee Qwon, who had volunteered to travel to the
tombs with him today. *Volunteered* was a rather benign
term—*insisted* was more like it.

"Bigger than I thought," Flenn answered. "Quite
beautiful."

"I hope you will allow me to show you some of the
highlights in addition to the Royal Tombs," Lee offered.

"Maybe another day." Flenn said as he watched a
group of school children in yellow-and-white uniforms
making their way toward a granite monument in the
center of a small park. "I suspect Sarah will have plenty for
me to do in the days ahead."

Lee laughed. "She is all business; not like Mr. Scudder."

Flenn raised an eyebrow. "What do you mean?"

"Forgive me," Lee said quickly, "I meant no disrespect."

Flenn pressed. "Don't worry about it. Between you and me, I don't like the guy."

"Mr. Scudder is very much distracted lately," Lee offered. "Maybe that is what your business is like… many distractions every day."

"Distracted? How?"

"He is on the telephone a lot, the one that is a direct link to Washington; especially when Miss Sarah is away. I am certain he has many responsibilities to call Washington so often."

Was the Korean trying to tell him something?

"I wouldn't know," Flenn said. "I haven't been given access to that phone yet." *In truth, he likely never would. Sarah Coverdale would be the lead investigator once Eric Scudder left. She'd be the only one permitted to discuss their progress with Washington.*

Flenn had never met Sarah's boss, Jeremy Schmitt; although rumors were that Schmitt might be in line one day for a top job in the agency. Sarah hadn't told him much about the man. Maybe he would ask her tomorrow night when Sarah dropped off her notes. She'd told Flenn she had her own theory about the theft, but so far had refused to discuss it. When pressed, all she had said was that her theory was far-fetched; but, she'd promised to let him read her notes and see if he would come to the same conclusion.

Sarah had allowed Flenn the afternoon off to visit the tombs. He had not told her, or Lee, about his mother's request. Truth was, Flenn seldom spoke about his family to anyone. Not that he wasn't close to them, he was, particularly his father. It had more to do with the Flenn family's basic rule: *Never discuss private matters—family, sex, religion, politics—with anyone.* It was a good rule, one which had helped prepare him for the work he'd be doing in the future, for Flenn was being groomed to be a spy, not just an investigator. The fact that he could easily use his own identity as the wealthy son of an American businessman gave him the perfect cover to go just about anywhere in the world. That, coupled with his penchant for Middle Eastern languages, would prove a huge advantage for the agency, not to mention his career. Flenn hoped to go far in the CIA, maybe as far as director. He smiled and thought, *"Well, everyone has to have a dream."*

Lee Qwon frowned. "Please understand, Mr. Scudder has always been kind to me." Flenn found that hard to believe. "That is why I did not mind when he asked me to help him mail some of his belongings to the States. He is very anxious to go home, I believe."

"I may be young, Lee, but I'm old enough to recognize a pompous ass when I see one. Scudder is what we call back home 'the Ugly American.'"

"Mr. Scudder is heavy, but I don't think he is so very ugly," Lee said, puzzled by the remark.

"It is an expression. It means an arrogant American who is rude to foreigners in their own country. Trust me, we aren't all like Scudder, or those jerks you read about in the papers like that actor, or that real-estate guy with the weird hair. In fact, most Americans are a bit humble. I hope that you'll have a better impression of us after Scudder is gone."

Lee opened his mouth as if to say something, but then saw the tombs ahead of them. "Ahh, we have arrived. May I accompany you around the grounds?"

Flenn smiled. "Thanks, but I'd rather have some time to myself, if you don't mind."

Lee smiled. "Of course," he said, looking as if he knew Flenn's motivation for traveling here, which of course he couldn't have. "I have some errands to run. How about I return for you around four this afternoon? That should give you plenty of time to see the tombs."

Flenn smiled in return, as if to say, *Perfect!*

CHAPTER *TEN*

Zack rolled over on the soft ground, opened his eyes… and quickly jumped to his feet. Flenn was gone!

Mango and kapok trees surrounded him on every side. He couldn't see through the thick, green underbrush for more than a few yards in any direction. Nor could he hear anything… the jungle was quiet this morning; *too quiet.*

Damn it, damn it, damn it! Flenn must have gotten up in the middle of the night and set off to find his way back to the village!

Zack had spent the day yesterday tending to Flenn, making sure they both stayed hydrated, and keeping an eye on the patch of sky he was able to see through the trees. Thankfully, Flenn had slept most of the day. Zack had hoped he'd be strong enough for the two of them to start finding their way down the mountain this morning… *but now Flenn was gone!*

Zack thought he heard something heading his way. Without a weapon, he picked up a large rock and got ready to hurl it.

"I hope you're not planning on throwing that thing at me," Flenn said, walking out of the large, leafy underbrush. He looked much stronger than he had the day before when Zack had spent the day watching him closely, giving Flenn water and protein bars, and keeping him covered in bug spray.

"You weren't the ex-agent I was expecting," Zack said, relieved to see his friend was feeling stronger.

"Why? You think Scudder's coming this way?" Flenn sat down on a stump, retrieving a water bottle from Zack's backpack.

"The thought had occurred to me," Zack said. "I still haven't heard from Sarah yet on where he is."

"Can't you just call her?"

"I follow orders," Zack said. "She told me to sit tight till I heard from her. Where were you just now?"

Flenn shot him a look. "Since when did *you* ever follow orders? And, for your information, I was answering nature's call. I figured you'd prefer me to do that somewhere away from camp."

"What I prefer is that you wake me up and tell me where you're going." Zack tossed the rock to the ground. "And as for not following Sarah's orders… well, she's special; you know that. She was our professor long before she started pushing a pencil for the deputy director."

Flenn rubbed his shoulder. "Must be a pretty impressive pencil for her to have found out about Scudder."

Zack nodded. "I wish I knew more, but when she told me your life was in danger, there just wasn't time."

Flenn looked off in the distance. "And you haven't called her?"

"No, she told me to wait."

Flenn grinned. "Can't get a signal, can you?"

Zack snorted ruefully. "Sounded better to say I was following orders."

"That'll be the day." Flenn sat down, wishing for a large carafe of coffee. "So, what's next, Lone Ranger?"

"Getting you down this mountain and to a doctor. I did the best I could, but your wound needs looking after."

Flenn looked away; he was quiet for a moment. "I almost wish you hadn't come."

"Why?"

"Those children. I'll never be able to get them out of my mind. They were just little kids. They didn't deserve this, they… " Flenn caught himself before the tears came.

Zack didn't respond; instead he reached into his backpack to retrieve a bottle of water. *Only two left. They would have to ration the rest. It was time to leave.*

"Can you walk?"

Flenn straightened. "Yeah; my shoulder hurts, but the rest of me is okay. How's the water supply?"

Zack shrugged. "We could stand to find more." Flenn nodded. They couldn't go back to the village, Scudder would be watching. Nor could they stay in the jungle much longer. The mangos and protein bars would last for a while, but they needed to find water soon. They wouldn't last long without it. "So, have you figured out how we get out of here?"

Zack pulled a GPS device out of his back pocket. "By following this." He pointed to the left. "It says we go that way. We can parallel the mountain road, but we need to stay off it so no one will spot us. He glanced up, "As long as we stay under this tree canopy we should be okay."

Flenn looked away. "I'm never going to be 'okay.'"

Zack set his face southward. He handed Flenn a sturdy walking stick he'd managed to find yesterday. "You ready?"

The pace was slower than Zack would have liked, but Flenn had to conserve energy, and the jungle floor was difficult to traverse. It took the entire day to find their way to the dirt road that led down the mountain. They were careful to avoid open spaces, staying under the cover of trees which ran parallel with the road. Both men were keenly aware that the drone might be still flying overhead, ready to strike.

Zack had managed to change Flenn's shoulder-dressing once, but there were no more bandages in the med kit. The kit was normally equipped with scissors, broad-spectrum antibiotics, analgesics, morphine, bandages, scissors, and a small bottle of Jack Daniel's— just in case. He'd grabbed it from his car, throwing out the scissors and whiskey to get through airport security. Fortunately, security had somehow missed the tiny scalpel which he'd used to dig the shrapnel out of Flenn's shoulder. Perched on a large boulder as night fell, Zack wished he'd kept the whiskey. Tomorrow, he reasoned, they'd make better time by traveling in the early hours. It had originally taken Zack two hours to reach the village from the airport by motorbike. At this pace, it was going to take at least another day to descend the mountain.

The jungle was full of sounds and snares which slowed their journey. Not only were they leery of potential danger from above, but plenty of less-sophisticated life forms inhabited the jungle, and were just as dangerous. As funny as it had seemed at first, trying to avoid getting hit by falling fruit was proving to be quite a challenge.

"Freeze!"

The command caught Zack off-guard, until he saw the reason for Flenn's alarm. Not six feet away was a bright green snake about two feet long. Unlike the harmless green snakes back home in Alabama, Flenn knew it to be a Green Palm Pit Viper. The yellow stripe and the triangular head were dead giveaways. "Don't move a muscle," Flenn whispered.

The snake blended in with the foliage of the palm fronds strewn on the ground and would have been impossible to see had it not been moving. The men watched as it slowly slithered past them. The snake paid no attention to Flenn but stopped when it came close to Zack's left foot. Zack would have noticed Flenn's lips moving in silent prayer had he been able to take his eyes off the creature. It surveyed Zack's sneaker closely, flicking its tongue toward a loose shoestring. A bead of sweat rolled from Zack's forehead down to the ground. At last, the snake moved on.

Zack inhaled deeply. "Just what was that thing?" he asked as it disappeared into the forest.

"A snake."

Zack poked Flenn with his walking stick. "I know it was a snake, doofus, what *kind* of snake?"

"A very bad one."

"You don't know the name? You used to learn all about the flora and fauna before we went somewhere on assignment. You'd read up for days about all that crap."

"Still do."

"So?"

Flenn shrugged. "It's a Green Palm Pit Viper, but down here the locals call it a two-step snake. If it bites you, you take two steps, and then you die."

Zack wiped more beads of sweat from his face. "Great! I've got missiles from the sky and two-step snakes on the ground. What else have I got to worry about?"

"That!"

Flenn pointed ahead at a dozen armed men in a clearing.

CHAPTER *ELEVEN*

Seoul; twenty years ago...

"There's only one logical conclusion," Flenn put down the stack of papers, and pressed his palms against his tired eyes.

"You think so, too?" Sarah stared at him from across the coffee table in his apartment. It was late. "Tell me."

Flenn sighed. "You're not going to like it."

"I already don't like it. Tell me anyway. That's why I brought you here. You were the best in my class at putting facts together without letting assumptions distract you."

Flenn sighed. "Those distractions were fabricated ones in the classroom, meant to disguise the obvious." He pointed to her notes. "This, on the other hand... " His eyes met hers, "but if I'm wrong... "

"I'm the lead investigator now, Flenn; I want to know what you think. I want to know if you came to the same conclusion—the one I keep trying to dismiss."

"The janitor's son did it."

"But we searched everywhere."

He pulled out her report from the file. "No, it says here *Scudder searched* everywhere. You joined the investigation already in progress. Your notes say that after you got here, the two of you started shadowing the son."

He searched through the report. "Scudder followed the man at night, and you took over during the day." He picked up a page and pointed to a paragraph: "Then on the fifth night, you wrote that Scudder came back early."

Sarah knew where this was leading; Flenn was confirming what she had already concluded. "That was the night before the son went on one of his hang-gliding jaunts—probably went to bed early. Nothing else for Scudder to do." She didn't believe that, but was waiting to see what Flenn had come up with.

Flenn looked at the file. "This says you were looking out the window of your apartment when you saw Scudder return that night. Did you ask him about why he came home early?"

Sarah pushed her hair back behind her ears. "I suppose I should have. I mean, we were just trying to get a feel for the son's routine, see if there might be someplace he could have been stashing the treasure."

Flenn looked down at the file. "No one leaves a stakeout early," he said, turning a page in her notebook. "The next day, Eric suggests you swap up, tells you he will take days from now on. And being the nice person that you are… "

"I said yes."

"Three days later, the son dies in a hang-gliding accident. The way I read it, either you or Scudder had something to do with that *accident*. Then, whichever one of you did it went back to where the son had hidden the artifacts and claimed them for yourself."

Flenn looked into her eyes. "You know what I'm going to say next, don't you?"

"Say it anyway, just so I don't feel crazy."

Flenn looked around the room. "How sure are you we're alone?"

"I'm not, but it concerns the Koreans too, so if they're listening maybe you'll be helping us both. Shoot." Sarah stared at him, marveling that in just two days he had managed to come to the same conclusion that had taken her weeks to derive.

"One of you found the bowls, killed the kid, then swiped them for yourself."

She smiled. "Which one of us do you think it was?"

He shrugged. "You, of course."

Sarah gave him the finger.

His grin vanished as he leaned back into the sofa. "Scudder. That's where all this is leading... right back to his big fat ass." Flenn grunted. "Of course, I can't prove any of it, so, it's not much more than a hunch. And I hate hunches."

"Hunches are for horseraces," she quipped.

Flenn nodded. "I remember you saying that in class. 'Hunches are for horseraces and the stock market.' I also remember how Zack Matteson used to argue with you."

"Matteson? I'd forgotten all about him. Whatever happened to that guy?"

"He was with me when that thing I mentioned went down in Ireland... and later in Kuwait."

Sarah nodded, then was quiet for a moment before turning back to her notes. "But, come on, isn't what we're doing now just playing a hunch?"

"Not from what I've just read in your notes. There was no sign of a break in at the museum, the janitor was asleep the night the artifacts were taken, hardly anyone had taken interest in the exhibition, and there was only one other set of keys. The most logical conclusion is that the janitor's son took his old man's keys, made a copy, came in that night and took them. Scudder found the artifacts while he was snooping around, rigged the glider to kill the kid, then went back and swiped them for himself."

Sarah sighed. "And that's *obvious*?"

Flenn raised an eyebrow. "To me it is."

Although Sarah had come to the exact same conclusion, she'd found it far from obvious. "Even if we could prove it, Scudder is leaving day after tomorrow," she said. "He's not dumb enough to take the bowls with him; so, here we are with a likely murderer and a thief amongst us—and no evidence."

Flenn got up and poured himself another cup of coffee. "Tell me something. You didn't really bring me here to find the artifacts, did you? You brought me here to validate your suspicions."

Sarah didn't answer.

"I take your silence to be a 'yes.' Okay, now that I've confirmed your theory, or at least supported it, I'm afraid I don't know what else to tell you… except one thing." He put down the cup and thumbed through his own notebook. Flenn's memory was excellent but he took copious notes anyway. "Here it is… Scudder told me he was arranging for Lee to mail the stuff he couldn't take with him on the plane." He looked up. "Lee must have the artifacts."

"No way!" She hadn't seen that one coming. "You really think Lee's in this with Scudder?"

"Don't know, but if I *did* play hunches," he winked, "then I'd say probably not. Lee doesn't seem the type. In fact, I think he was trying to clue me in on some of this the other day at the tombs."

He set Sarah's notes aside. "You've got a real problem here. You're lead investigator now. If you turn Scudder in without evidence, and neither he nor Lee are in possession of the artifacts, then Scudder will crucify you. Without hard evidence, he'll play you for a fool back home. He'll find some sympathetic big-wig and have you blacklisted from any future promotion—but you *already* know that, don't you?"

He leaned back and stared at her. "Is that why I'm here?"

Without answering, Sarah stood up, walked into the kitchen, and came back with a beer. She flopped down on the sofa next to Flenn. "So, now that you've confirmed both my conclusion and my dilemma, what do we do? I mean, my gut tells me Scudder killed the son after he followed him to the artifacts, but there's no proof." She sighed. "I don't know, Flenn, maybe it's just because I don't like the guy. Maybe I *want* him to be guilty."

Flenn took a slow drink of coffee then set his mug

down carefully on the coaster, and pinched the bridge of his nose. "The janitor's son is most likely the thief. He has a record of petty theft, no job, and mooches off his father. Scudder's own notes say that the son began spending money lavishly after the robbery. He bought a hang glider, which he kept in a garage behind the old man's house."

"More like a shed," Sarah interjected. "I went snooping around there one night, thinking maybe he might have hidden the artifacts in there. The shed wasn't even locked. Nothing much in there but the glider. If he did still have the bowls, where'd he come up with the money to buy the glider?"

"Probably spending on credit in anticipation of selling the bowls," Flenn said.

They sat quietly for a moment; both lost in thought. At length Sarah spoke, her words more of a lament than a question. "So, what do we do now?"

"Has it occurred to you that there may be nothing we can do?"

She leaned forward. "What do you mean—we just let Scudder walk away?"

"For now."

She scowled. "No way in hell I'm letting that jerk get away with this! He's walked over everybody since he first got here; he's given the agency a bad name."

Flenn snickered. "I don't think the CIA needed Eric Scudder to give it a bad name—we've sort of done that to ourselves over the years."

"Believe me, Scudder's made it worse. The man is a Neanderthal with a badge."

Flenn picked up Sarah's notes and thumbed through them again. "I can't see a successful way out of this without more evidence, and that's going to be hard to come by once Scudder leaves."

Sarah nearly slammed her beer on the coffee table. "Damn it, Flenn! There's got to be something we can do!"

He scratched his head. "Well, I suppose we could search Lee's apartment. I mean, without his knowing about it, of course."

She shook her head. "I'm not good at breaking and entering."

Flenn patted her knee. Not for the first time, she wished she wasn't his senior.

"I'm not so good at breaking, but I'm really good at entering," Flenn said. She raised a hopeful eyebrow. "I'm talking about doors, Sarah."

"Story of my life," she said with a sigh. "I suppose I could call Lee to the office tonight, invent some excuse so you can go snooping." Flenn looked at his watch; they both decided it was too late. Instead, they agreed Flenn would go to Lee's flat the next morning after Lee left for work. He would call Sarah if he found anything.

"You know," she said, "even if you do find something, all it proves is that *Lee's* involved, whether wittingly or not. Scudder could still walk away."

Flenn shook his head. "If that's the case, and Lee is involved, I imagine he'll sing like a bird to implicate Eric."

Sarah shrugged. "Maybe, but it would look like he was just trying to shift the blame. In fact, if I know

Scudder, he's already got a contingency plan based on that very possibility."

Flenn raised his coffee mug. "Well, you've got one thing now that he doesn't have a contingency plan for."

She raised an eyebrow. "What's that?"

He winked. "Me! He may be smart, but we're smarter. I've got an idea… "

CHAPTER *TWELVE*

Sarah Coverdale despised rush-hour traffic. Washington D.C. was nearly as bad as Seoul had been twenty years ago. Her commute to Langley from Arlington was an hour each way. Up at 5 a.m. and out the door by 6:30, she barely had time to kiss the kids goodbye most mornings.

Thankfully Alan was a great dad. He took care of their kids, the house—everything. Sarah had been lucky to find him, and she knew it. They'd met 15 years ago at a seminar where she'd been lecturing on the politics of law enforcement. He'd been a reporter at the time, working for a small newspaper in Roanoke. When it came time for questions, Alan Stabler had stood and insisted that her entire premise—'Politics has no Place in Law Enforcement'—was Pollyannaish.

"Politics permeate everything, including law enforcement," he had argued, "from when a cop arrests an immigrant to the handling of protestors in front of the White House." Sarah had debated him from the podium, and then afterward when he insisted on buying her dinner. They had continued the debate over breakfast the next morning in her hotel room.

Sarah and Alan still argued over ideas, politics, education, even religion—he was a devout Catholic, she was a lapsed Presbyterian—but always good-naturedly, and never in front of their kids. Despite their ideological differences, Alan was forever and always her soulmate. This morning, Sarah had kissed him while he lay sleeping, then left two hours early to be in the office before Jeremy Schmitt arrived.

Schmitt technically worked under her, but it rarely seemed that way around the office. He pretty much did his thing and she hers. At times, they cooperated on assignments handed them by their boss, Deputy Director Carl Moore. Otherwise, their contact with one another was sporadic at most. She still had no idea why Schmitt had arranged for Eric Scudder's life-sentence to be commuted by the South Koreans. She wouldn't have known about it at all had she not been in the habit of checking Scudder's status every year on New Year's Day.

Sarah had loathed Eric Scudder from the first time they'd met 20 years ago; the world was a better place with him behind bars. But now, for some reason, Schmitt had gotten him out of jail, and had gone to great lengths to keep Scudder's release under the radar. Whether or not Schmitt had gained Director Moore's approval she didn't know, any more than she knew Schmitt's reason for wanting Scudder back in the States.

It had taken her weeks to figure out who had convinced the Koreans to let Scudder go; but once she learned he'd been freed, she had quietly assembled a team of three former students to help find Scudder and to monitor his communications. The first member of Sarah's team was Emily Colbert, who'd been at the top of her class and was currently on assignment in Seoul. Colbert's lover worked within the NIS, which was how Sarah had found out that Jeremy Schmitt was behind the release.

The second member of Sarah's team was a deep-cover operative in Latin America. Sarah had secretly reassigned him, giving him a convincing identity which had fooled both Scudder and Schmitt. He was even now feeding her information on Scudder's every move.

The third was the man she was on her way to see this morning.

As she stopped her car at the first checkpoint, a young guard expressed surprise to see her. "Ms. Coverdale, you're here awfully early," he said.

"You know how it is, Jake. The early bird catches the worm."

Jake cocked his head. "Huh?"

Sarah offered a wan smile. "It's an old expression." *He couldn't have been much more than a toddler when she'd first met Scudder.* The guard grinned politely as he waved her through.

Hollywood likes to depict actors walking through the entrance at Langley across a marbled eagle and shield, the symbol of the CIA, as if they were heading straight for some clandestine meeting. In truth, hardly anyone entered by the front hall of the old building except for tourists. Most employees used one of a dozen other entryways to start their workday. Today, instead of heading to her seventh-floor office, Sarah made her way to an entirely separate building, where a few weeks ago Mohammed Raiji had played her a phone conversation he'd recorded. In it, she had been able to clearly hear

Schmitt's assistant, Gerald Rudolph, tell Scudder that *Operation Clean Slate* was a 'go'.

Clean Slate... the phrase still sent a shiver down her spine. Thanks to Mohammed, Sarah knew Scudder had been trailing Scott Flenn online, and that he'd booked a flight to Honduras within a day of Flenn's posting information about a mission trip the priest was planning. It wasn't difficult to put it together. Scudder still blamed Flenn for putting him in prison. *Operation Clean Slate* was about killing Flenn in Honduras.

Whatever Schmitt's plans were for Scudder, his cooperation had obviously been secured by offering the fat man what he would have wanted most—revenge. No doubt Scudder had been planning how to eliminate Flenn for years; but, what he hadn't planned on was that Sarah Coverdale would be shadowing his every move. Sarah had to be careful though, especially now that she knew Jeremy Schmitt was pulling Scudder's strings.

Sarah had debated warning Flenn, but Scott was not the student, or even the young spy, she'd known so long ago. She couldn't be certain of how he'd respond now that he had left his old life behind. Plus, Flenn's telephones and email were likely being monitored; she couldn't risk Schmitt discovering that she was on to him. She'd wrestled for days with how best to protect Flenn before it dawned on her to contact his long-time partner, Zack Matteson.

However, today was now March 5, two days after Zack had landed at San Pedro Sula to try and save Flenn, and still no word!

Sarah couldn't request satellite reconnaissance to check if there'd been a strike at the village; Schmitt was undoubtedly checking to see if anyone in the agency was on to him. No, all Sarah could do was wait—wait, and keep trying to contact Matteson. It was driving her mad. It had been simple enough to figure out that Scudder would seek revenge—though she hadn't expected it to be as dramatic as using Hellfire missiles—what had not been so easy was to determine why Schmitt had Scudder released in the first place.

What was Schmitt up to? she asked herself for the hundredth time. Hopefully, Mohammed Raji was about to shed light on just that. Mohammed had called last night while she was at her eldest daughter's soccer practice.

After passing her class, Raji had gone on to specialize in *communications oversight*—eavesdropping. It was Raji who had discovered Scudder was on his way to Central America ahead of Flenn. When Sarah had asked him to monitor all communications between Schmitt and anyone in Honduras, Mohammed hadn't even blinked an eye. *If his favorite instructor wanted him to listen in on the chief resource director, then there must be a good reason,* he had told himself.

There had been only one communication to Honduras, and that had been to a Gen. Rodriguez at the Soto Cano Air Base. Schmitt had telephoned the general with a request to "borrow" their drone, which was a bit misleading since the drone was on loan from the CIA in the first place. The Hondurans were using it in their war with drug cartels.

Sarah knocked before entering Mohammed Raji's unmarked, 8-by-8', windowless office. Floor-to-ceiling electronic equipment barely allowed enough space for a small desk and a single chair. Sarah knew this was one of many similar rooms throughout the building where teams of experts listened in on digital communications across the globe, *even here at home*, albeit illegally. Supposedly, the CIA never worked within the United States—that was the FBI's territory—but technicians like Mohammed violated those boundaries frequently. There was even a secret academy in Florida where agents were taught the ins and outs of working around the FBI. Mohammed had trained there, as had Sarah for that matter—but that was another story.

Mohammed Raji was one of several technicians referred to as *freelancers*: particularly skillful people who were assigned by various departments to help with high-level investigations. Sarah had given him authorization to tap into her own department's server to keep an eye on Jeremy Schmitt, with the understanding that if discovered this could mean the end of both their careers. Mohammed had simply grinned and winked; she caught his meaning: *No one was going to catch him!*

"So, what've you got for me?" Sarah said, closing the door behind her. She wasn't wasting time on pleasantries today, not with Matteson and Flenn still missing. Mohammed stood to greet her, accidentally knocking one of the keyboards off his desk. He bent down awkwardly to retrieve it, having to wind himself around several cords and wires in the process.

He was a tall man in his early 30s, and unhealthily thin. Sarah remembered that as a student, Mohammed seemed to exist solely on sugary drinks. Sure enough, there was a large grape-slush on his desk. "I thought you'd want to see this," he said, reconnecting the keyboard. Three terminals were flashing various numeric codes at phenomenal speed. Sarah had no idea what the codes meant. Computers weren't her thing.

Mohammed typed in a command. *Nothing.* He disconnected the keyboard and tried again. *Still nothing.* The third time he picked the keyboard up and banged it on the corner of the desk. *Bingo!*

He offered Sarah his chair and stood behind her, crammed against one of the large computer consoles. "Schmitt has frequented this webpage a lot over the past six months," he told Sarah, pointing to the screen in front of her. "I did some checking on why Scudder was arrested in Korea years ago, and may have found a connection. Take a look."

He clicked the mouse and the image of a once-familiar building appeared on the screen. It was the Seoul Museum of Art and Antiquities. She glanced up at Mohammed. "I know this place." He reached over her and clicked on a link; the web page faded away and another took its place. Sarah gasped. "No way!"

"This is what Schmitt keeps looking at," Raji said. "Judging from your reaction, I'm guessing you know the reason why?"

Sarah didn't answer. She just sat and stared at the image of several ancient incense bowls. The last time she'd seen them had been in the shower of a flat in South Korea, right after the police had arrested Eric Scudder. Mohammed stood, peering over her shoulder. His job didn't include asking the Director of the Effectiveness Office questions about an investigation she had undertaken, even if she had solicited his help.

His only comment was, "They're beautiful."

Sarah nodded. "And priceless." She read the information beneath the photograph. The bowls were currently on an international exhibition tour, which would be stopping in Mexico in just a few weeks. It all clicked. *This was why Schmitt wanted Scudder out of prison!*

"That bastard wants Scudder to steal them for him… " she slammed her fist on the desk, almost dislodging the keyboard… "Again!"

"Ma'am?" Mohammed's eyes traveled from his former professor to the screen and back to Sarah again.

It was all coming together; and, unlike the art depicted on the screen in front of her, this picture was an ugly one. Schmitt had been their contact in Korea 20 years ago. He was known to have an appreciation for antiquities. That was why the military had specifically approached him when the Koreans asked for help with their investigation. They figured Schmitt would have a unique appreciation for the situation.

Sarah remembered how Schmitt and Scudder had been in constant contact back then. She could still recall the conversation she'd had with Schmitt that day, March 3, after waking him at home. He had been noticeably shaken to hear that Scudder had been arrested. He'd kept asking her what Scudder had said, and whether he'd divulged if there had been any other accomplices.

Schmitt was in on this from the beginning! It all made sense now! Schmitt would have known people who would have paid millions for these relics.

Sarah closed her eyes and began rubbing her temples. *Or, had Schmitt simply wanted the collection for himself?*

Sarah felt her blood begin to boil.

Schmitt must have found out that the artifacts were on tour. This would be his last chance to swipe them, but to do that he needed Eric Scudder. That weasel, Gerald Rudolph, was obviously in on it as well; but, it was Scudder who was the key player. For whatever reason, Scudder had never ratted Schmitt out. Or maybe he had, but the Koreans simply hadn't cared. Either way, Schmitt had cut a deal with Scudder for his freedom—The artifacts in exchange for Flenn's life!

Sarah needed more time to put all this together, and desperately needed to hear from Zack Matteson. She had called numerous times, but with no response. *God, please let him still be alive!*

Mohammed looked up. "Ma'am, there's something else."

"Yes?" Sarah opened her eyes.

Mohammed shifted his weight. "It's what I called you about last night."

Sarah nodded toward the computer. "I thought *this* was what you called me about?"

"Yes, ma'am. I mean, sort of… well, this is part of it."

Sarah leaned back in the chair. "Go on."

"Rudolph made contact with Schmitt yesterday."

Mohammed pulled at his shirt collar. "Apparently, they still have the drone and two of the missiles."

She shook her head in disbelief. "I assumed they'd returned it by now."

"Schmitt said something about Scudder having it for a week," he answered, "I'm guessing that means through next Wednesday."

"So, if Matteson and Flenn are alive..."

Mohammed finished her sentence. "Then they're still in danger."

Sarah Coverdale looked back at the image on the computer screen. She wasn't religious, but she said a silent prayer for Scott Flenn and Zack Matteson— wherever they were.

CHAPTER *THIRTEEN*

Zack and Flenn ducked before the men in the clearing saw them. "Who are they?" Zack whispered.

"How the hell should I know? Could be anybody. Hunters, drug cartel, paramilitary… "

"Or Scudder's people," Zack added.

They raised their heads only enough to see if they'd been spotted. The men were standing in a circle, looking at something on the ground. "Wish I could reach Sarah," Zack whispered, "then maybe we could get some goddamn answers."

Flenn elbowed him in the ribs. "Don't use that word in front of me."

"Great! I almost got blown out of existence, bitten by a deadly snake, and now I may be shot by some of Scudder's men, and you're worried about my language?"

"*Shh!*"

One of the men turned in their direction. Flenn and Zack knew that movement was what usually caught a predator's eye, so they both froze. The man surveyed the surroundings, then returned to whatever it was that had caught the group's attention. A moment later, four men hoisted the carcass of a gigantic animal on their shoulders and began to walk in the opposite direction.

"Hunters," Zack said, letting out a sigh. "Looks like they've killed some sort of mountain lion."

"A jaguar," Flenn corrected, his eyes never shifting from the hunting party.

"Funny, I didn't hear a shot."

Flenn watched the men move eastward toward the road, carrying the large animal. "They build pits, place stakes in them. Quite cruel, really."

"People eat jaguars?"

"Sometimes." Flenn watched until the men were out of sight. "Mostly, smugglers kill them for protection. A single cat can roam hundreds of acres. They play havoc with those traveling at night or waiting around makeshift landing strips. Dope dealers are more afraid of the jaguars than they are of the local police."

"So, are these guys hunters or smugglers?"

Flenn shook his head slightly. "The fact that each one has a rifle says they aren't your average hunters. Most people can't afford rifles down here. They have machetes instead; not really a weapon, mostly a tool for cutting down vegetation, chopping up fruit... I've even seen a guy using the tip of his machete as a screwdriver."

"Those guys didn't exactly look like mechanics. My money's on drug dealers."

"Yeah, probably." Flenn rolled slightly to take the pressure off his left shoulder. "Most villagers don't *buy* rifles; they're *issued* them. And the only people issuing weapons down here are the military and the drug lords."

Zack sat up. "Those weren't soldiers." He took a swig of water and passed the bottle to Flenn. They rested for an hour before pressing on. Zack took the lead, keeping an eye out for any sign of the smugglers. *If only he could have gotten his hands on one of those rifles!*

Flenn followed a few yards behind. His shoulder ached, but he didn't complain. Zack had been giving him antibiotics—*Amazing what Zack kept in that med kit!*—but the only pain reliever left in the bag was aspirin. Not that he would have taken any more morphine; he wanted to keep his wits about him. He reached up and lightly pressed around the wound, hoping the antibiotics would hold back any ensuing infection.

The shade from the palm and pine trees kept them from melting in the Honduran sun; but their water supply was running critically low. Flenn reached down and patted his pocket, checking to see if he still had the purification pills he'd wrapped in a foil pouch days ago. He did. He'd thought to purchase several from a *pharmacia* in San Pedro Sula. Water-borne diseases and illnesses down here were crippling. If he and Zack could just find a stream, he could use the pills to make the water safe for drinking.

As he stepped over roots and fallen limbs, Flenn recalled how most of the children in the villages had intestinal worms, something he'd convinced his brother, David, to help him rectify at San Jose de la Montaña last year. Thanks to Flenn Industries, the new water treatment facility had improved the health of nearly everyone in the village. Flenn smiled. *This year when he had come he'd found the children looking much stronger.*

The smile vanished.

Many of those children were now dead; murdered by a madman bent on revenge; with the assistance of the CIA!

Why would anyone possibly want Eric Scudder out of prison? It couldn't just be to murder him. No, Flenn reasoned, *someone had a job waiting for Scudder, and had agreed to this as payment.*

A vibrating sound came from Zack's backpack. They both froze. Zack pulled his backpack around and reached in for the satellite phone. He stood perfectly still, afraid of losing the signal. "Hello?"

Flenn could only hear Zack's part of the conversation.

"No, we're alive... Yes, ma'am, I figured you'd be worried. I haven't been able to get a signal... No, we're making our way back. I'm afraid it's going to take a while... He's hurt, but you know him, tough as nails." Zack lowered his voice. "There was a lot of collateral damage... children... Yeah, we feel that way too." He glanced at Flenn. "I think he'll be all right. Are you any closer to finding how Scudder got out of prison or who he's working for?" There was a long silence as Zack listened to whatever it was Sarah was telling him.

Flenn wondered if Sarah had fully understood what Zack had meant about collateral damage. *How could she? How could anyone, other than those poor parents who were even now going through unimaginable grief?*

"I got it," Zack finally said. Just let me know when you locate him. We'll take care of the rest."

Zack glanced at Flenn. "I don't know if I can promise that. He's pretty upset. I'd say if he has his way, Scudder's days are numbered... Yes, ma'am; I'll do what I can... Yes, I understand."

Zack pressed a button and returned the phone to the backpack. Flenn recalled the last time they'd used a satellite phone; it had only been a few months ago—the night he and Zack had turned the tables on the Iranians and Daniel Romero. That particular phone had helped them prevent an all-out war in the Middle East, as well as save America from a rigged election that would have brought two psychopaths to power.

"So," Flenn asked, "what did Sarah say?"

Zack picked up the backpack and walked past him. "She said to tell you hello."

CHAPTER *FOURTEEN*

Seoul; twenty years ago...

Lee Qwon left his flat for work at exactly 7:40 every morning to be in the office by 8:30. Flenn put down the newspaper he'd been pretending to read in the coffee shop across the street only after the bus pulled away from Lee's stop. He left the waitress a generous tip and walked across the busy street to the apartment building, then trotted up two flights of stairs. Lee's flat was at the end of a long hall, on the left. Fortunately, there were no security cameras in the hallway.

Flenn tried the passkey Sarah had given him. Everyone working for the agency was required to register all computer passwords, leave detailed information about their next of kin, and provide a key to their home in case of emergency. The keys were locked in a safe in Sarah's office. They'd gone last night to retrieve Lee's.

Flenn turned the key.

Nothing.

He tried again. It still didn't work. Making certain no one was watching, he retrieved a small tool from his wallet and inserted it into the lock. A few seconds and a couple of soft clicks later and Flenn was inside.

Lee wasn't much of a housekeeper: newspapers and

books were scattered everywhere, dirty dishes stacked in the sink, the microwave door left open with the hardened remains of the last dozen or so meals caked onto its walls. *So much for Asian stereotypes of tidiness!* Flenn walked into the master bedroom to find an unmade bed, a simple bamboo chest, and a few framed pictures on the wall, presumably of Lee's family. An empty pizza box sat open on a wicker chair in the corner.

Flenn found Scudder's packages in a smaller, second bedroom. Four large and two small cardboard boxes had been sealed and addressed to a post office in Arlington, Virginia. The top line of the address listed a number instead of a name. Flenn recognized the zip code; it was a special post office used by the CIA.

Clever, Flenn thought. No one would suspect an agent with Eric Scudder's clearance picking up a package at a drop for clandestine operations. All an agent had to do was present proper identification and know the number printed on the package.

Flenn studied the boxes. The largest appeared to have been opened and re-sealed as if someone had checked its contents. He reached in his pocket for a pair of latex gloves, then carefully peeled back the packaging tape and found... piles of folded clothes and towels.

Who packs towels to send to the States?

Digging deeper, Flenn's hand brushed against something hard. He pulled out a padded package, the inside of which had been lined with a thin layer of lead.

Protection from x-rays, he presumed.

Inside was an ornate golden orb. Flenn recognized it as part of the missing collection. Scudder was undoubtedly planning to have Lee mail the boxes through special U.S. envoy, avoiding standard postal inspections. He took his time opening each box and jotting down a description of every piece.

Finally, Flenn glanced up at the clock on the wall. He'd been here all morning. He spent the next couple of hours rearranging the boxes, careful to leave one of them open. Lee's phone was attached to the wall next to the sofa. He called Sarah and told her what he'd found, then dialed a second number, but got a recording. He left a message: "Eric, have I got a present for you! You won't believe what I've found. Looks like you won't have to leave Korea emptyhanded after all!" Flenn sat on the sofa and waited for the phone to ring. It didn't take long.

"Scott, what the hell are you doing at Lee's apartment?" The voice belonged to Eric Scudder.

Flenn smiled. *Bingo!*

"Eric, how did you know I was… "

"It's called Caller ID. Surely you've heard of it." Flenn had not only heard of it, he was counting on it.

"So, what are you doing there?"

"I'll tell you when you get here. I tried calling Sarah but no one answered," Flenn lied. "Anyway, I guess you're still lead investigator, so get your ass over here right away. I'll wait."

Scudder arrived within the hour. He was out of breath, probably from vaulting up the steps two at a time, Flenn thought.

"Geez, Eric, you didn't have to run." He pointed to the boxes. "This stuff isn't going anywhere."

Scudder looked around the living room where Flenn had pulled all the boxes. "What's so special about those boxes?"

Flenn grinned. "Aha... they appear to be ordinary boxes, but when you dig deep inside you pull out a prize, just like in a box of cereal when we were kids."

Scudder shook his head. "You're babbling, Junior. What is this all about?"

Flenn pulled out one of the lead-lined packages. "Looks like Lee was our man all along! I mean, look at this!" He opened it up to reveal one of the missing incense bowls.

Scudder shook his head. "Unbelievable," he said. "So, Lee's our man?"

Flenn set the first of the ancient incense burners down and reached in to pull out another package. "Can you believe this guy? He was sending it straight to the States in *your* boxes."

"My boxes?" Scudder's eyes narrowed.

Flenn pulled a third package out but dropped it on the linoleum floor. Scudder was visibly shaken when they both heard the contents break.

"Be careful with that!"

Flenn shrugged as he reached inside his pocket. Scudder flinched as Flenn popped open a switchblade.

"You know what I can't figure out?" Flenn cut the tape he had carefully replaced on the second box. "These numbers above the address."

He opened the box and pulled out another package, which he also dropped on the floor. Scudder's face was turning red. "Damn it, Flenn! Quit that! Those are irreplaceable!"

Flenn just smiled. "Oh, well, not our country's artifacts, huh?" Scudder looked like he was about to come unglued.

"You know, what I'm thinking, Eric? That these numbers must be some kind of a code." Flenn put the knife back in his pocket. "Interestingly enough, they're all going to the same zip where I get my issues of *National Geographic*. I like to read those now that my subscription to *Boys' Life* has expired."

Scudder looked down at the boxes and then up at Flenn who was still digging through them. Flenn pulled out yet another parcel and then looked straight at Scudder. "What's even more interesting is that only someone like you or me with possession of this exact code could pick up these packages from that post office." He began to toss the package from hand to hand. "I wonder how Lee expects to get them?"

Eric Scudder had finally had enough. He pulled out his .38 and pointed it directly at Flenn. "Put that down, right now! And, carefully!"

"I guess this is where I'm supposed to say something cliché, like, 'Did you really think you'd get away with it, Eric?'"

"Shut up!"

Flenn grinned. "Know what time it is, Scudder?"

"It's time for you to shut up!" Scudder's mind was racing.

"No, seriously. According to that clock behind you it's three p.m."

"So?" *Surely this kid didn't think that he'd turn around to look at the clock!*

"You know the Koreans... lots of mystery behind the number three. And today's March Third. Hmm, three o'clock on the third day of the third month. Doesn't that intrigue you at all?"

"Not in the slightest, now shut up!"

"I mean, maybe there *is* something to all of that numerology stuff. You'd be surprised how many cultures have assigned something mystical to the number three. The Mayans built a complex astronomical calendar based on it. Christians have the Holy Trinity; the Celtic people venerated the number three; the Chinese think three is lucky, oh, and... "

Scudder waved his gun. "Would you shut up?"

Flenn ignored him. "I mean if I were you, I don't think I'd want to anger the entire cosmos by doing something like shooting me on such an auspicious hour and day."

"Don't worry, I'll just shoot you three times; now quit trying to rattle me. It's not working."

Flenn tried a different tack. He needed to keep stalling. Sarah should be here any minute.

"So, how'd you talk Lee into it?"

Scudder's plans had just gone down the toilet. He had to think fast. Shooting Flenn wasn't the problem; getting his body out of the apartment without being seen was.

"I gave him five hundred bucks to mail it all for me. Lee doesn't know what's inside."

"You sure about that?" Flenn kept lobbing the package from hand to hand.

"What?"

"That Lee doesn't know. When I got here, the packages looked like they'd been opened and taped back up."

Scudder shook his head. "He wouldn't… "

"Maybe he just took a little peek. I mean, if he figured out that you had killed the janitor's son, he might have been too scared to report you, even if he does actually moonlight for Korean intelligence."

Scudder was having difficulty keeping his focus, what with Flenn's constant juggling of the package. "Only Coverdale thinks Lee Qwon works for NIS. The man is a simpleton, just like that hang-gliding moron. He never checked the bolts on that new glider he kept in his old man's shed."

Flenn frowned. "It doesn't bother you at all? Killing innocent people?"

"Nobody's innocent, kid. That gook was a thief. Probably was going to try and hock the whole collection to someone in Japan." Scudder smirked. "He'd have only gotten pennies on the dollar."

"So, will you, Eric. Pawn shops in D.C. wouldn't know what to do with this stuff."

Scudder smiled. "I've already found a buyer. Paying me royally!"

Flenn stopped tossing the package. "Ah, there's that number again. How about cutting me in for half?"

Scudder blinked. *Had he heard correctly? Was this kid simply an entrepreneur like himself?*

"You don't need money; your family's loaded."

Flenn thought a moment. "You have a point. Tell you what. Why don't I give you five million? Some of this stuff would look great on dad's credenza at home."

Scudder considered the possibility. Selling to Flenn was certainly more profitable and less messy than killing him. He could tell Schmitt that Flenn had stolen them off Lee.

"Five million—you're kidding?"

Flenn rolled his eyes. "Of course, I am." He tossed the package straight at Scudder. "Here, catch!"

Scudder's eyes widened as he frantically reached for the package. Flenn's hand dropped straight down into the open box and he pulled out his .45. "Drop them both, Eric! From this distance I can't miss." Scudder reluctantly let go of his pistol but embraced the package. He looked at Flenn as if he were about to charge. "I'm telling you, Eric, I can't miss!"

Scudder nodded slightly. "True, but I'm guessing you won't shoot an unarmed man." The corners of his mouth turned up slightly. "You ever killed anyone, kid? It ain't pretty."

Before Flenn could respond, Scudder turned and bolted out the door. Even as he bounded down the stairs, Scudder was already thinking about how to pin this on Flenn and Coverdale, once he'd found a way to kill them both. His boss, Jeremy Schmitt, would help; after all, he'd been the one paying him to swipe the artifacts in the first place.

Scudder could hear Flenn on the steps behind him as he hit the ground floor and ran into the street… straight into three armed policemen.

Even if Flenn hadn't understood Korean, anyone would know that the cops pointing their weapons at him were ordering him to drop his pistol, which he did immediately. Scudder was nervously trying to convince them to check his identification, while telling them that Flenn was a thief and a murderer.

The officers took the package out of Scudder's hand.

"Careful with that!" Scudder shouted.

"Why?" asked Flenn. "It's only Lee's dirty breakfast dishes. I unpacked the rest of the artifacts while I was waiting for you to get here. I've already told Sarah that the real ones are in Lee's shower. It seemed the best place to stash them where you wouldn't possibly find them," Flenn said. "You really should bathe more often, Eric."

Scudder looked like he was about to burst out of his skin. "You said you couldn't reach Sarah!"

Flenn smiled. "And you believed me... now tell me, who's the kid?" The police pushed them toward separate squad cars. Scudder flashed Flenn a look of unbridled rage as they patted him down. The cops were shoving Scudder into the back seat when a white Renault sped toward them, causing them to draw their weapons a second time. Sarah Coverdale jumped from the car waving her badge as Colonel Akiko Kasai stepped out of the passenger side in full uniform. Onlookers were gathering, but keeping a careful distance. Flenn wondered if things like this happened often here. He guessed not.

The officer in charge holstered her weapon and spoke at length with Col. Kasai before releasing Flenn into

Sarah's custody. "Glad you finally got here," Flenn told Sarah. "What took you so long?"

Sarah cut her eyes toward the colonel.

"I insisted on coming," Col. Kasai interjected. "After all, the Koreans came to the military first."

"She's already contacted NIS," added Sarah. "They're sending people over, along with the museum curator to authenticate what you found."

They headed back up the steps of Lee's apartment building as the police drove off with Scudder. Flenn watched as the car drove away. "You're not taking him with us?"

Colonel Kasai shook her head. "I never liked that man; let the South Koreans deal with him."

Flenn looked at Sarah. "Sounds okay by me."

Sarah agreed. "Let Langley come get him… if they want him."

Flenn turned back toward the apartment. "Doubt they will. You know how they don't like to be embarrassed."

Sarah followed Flenn into the apartment. "The embarrassment is that they ever hired the jerk in the first place."

Colonel Kasai came up behind. "No," she said quietly. "Never liked that man."

CHAPTER *FIFTEEN*

"Damn it, Zack! Are you going to tell me what Sarah said, or not?"

"You sure you want to know?" Flenn wasn't, but he nodded just the same.

Zack stepped over a fallen tree branch and turned to help his friend, careful not to touch Flenn's wounded shoulder. "She said Scudder was released in a deal organized by Jeremy Schmitt."

Zack let that sink in for a moment.

"Sarah didn't say, but I get the feeling she's investigating Schmitt. Anyway, Scudder has apparently agreed to do something in exchange for this elaborate plan to get rid of you."

He let that sink in, too.

"She didn't tell me what, but it sounded like something Langley wouldn't approve of. Sounds to me like Scudder's working for Schmitt—not the agency. Sarah said Scudder has a team down here on something he's calling *Operation Clean Slate.*"

The words made Flenn see red. "Son of a bitch killed a dozen children! There's nothing *clean* about it!"

Zack went on. "Scudder has a team of four men; two he brought with him, and two more he found down here.

Probably needs them to help with the terrain and for extra protection."

Flenn stopped walking. "Protection? Against what?"

"I'd assume *you*, if he wasn't successful."

Flenn rubbed his shoulder. "He *wasn't* successful."

Zack pulled out a water bottle and offered it to Flenn. "Yeah, but he doesn't know that. He's probably gloating right now, sure that he killed you."

Flenn thought about that. "So, who's Sarah's informant?"

Zack shrugged. "All I know is that he can only get away from Scudder to call Sarah every now and then. Apparently, Scudder's been on cloud nine the past couple of days; no doubt celebrating your demise."

"Sounds like him."

"Glad I never met the weasel. Anyway, he only has the drone for a few more days. Sarah said it's due back next Wednesday."

"What's today?"

"Saturday... I think."

"So, we have until Wednesday to find him."

Zack looked over at him. "How did you know that's what Sarah wants me to do?"

Flenn's eyes flashed fire. "I don't give two cents about what *she* wants you to do. It's what *I* am going to do!"

"Now, *that's* the Flenn I know!"

"Maybe that's who I've been all along." Flenn gazed into the jungle. "I'm going to find Eric Scudder... and I am going to kill him!"

CHAPTER *SIXTEEN*

Two weeks earlier...

Tegucigalpa Airport was seldom crowded, but the terminal was practically deserted two weeks to the day before Flenn was scheduled to arrive in Honduras. Two white men—one fat with thin, gray-black hair, a mustache and soulless eyes; the other, pencil thin with glasses and thick white hair—walked briskly in front of a stocky brown-skinned man carrying their luggage. Eric Scudder looked around and scoffed, "God, this place is almost as bad as that prison in Korea."

After clearing customs, the trio went outside to find directions to the nearest car dealership. It turned out there weren't many. A beggar, with neither a right hand nor a left, called out to them. A bucket was strapped around the man's neck with a few coins inside. Scudder made a face and walked away. The dark-skinned man set down one of the suitcases and reached into his pocket.

"What's with that guy?" Gerald Rudolph asked Carlos Hernandez, after Carlos had dropped a few dollars into the man's bucket. Rudolph had only met Hernandez a few weeks ago, but it had turned out to be fortuitous. Carlos was from Guatemala, but had lived in D.C. for the past 11 years. Gerald and Carlos had met in

Gerald's favorite bar; the physical relationship had been intense.

Gerald Rudolph, who worked in the CIA's home office at Langley, had done a background check and found that Hernandez had a record of smuggling drugs and people across the border. Ordinarily, he would have ended the relationship right there, but it had occurred to him that a man with such skills might prove useful to his boss for an upcoming mission in Honduras. *This mission.*

Carlos glanced back at the man with the bucket. "Him? He is sent to the airport," Carlos said. "Someone cut off his hands, and now brings him here to beg for money. I've seen it before."

Gerald's jaw dropped. "You're kidding, right?"

Carlos shrugged. "Some of the local crime lords cut off the hands of weak men, usually dope-heads or alcoholics, then send them to the airport to try and get the sympathy of foreigners. They take the money back to their bosses and are paid just enough to keep them in drugs and cheap booze."

"My kind of people!" Scudder said. "Carlos, go back and give that sap a hundred bucks and arrange a meeting with his boss, but only if his boss speaks English. Jerry," he said to Gerald, "go find us a taxi so we can go buy a set of wheels." Scudder rubbed his hands together gleefully. "I feel like something big! Red, I think."

The beggar was reluctant at first to give Carlos any information—until he saw the $100 bill. The local currency was lempira, but everyone here coveted American money. Carlos caught up with his companions.

"He won't give me any names, just that he works for two brothers, both of whom speak English."

Scudder smiled. "Arrange a meeting. Tell no-hands over there to have his bosses come to the Sheraton tomorrow morning at eight o'clock sharp. Oh, and give him *your* name, not mine."

Less than two hours after leaving the airport, the trio drove off a nearby car lot in a brand-new Nissan Titan— fire engine red. Scudder had been like a kid in a candy store. Gerald figured 20 years in prison, and an expense account provided by none other than Uncle Sam, could have that effect on a person.

Scudder took a left out of the lot and drove toward the tallest building he could see on the horizon. "Now gents, let's take a look around this god-forsaken town before we go find our hotel."

They drove for over an hour as Scudder made non-stop derogatory remarks about the city and its inhabitants. "Okay, I've seen enough of this slum," he said at last. "Carlos, where can we get ourselves some guns down here? Jerry tells me you can arrange all that, which is why I let you come along." In truth it had been Rudolph's boss, Jeremy Schmitt, who'd approved that.

"Already have it worked out, boss," Carlos answered. "I called some people I know before we left the States. They're supposed to be delivered tomorrow at noon. Of course, you can find guns just about anywhere down here. Reliability's the thing you have to worry about."

Scudder frowned. "I presume we won't have to worry about the reliability of the ones coming tomorrow?"

Carlos shook his head. "Brand new. Three .45's, and two fully automatic assault rifles, just like Gerald said you wanted."

"Good," Scudder said, his mood brightening. "I think I'd like a few knives too." He pointed to a man in a dirty white tee shirt walking down the busy street. "That fellow over there sure has a long one."

Carlos looked out the window. "That's a machete, boss."

Scudder pushed his glasses further up on his nose. "I'm not an idiot, Hernandez. I may have spent the past two decades in a Korean prison, but I still know a machete when I see one!"

"Sorry, boss."

Scudder glared at him. "Never mind. I just don't like people talking down to me. Got it?"

"Won't happen again, boss."

"Good, now about those knives? I don't like the idea of being unarmed at breakfast with a couple of spicks who cut off people's hands for a living."

Carlos ignored the insult. "Believe it or not, Ace Hardware has a few stores down here. They should have what you want."

Scudder pulled into a gas station, sent Gerald to fill up the tank, and then told Carlos, "Go inside and get a case of the local beer—something good—then ask them where the closest Ace Hardware is."

Scudder took a deep breath and smiled. Sitting alone in a beautiful new truck, ordering people around, buying weapons, drinking beer—*God, life was good!*

CHAPTER *SEVENTEEN*

Two weeks earlier...

Scudder sat perched on a wrought iron chair in the hotel's garden café gorging himself on two different kinds of sausage, an order of bacon, a slice of ham, three eggs, and a stack of pancakes with maple syrup. Knowing that Scott Flenn would arrive in Honduras in less than two weeks had given him quite an appetite.

It had been like a gift from the gods, Scudder thought, and not for the first time. *Flenn had stupidly posted detailed plans of his upcoming trip on Saint Ann's website a month ago. Jerry Rudolph had convinced Schmitt to give the go-ahead, and now he was about to fulfill his ultimate fantasy of blowing Scott Flenn into a million tiny bits!*

Rudolph sat across the table nibbling on a plate of cheese. Carlos was three tables away eyeing two locals who'd just entered the portico. Dressed in torn blue jeans, sunglasses, and worn tee shirts, the men were trying to convince the maître d' that they had been invited here. Carlos signaled the maître d', gave him a twenty, and asked for the men to be seated at his table. Carlos offered breakfast, but both men just ordered beer.

Even though they were out of earshot, Scudder knew what the three men were discussing. The 'hand-choppers,' as he had dubbed them, would want to know what kind of job they were being asked to do and for how much. Scudder hoped the two skinny thugs were tougher than they looked, just in case things turned sour. He might not need the extra muscle, but he'd waited a long time for this and wanted to be prepared for anything... *just so long as they understood who was boss.*

Scudder could smell loyalty a mile away. Jeremy Schmitt had taught him that years ago. He looked across the table at Rudolph. Jerry was loyal, of that he had no doubt; but, not to him, to Schmitt. Scudder knew Schmitt had sent the skinny clerk here to keep tabs on him. He didn't mind, just so long as Jerry helped him secure the drone next week.

Scudder stuffed a sausage in his mouth. The plan had come to him almost immediately after discovering Flenn's plans to travel to Honduras. *A drone strike would be so much more fun than merely lobbing a hand grenade, which was what he'd fantasized about in his cell all those years in Korea. Plus, here in Honduras, there would be little risk. Nobody cared what happened down here.*

It had taken some time to persuade Rudolph, but in the end, Scudder had insisted that taking Flenn out in Honduras was the only way he'd do what Schmitt wanted him to do in Mexico next month. Scudder knew he had the upper hand. Schmitt had gone to a great deal of trouble to convince the Koreans to release him. He obviously didn't want to risk bringing in anyone else; but then, who else was there? Nobody, except for Jerry Rudolph. Scudder didn't particularly like Rudolph. It wasn't the fact that Jerry was gay, Scudder couldn't care less; it was that he never liked pencil-pushers coming along on an assignment. They did nothing but get in the way. Still, so long as Jerry kept paying the bills, Scudder would put up with the man.

On the positive side, Jerry *had* managed to find Carlos, who'd already proven useful. Scudder was beginning to think that Carlos might even come in handy when they went to Mexico. *It would be in Mexico that he'd complete the assignment that had won him his freedom and get Schmitt those damn incense bowls.*

Scudder watched Carlos as he proposed the deal to the hand choppers. *Carlos certainly seemed loyal, and he had happened along at just the right time. Jerry probably meets lots of men in bars,* Scudder told himself, *but this guy speaks Spanish, blends in well with the locals, and has a history of certain business dealings which will make him the perfect accomplice for Mexico.*

Several minutes passed before Scudder got up and strolled over to Carlos and the hand choppers. "Either of these greasers speak English?" he asked Carlos.

"We both speak English," said the bigger of the two as he stood to face the stranger. "And just who the hell are you?"

Scudder pushed his glasses further up on his nose. *They would have to learn to be more respectful.* "Who am I? I'm the man who is going to make all your dreams come true. So sit down and shut up!"

Carlos nodded and the man sat back down.

"I'll pay you each five hundred a day in American

money. Only one thing... and this is very important, so listen carefully." Scudder leaned in and glared at the men over the top of his glasses. "I'll kill you both if either one of you double-cross me. Do what I say, and don't get greedy and you'll make a fortune, plus a bonus at the end when this is all done."

The men looked at each other, then back at Scudder. "How long will you need us?"

Scudder stood back up and grinned. "Two weeks, maybe more," Scudder said. Their eyes grew large as they did the math. "I'll start you off with a thousand each. I just need to know that you'll do whatever I say, no matter what."

The smaller man looked at the other, then said, "My brother and I will kill whoever it is you want killed as long as the money keeps coming."

Scudder glanced at Rudolph, who'd just joined them. "Who said anything about killing?"

The bigger of the two men smirked. "No one pays that much money unless someone is going to die."

You have no idea, thought Scudder.

He pointed at Rudolph. "This is Jerry. He's my banker. He'll pay your advance when you come back here day after tomorrow."

"My name is Gustavo," said the larger man, offering his hand, "and this is my brother, Emmanuel."

Scudder ignored the offer of a handshake. "I'll never remember that." He looked at the man. "You're Frick, and," he said to the other, "you're Frack." They exchanged glances and shrugged. Scudder glanced down at their choice for breakfast. "I don't care about an occasional beer, but no drugs, or I'll do the same thing to you as I would if you double-cross me. Gotta' problem with that?"

"No, señor," they said in unison.

"Good. I assume you have your own transportation?"

"Sí," Frack said. We have a Jeep."

Scudder nodded. "That'll do. You'll need to bring it; I don't expect to play chauffeur while I'm down here." He scratched his head. "I don't suppose either of you know anyone in San Pedro Whatchamacallit?"

"San Pedro Sula?" Frick answered. "That's a long way from here."

Frack looked at his brother. "What about Juan?"

Scudder cocked his head. "Who's Juan?"

"We have a distant cousin who heads up a small gang there," Frick said.

"Perfect. Contact him and bring him when you come back. I want to talk with him. I guess it's too much to expect that he speaks English."

"Juan speaks some English, señor," Frick said glancing at his brother, "but he isn't very, how you say... intelligent."

Scudder studied the brothers. "Yeah, there's a lot of that going on down here. Just bring your cousin to me. Tell him I'll make it worth his while." Scudder hadn't felt this excited since he was a frat boy looking forward to spring break. "By the way, do you have any beaches down here with cliffs overlooking the water?"

"Sí, señor," the larger man said. "There are several of them."

"Good, good!" Scudder looked at Frick. "We've got a few things to prepare. Pick out one of the less crowded beaches and bring directions after you come back. Now, get out of here. Bring decent clothes and shoes if you've got any, but don't come armed. You'll only use what I give you, understand?"

The brothers nodded, then got up to leave.

"Oh, and one other thing," Scudder said. "I've seen your work... leave the machetes at home."

CHAPTER *EIGHTEEN*

Zack and Flenn had come across the stream by accident late in the afternoon. Zack had heard what he thought was running water off in the distance; they'd followed the sound until they came across a tiny cascade heading down the mountain. They filled their water bottles, placing a purification tablet in each.

The stream widened a few hundred yards away, veered slightly to the right then cut a wide path down the mountain. According to Zack's GPS, it appeared to run into a small neighborhood on the outskirts of San Pedro Sula. All they had to do now was follow it down the rest of the way. That, and talk about Flenn's plan for revenge.

"You know, Flenn, there's nothing stopping Scudder from returning that drone to the base earlier than expected."

"Yes, there is." Flenn swallowed three aspirins and chased them with water from one of the bottles they'd refilled from the stream.

Zack raised an eyebrow. "And that would be... ?"

"His ego, for one thing. and the fact that he's been locked up for twenty years. He'll want to play with his new toy as long he can. It wouldn't surprise me if he's scoping out some bank somewhere."

"I thought he preferred art?"

Flenn shook his head. "He prefers money. That's why he was stealing those treasures from the Koreans. I doubt he knows anything about art. I'm sure he was simply planning to sell those incense bowls to someone."

"Until you turned him in?"

Flenn pointed to the GPS. "If *your* toy is correct, looks like we can be back in the city early tomorrow—that is, if we keep moving." He stooped to pick up a fallen branch to use as a fresh walking stick, trying not to grimace from the pain.

"How's the shoulder?" Zack brushed aside a lizard that was examining his backpack. The reptile turned and hissed, then did a lizard-stomp of indignation into the underbrush.

"I'm fine. Can we go?"

"Maybe we ought to rest a bit longer," Zack offered.

"Quit treating me like a baby."

"Well, Flenn, I mean you aren't out in the field anymore. I doubt the life of an Episcopal priest is all that demanding."

Flenn shot him a look. "You haven't met some of my parishioners."

"I mean physically demanding."

"Oh, yeah? I run five miles every day, work out three times a week and watch my diet. I could still take you!"

"Sure, sure, blindfolded, with a wounded shoulder, and the other hand tied behind your back, right?" Zack winked and tossed the water bottles into his backpack. Zack was dubious; he wanted to give the pills plenty of time to work their magic. The last thing he needed was to end up with Montezuma's revenge.

They followed the stream downhill. Instead of meandering as most mountain tributaries do, this one traveled pretty much in a straight line. They walked until dusk, ate a couple of mangos they found along the way, and then drifted off to sleep. Once again, Flenn was tormented by nightmares of the village children, all looking up at him with questioning eyes. *Why did you bring this to us?*

Flenn awoke with a start. Something had bitten him.

The light from a full moon filled the forest. He reached for Zack's backpack and the bug spray. Zack was awake, staring at something off in the distance. "What's out there?" Flenn whispered.

Zack pointed about 50 yards off to where the stream descended into a small waterfall. The trees broke just above the cascade allowing them to see a large patch of the night sky. Right in the middle was the full moon, shining as brightly as Flenn had ever seen. "Look," whispered Zack.

Three jaguars, silhouetted by moonlight, were drinking from the stream. An anteater walked up beside them and it too began to drink. On the opposite bank, what appeared to be two white-tailed deer came out of the forest. *Like something from a C.S. Lewis tale,* Flenn thought as he and Zack sat motionless, mesmerized at the tranquil scene before them. Zack whispered, "Why don't they attack the deer or the anteater?"

"Must not be hungry," Flenn whispered back. "They only kill for food or to protect themselves. Man is the only creature that kills for sport—or out of anger," he added.

"I'm not so sure about that. Donna had a cat who would torment its prey, but never eat it."

"Housecats are the exception." Flenn thought of his own four at home. He'd found a mother cat and her kittens right before Christmas, but had never found homes for them, not that he had tried all that hard. His secretary, Iriana Racks, was taking care of them while he was away.

They watched until each animal finished drinking and disappeared into the forest. "You know," teased Flenn, stretching back on the ground. "Those jaguars will probably get hungry later, and they do like to hunt at night."

Zack peered into the forest, but he didn't see anything moving their way. "Good thing they don't know we're here."

"Oh, they know," said Flenn. "They've known all along. They have a great sense of smell."

"Oh, great! Maybe one of us should stay awake?"

Flenn closed his eyes. "Not a bad idea. Night."

CHAPTER *NINETEEN*

Two weeks earlier...

The morning humidity was rising as Carlos sipped a cappuccino in the garden café. Gerald Rudolph sat next to him, finishing off the last bites of a vegetable omelet. Rudolph wiped the corners of his mouth before reaching into his back pocket for his wallet. "So, how much do we owe you for last night?"

"They were expensive," Carlos said as he finished buttering his toast. He was referring to the two prostitutes Gerald had asked him to find for Scudder last night. Carlos reached for the mango jam. "Very expensive."

During their stay at the luxury hotel, as Scudder made plans for Flenn's arrival to Honduras, Carlos had learned that Gerald—only Scudder called him Jerry—not only controlled the pocketbook but was also there to keep Scudder from going off the deep end. For someone who worked for the CIA, Gerald wasn't all that good at keeping secrets.

Gerald had promised Carlos 50-grand just so long as Carlos did what he was told. Fifteen thousand of that had been paid in advance. Plus, Gerald had made overtures for a renewed relationship once all this was over. Carlos told Gerald how much the girls had cost, but Gerald only shrugged. "Well, the man *has* spent 20 years in prison."

It was already mid-morning and neither one had seen Scudder emerge from of his room. "Suppose we ought to go check on him?" Carlos asked.

Gerald snickered. "Not unless you want to get shot." The guns had arrived yesterday. Six Heckler and Koch pistols—one for each of them—plus a spare. Two Austrian-made Steyr assault rifles, and a gold-plated, two-shot derringer which Scudder had pocketed for himself. The weapons had cost Gerald a small fortune.

"Somebody has deep pockets," Carlos had remarked after the gun dealer had departed.

"Deep enough that they could have you killed for asking too many questions," Gerald whispered as Scudder had stood over the cache, rubbing his hands together like a kid at Christmas.

Carlos signaled the waiter for another cappuccino. "So, what's next?" he asked Gerald.

"Remember what I said about questions? Scudder will tell you what to do next; just wait for instructions."

Gerald reached for the sugar, intentionally brushing his hand against Carlo's. Nothing physical had transpired between the two since they'd arrived. *Too bad,* thought Gerald, hoping that Schmitt would allow Scudder to keep Carlos around when the inevitable order came to liquidate witnesses. Carlos was attractive, in an exotic, dangerous sort of way. The nights they'd spent together when they'd first met had been electric; however, if things got crazy toward the end of all this, Gerald was

ready to make the sacrifice, just so long as it was Scudder
who pulled the trigger and not him.

Carlos pointed toward the café entrance. "Here he
comes now." Both men scooted over so the big man could
sit down at the tiny table. Gerald couldn't resist asking.
"Sleep well?"

Scudder rubbed his forehead, obviously hung over.
"God no! But, I did everything else well." The way he
smirked sent a shiver down Carlos' spine. Eric Scudder
looked like one of the slobs he'd seen coming out of strip
joints in the middle of the day. The boss was, what a
friend of his called, "smarmy." *Put a cowboy hat on the man
and set him up on a large covered wagon and Scudder could
have sold snake oil to the Indians.* Of course, Carlos kept that
thought to himself. He was here for one reason only.

"Money?" Scudder looked across the table at Gerald.
"Did you get the extra cash?"

"We went to the bank before breakfast," Gerald
answered. "I got what you asked for, plus a bit more for
extras like last night. I just reimbursed Carlos here for
those two girls."

Scudder rubbed his head. "No more talk about last
night," he said as the waiter approached the table. "There
aren't going to be any repeats of that on this tour." He
ordered a Bloody Mary and fried eggs. "Last night was
just for old time's sake." He glanced up at Rudolph.
"What about your contact at Soto Cano? Will everything
be ready for us at the airbase?"

Gerald reassured him, "Our friend back home says it
will be, but…"

Scudder shook his head. "Damn, there's always a *but*."

"We can only have it for seven days. That was the most he was able to negotiate. From what he told me, it wasn't easy."

"Nothing worthwhile ever is. Just so long as we have the drone when our friend arrives. Make whatever arrangements you need to, I don't want any screwups. This absolutely must happen on the third of March!" Scudder peered at Carlos through bloodshot eyes. "Have you made any headway in finding us a place to stay?"

Carlos nodded. "I've got it narrowed down to two houses. I'm heading off with a man in about an hour to check them out. Should be back by midafternoon."

Scudder nodded approvingly. "Jerry, that leaves you to fill in Frick and Frack. Make sure they know never to question me on anything, and that they understand the chain of command. They are to come to one of you guys first. Carlos, if they come to you, then talk to Jerry before approaching me. Understood? I want this to run as close to an official operation as possible."

Gerald knew what Scudder actually wanted was for everyone to understand that he was in charge of everything from this point onward. *The man had a score to settle, and he wanted no dissension in the ranks.*

"Oh, and make sure they only have a weapon when I say so, and never simultaneously." The waiter set Scudder's drink in front of him. "I don't want them getting any fancy ideas." Gerald and Carlos both nodded. Carlos was glad Gerald had allowed him to keep one of the .45s. It would likely come in useful soon enough.

Scudder downed the Bloody Mary, then ordered another. "You both clear on the day's assignments?" They nodded. "Good. After breakfast, I'm going back to bed... this time to sleep."

****

Real estate agents in Honduras are few and only used by the wealthy. Carlos had spent the previous afternoon with one eager to make a sale. The man was visibly disappointed when Carlos explained that his associates only wanted to rent; however, the agent brightened when informed that there would be an additional $5,000 in it for him, just as long as he kept the deal confidential.

Carlos had accompanied the man today to view two more haciendas. The first was a virtual palace, just outside of the city. Tall granite walls crisscrossed with razor wire made the place seem more like a fortress than a home. Inside, however, polished white marble floors gave way to creamy silk carpeting as the foyer branched off into a magnificent ballroom. No doubt Scudder would love this place, but there were way too many other houses nearby—too conspicuous. And that was the one thing Scudder had said he did *not* want.

The second house was 30 miles outside of the city, on a 40-acre plot of land, which had once been used to raise thoroughbreds. The agent explained that the owner seldom used the place anymore, though they kept it maintained for occasional family gatherings.

Carlos and the agent turned off a two-lane highway onto a paved drive, where a small guardhouse and a gate were affixed between two long sections of fencing. The fence needed repair, if not replacement. An old man wearing a holstered revolver stopped them at the gate. The agent pressed a few lempiras into the guard's hands and explained that they were there with the family's consent. The man nodded and waved them through. They drove up a small hill, topped by a two-story brick house, two outbuildings, a garage, and what looked like stables. The last of the horses had been sold years ago, the agent explained.

The grounds immediately around the house were trim and neat, while the outlying pastures were overgrown from years of neglect. This house was more modest than the first, but it was isolated. Nothing around for miles. Inside, the décor was simple, but comfortable: plush sofas, leather chairs, a baby grand piano, five bedrooms, and a well-stocked kitchen with a door leading to the driveway.

"How much?"

"Four-thousand American dollars a week," the agent answered.

Carlos negotiated the price down to half, with an agreement that the agent would stock the refrigerator once a week, plus bring anything else they might need.

"One more thing," Carlos said as the agent dropped him off at the Sheraton, "we won't need your guard. Tell the old man he's got the next few weeks off."

CHAPTER *TWENTY*

Flenn opened his eyes. It was daylight. Zack had fallen asleep without waking him to take a turn at night watch.

Without thinking, Flenn stretched his limbs—a horrible pain shot down his shoulder and across his back. He gingerly peeled back the bandage; the wound was red and angry-looking—signs, he knew, of an infection. He needed a stronger antibiotic. His experience with Honduran medicine and those who dispense it had been limited. The villagers had told him last year that their local hospital was basically a place people went to die. He understood. Doctors cost money, something the people of San Jose de la Montaña didn't have. Their only experience with a hospital or a clinic had probably been in extreme situations where a loved one was already too far gone to be saved. Undoubtedly, somewhere in Honduras there were better hospitals for the wealthy. Although he bristled at the injustice of it, he knew he might need to find just such a place, and soon.

"What's that smell?"

Flenn looked to see what his friend was complaining about, then began to laugh. Inches from Zack's head was a large pile of dung. "Look to your right."

Unfortunately, instead of sitting up to look, Zack turned over and managed to roll right into it. "Oh, Jesus

H. ... " Zack stopped himself. "Damn it!" He tried slinging the stuff off, but it was too sticky. Flenn laughed even harder. The more Zack thrashed about, the funnier it got.

"I'm glad I'm such a source of entertainment!" Zack sniped, as he used a giant banana leaf to try and wipe off the goo. A second later he screamed like a little girl as a tarantula jumped out of the banana tree and scurried away.

Flenn rolled over, holding his sides. He laughed so hard that tears poured from his eyes. He always hated when he did that. Flenn never let himself cry in front of anyone; never had, not even when his parents had died.

Zack made his way to the stream and washed off. "You realize what must have happened, don't you?"

"What... " Flenn could hardly speak for laughing. It felt good; cleansing in a way. He took a breath. "What... what happened?"

"One of those blasted panthers came up last night and took a giant dump right by my head!"

"Jaguars," Flenn corrected, "and yeah, that's exactly what must have happened."

Zack stared incredulously at his friend until he too started to laugh. Finally, he stood up, dripping wet, and said, "We need to get moving. I'm getting tired of mangos for every meal."

Flenn pointed to the banana tree. "Well, you could always have a banana."

"I'm not ever going near a banana again! Those things can kill you!"

Flenn and Zack had nursed one another through a lot: war zones, gun runners, terrorists, Zack's ex-wife...; they'd been each other's closest ally and confidant through thick and thin, and had learned to treat almost everything with humor. Even now, years after he had left the CIA, Flenn had to admit that it felt good to be with his old friend. Once again, Zack Matteson had saved his life; and, once again, Flenn felt the subtle seduction of the old ways. Flenn picked up the backpack as Zack slipped his shoes on. "I'm ready if you are, Tarzan," he said.

Zack was glad to be on his way. *Once they got out of the forest, they'd check into a nice hotel, have a proper bath, get a good night's sleep, and then check in with Sarah. After that, they'd start looking for Scudder. Flenn had probably meant it when he said he was going to kill Scudder; but Sarah hadn't authorized that... at least, not yet.*

From what Zack had heard about the man, Eric Scudder wasn't stupid. If he was running some sort of a secret mission for Jeremy Schmitt, he wasn't going to put all his cards on the table. Which meant that, even with an informant hiding among Scudder's people, neither capturing nor killing Scudder would be a simple matter.

Sarah hadn't told Zack why Schmitt wanted Scudder, just that there was some sort of quid-pro-quo thing in the works. *Schmitt must have wanted Scudder awfully bad to convince the South Koreans to let him go. Scudder was a murderer and a thief. What could Schmitt be after? Was it something the CIA needed, or was it more personal than that?*

Zack guessed the latter.

CHAPTER *TWENTY-ONE*

Three days before Scott Flenn was scheduled to arrive in Honduras, Scudder and Gerald stepped onto the air base at Soto Cano and were met by two Honduran captains, neither of whose names Scudder bothered to remember. The captains took them past several barracks to a small building near an enormous hanger. The CIA and the Pentagon had both pumped billions into the Honduran military since the Reagan years, bolstering relations and maintaining close ties.

The two men were escorted inside a spacious, though spartan, office, where the captains saluted a major who was waiting for them. The major shook hands with the visitors, then took them to an adjacent office where they were then met by a colonel, who offered them coffee and sweet rolls. "The general will be with you shortly," the colonel said, dismissing himself from his own office. Gerald sipped the coffee, while Scudder finished off the plate of pastries. General Rauel Rodriguez showed up five minutes later, dressed in full uniform and accompanied by the same two captains who'd met them earlier. He dismissed the captains, and then, in perfect English, addressed the two Americans. "I am sorry to keep you waiting, gentlemen; as you might imagine, I stay fairly busy around here."

They shook hands and made a modicum of small talk. When Scudder complimented the man on his English (at least, Scudder had *thought* it was a compliment), Rodriguez told them he'd studied at the University of West Texas. After joining the Honduran military, he had been selected to study for two years in a special international program at the U.S. Air Force Academy in Colorado. From there, he'd spent nine months at the War College in Montgomery, Alabama, before returning to Honduras, where he'd overseen operations at Soto Cano Air Base for the past seven years.

Scudder began drumming his finger against the armrest, uninterested. "So, I understand you have a drone ready for us?"

The general nodded, "Yes, but may I offer you more coffee first?" He glanced down at the empty platter. "Perhaps more to eat?"

"No, thank you," said Gerald. "Perhaps you can take us to see the drone and its support vehicle?"

"Please," said the general, looking from one to the other. "I mean no offense, but are you sure you two can handle her? We usually use a team of five specially trained technicians." General Rodriguez had questioned the wisdom of lending what he had come to consider to be *his* drone; but in the end, he hadn't been given much of a choice. Jeremy Schmitt had reminded him that it was still U.S. property, and only on loan to Soto Cano.

"How many missiles can you give us?" Scudder asked.

The general was surprised by the fat man's brusqueness. He smoothed the medals over his left breast, feeling as if somehow they'd all just become askew. "As agreed, there will be one drone and four missiles. I take it one of you knows how to operate the drone's command vehicle?"

To the general's great relief, it was the skinny man who spoke next. "I've been well trained," Gerald said. And he had; Schmitt had seen to it.

"Yep, and he's going to teach me everything he knows, aren't you, Jerry?"

Gerald didn't answer. "I assure you, General Rodriguez, we will take very good care of it, and will return it to you undamaged."

The general stood up. He couldn't put his finger on it, but there was something about this that didn't feel right. Still, a deal was a deal, and there might be further appropriations from the United States in exchange for his cooperation. "No sense delaying further then, gentlemen, let me take you to the vehicle."

They walked outside a different door from the one they'd entered to where a camouflaged Humvee awaited. When a short, thin lieutenant opened the back of the vehicle, Scudder saw that the interior walls of the truck were lined with computers, SAT/NAV screens, and loads of equipment he'd never seen before.

Drones were relatively new when Scudder had been imprisoned, but his Korean guards had allowed him to read American magazines over the years. He'd been especially impressed to read news reports about the use of drones in the Middle East. He often imagined himself sitting in some control room, watching his unsuspecting prey from above.

Scudder climbed into the back of the Humvee. Two swivel chairs were bolted to the floor. "Most of this you won't need," the lieutenant explained. "It is for very advanced operations with much heavier missiles than the ones you will be carrying. You will have newer and smaller versions of the forty-five-pound ones your people use in Pakistan. But, believe me, these little ones pack quite a punch."

Gerald listened as the lieutenant gave an hour-long rundown on the equipment. He knew most of this already but did not want to insult his host. Scudder paid close attention, especially when the man turned on an active radar screen showing that the drone was currently flying overhead.

"How long can it stay up before refueling?"

"The larger ones, fully armed, can fly for 26 hours. The newer, lighter ones, like this one, can stay up for 72, armed with two missiles. When it is low on fuel, the onboard computer will direct it back here. Once refueled, it will automatically return to its last position.

Scudder stuck his head out of the vehicle and looked up into the sky. "I can't see it."

The lieutenant smiled. "No, but it can see you." He pushed a button and instantly offered them a bird's eye view of all the buildings on the base. He entered a command and an altimeter appeared at the top of the screen showing the drone circling at 22,000 feet. Scudder was impressed by how clear the picture was. He easily picked up on how to zoom in and out with a simple mouse-like device.

"The picture is amazing, he said, "especially at that altitude. And it can handle the weight of both missiles that high up?"

"No problem, señor. As I said, these are the lighter ones. They are not as powerful as the big ones used by your military, but the damage will be tremendous, so make certain you are careful. They cannot be fired simultaneously, but they can be fired in quick succession."

"How do we arm the missiles?" Scudder asked. This time it was Gerald who explained the process.

The lieutenant was impressed. "You have handled drones before, señor, no?" Gerald nodded, but didn't elaborate. When he was finished explaining the process the lieutenant handed Gerald the key, shook hands with both men, and walked away. He had no idea how they were planning to use the drone; and it wasn't his place to ask.

CHAPTER *TWENTY-TWO*

Flenn and Zack made it down the rest of the mountain faster than they anticipated. The stench of an open sewer told them they were near the city before they saw any sign of life.

The first shanty they spotted was no more than a few pieces of rope strung between three trees holding up a rectangle of rusted tin. The sound of children playing nearby was like a dagger twisting inside of Flenn's heart. Zack took the lead, avoiding eye contact with residents surprised at seeing two gringos emerge from the jungle. Some of the younger children began to fall in behind them as they made their way past open firepits in front of what passed for houses—sticks with bits of plastic and tin. One curious little girl ran in front of Flenn. Pointing to his shoulder, she asked, "Estas bien?"

"Estoy bien," he answered, lowering his eyes. She reminded him of one of the girls from the village. *She might have been one of those children had her family lived a few miles up the mountain!*

Zack intuited what Flenn was thinking and quickened the pace. The children fell behind, before turning and scurrying off.

Flenn and Zack crossed a road—red and yellow bricks laid in purposeful patterns that led off to both the left and right. Bricks and labor were inexpensive here. Streets that would have been the envy of millionaires'-row back home were lined on either side with nothing but shacks and shanties here. A roadside stand was selling bottled water, juice and meat pastries. Flenn and Zack stood silently and ate and drank their fill. A squat, dark-skinned man standing next to a dilapidated pickup truck called out to them. "Taxi? Taxi?"

Zack looked over at Flenn, who nodded. They crossed over to the man in the truck. "Habla Inglés?" Flenn asked.

"A little," the man answered.

"Can you take us to a hotel?"

"Sí, señor, which hotel?"

Flenn answered. "El Marcositas."

The man looked dubious, wondering if he had heard correctly. "Marcositas? You stay there before, señor?"

Flenn simply repeated the request... "El Marcositas." The driver shrugged, then turned around and climbed into the truck.

"So, *have you* stayed there before?" asked Zack.

"No, but I've seen it passing by," said Flenn. "It's a dump. I figure Scudder might be watching the better hotels, if he's not convinced I'm dead."

Zack nodded. "You're thinking like you used to do back in the day."

Flenn knew Zack meant it as a compliment, though it was anything but. "I know," was all he said.

CHAPTER *TWENTY-THREE*

The day of the drone strike...

Scudder was up before dawn. He'd prepared a pot of strong coffee and raided the fridge of two pounds of bacon and three-dozen eggs. He hadn't cooked breakfast in more than 20 years, and of all the smells he had missed in that God-forsaken hole Scott Flenn had left him in, the smell of bacon was the one he'd missed the most. He looked out the kitchen window at the Humvee, which they'd parked outside the door. The drone had allowed Scudder to follow Scott Flenn's every move ever since he had landed in Honduras.

Gerald came down first, and poured himself some coffee. "So, today is the big day."

"Christmas morning!" Scudder exclaimed with glee.

Gerald sighed. "I talked to Schmitt last night. He wanted me to remind you that you don't have to do this, the mission is not contingent on it."

"*His* mission may not be! *My* mission is different. If he wants me to steal those damned incense burners next month, then this is my price." Scudder began to look around the kitchen for something. "Salt, do you see the salt?"

Gerald picked up a shaker from the table and handed

it to him. "Seriously Eric, we could just hang out here for a few more weeks, then head up to Mexico."

Scudder poured a liberal helping of salt onto the frying bacon. "You and Schmitt have been trying to talk me out of this since I came onboard, but it is like I told him, 'If you want the treasures of King Muryeong, you're going to have to offer me something I want just as much... *my own treasure*. By the way, your boss was the one who came up with the name, *Clean Slate*. I wanted to call it *Pop a Priest*. I guess it wasn't in keeping with CIA protocols."

"None of this has been sanctioned by the agency," Gerald reminded him.

"No," Scudder said, looking up from the frying pan, "but it sure feels like old times." The meat sizzled in the pan, the aroma spreading through the rest of the house. "Have you figured out how to dispose of the Bobbsey twins upstairs when this is all done?"

Gerald poured himself a cup of coffee. "Like I said before, let me take care of it. You still haven't told us how you're going to handle Mexico. All you've given us is a rough sketch; Schmitt wants details."

Scudder turned off the stove. "First things first. Sit down, have some breakfast. Let's just enjoy the morning. Tomorrow, I'll give you details. As for Frick and Frack, I don't think we'll need them after we leave here."

Gerald took a sip of the coffee. "What about Carlos?" he asked, trying to sound detached.

Scudder thought for a moment as he picked up a piece of bacon, dripping with grease. "I may have changed my mind. I've gotten to where I like him. Who knows, he may be of some use in Mexico. Still, I don't like loose ends, and I know your boss certainly doesn't." He popped the bacon into his mouth as Carlos walked into the kitchen. "Ask me again when this is over."

CHAPTER *TWENTY-FOUR*

The night of the drone strike…

"I'm telling you, nobody beats Clapton!" Scudder banged his beer on the poker table for emphasis. Tonight was a night for celebration. At long last, Scott Flenn was dead. He had watched it on the Humvee's screen earlier today when he had fired two missiles into the village.

"No offense, boss," said the man Scudder had renamed *Frick*, "Clapton is good, but Jimi Hendrix was the best guitarist ever."

"Yeah, yeah," Gerald said, staring at his cards. "My money is on Steve Howe of Yes. That guy has got to be in his 70's, but he's amazing. He can still outplay just about anyone."

Carlos took a long drag from his cigar. "You guys ever heard of Steve Morse? Played for the Dixie Dregs before he started touring with Deep Purple." Carlos looked across the table at Gerald. "Even Steve Howe said Morse was amazing."

"Not better than Hendrix," Frick said, looking down at his cards, "only an idiot would say Hendrix wasn't the best guitarist of all time."

Eric Scudder slowly put down his cigar and placed his cards on the table. "You calling me an idiot?"

Frick shook his head. "No, boss, I'm just saying... "

Scudder pulled out his derringer. "You just called me an idiot."

Everything stopped. All eyes were on Frick. "No way, boss! You're one of the smartest men I've ever known! I swear on my mother's life."

Scudder frowned as he pointed the tiny pistol directly at the man's face. "I never met your mother."

Carlos interjected, "Boss, he meant no offense."

Scudder swung the gun toward Carlos. "You challenging me?"

Gerald spoke up: "Eric, put that thing away. We've all had too much to drink tonight."

The pistol now swung toward Gerald. "You know, Jerry, no one is expendable."

Gerald didn't bat an eye, which surprised Scudder; he hadn't thought the skinny pencil-pusher Schmitt had sent to babysit him had that kind of nerve.

"Nobody's questioning you. It's just a friendly card game. But if you pull that trigger, our friend in Washington is not going to be very happy. Trust me, I've seen him when he's angry. It's not a pretty sight."

Scudder stared at each one of them in turn, then suddenly burst out laughing. "Had you all going there for a minute, didn't I?" He set the derringer on the table.

Carlos was the first to laugh. "You sure did, boss!" He looked back at his cards. He had three aces. He placed them face down on the table. "Nothing here but junk. I think I'll go outside for a smoke." He got up and walked through the kitchen door and out into the driveway where he leaned against the Hummer and lit a cigarette. *What a wild few weeks this had been! From tracking Gerald Rudolph to a bar in D.C., to being hired to travel as a translator and bodyguard, and then to what had happened earlier today. Scudder and Gerald had spent half the afternoon in the Humvee. Unlike Frick and Frack, Carlos knew exactly what the vehicle's purpose was. However, he hadn't been instructed to prevent anything, only to keep his former professor informed of Scudder's movements.*

Scudder was drunk; he'd been celebrating ever since mid-afternoon. *If Gerald hadn't reined him in just now, who knows what might have happened. Frick would probably be dead.* Carlos took a breath. *He might be dead soon too, if he wasn't careful.*

Unlike Frick and Frack, Carlos was no fool. He assumed the fat man would eventually come to the conclusion that he was a liability, which was why Carlos kept his .45 with a round in the chamber. He slept lightly at night, and always with his door locked and a chair wedged against it. Not for the first time he wondered if Gerald would intervene should Scudder want him out of the way. *Probably not,* he told himself. *The bond between those two was stronger than any sexual attraction Gerald had for him—lust for power usually is.*

Carlos wasn't sure what was next on Scudder's agenda. Mexico had been mentioned, but neither Scudder nor Gerald had shared any details. Frick and Frack had been hired to serve as cannon fodder in case things got ugly, that much was obvious. Carlos was here because he spoke Spanish and was street-smart, not to mention the attraction Gerald thought was mutual. Gerald had insisted Carlos accompany him to the beach resort town of Rio Corto last week, leaving Frick and Frack to guard the hacienda. Scudder had stayed at the beach for only a few minutes before leaving the two of them and driving off toward the surrounding cliffs. He heard Scudder say something to Gerald about 'working on Plan B', whatever that was.

Carlos had managed to enjoy the day at the beach. Tourists were few, and the sun and the waves had been perfect. It reminded him of his home in Guatemala. Plus, he hadn't had to fend off Gerald the way he thought he might. Rudolph had spent most of the day on his satellite phone, presumably talking to Jeremy Schmitt back in Washington. Carlos knew who Schmitt was. He should— they both worked for the same agency.

Jeremy Schmitt had bought Carlos' cover from the beginning. And, why not—Sarah Coverdale knew better than most how to be thorough. Schmitt would have easily figure out who Carlos was had Sarah not changed his name and built a believable background story around him.

Carlos threw his half-finished cigarette on the ground and looked inside the Hummer. Scudder and Gerald had spent half the afternoon inside the vehicle while he had been ordered to keep watch down by the gate with both Frick and Frack.

He lifted the door handle. Locked.

"Looking for something?"

Carlos jumped. *How can such a big man be so quiet?*

"Just admiring the wheels on this mother, boss. This would make one cool monster truck, if it were a little bigger!"

Scudder looked at him. "What's a monster truck?"

Wow, you have been gone awhile, he thought of saying; instead, he explained to Scudder about monster truck rallies.

"Sounds pretty stupid to me." Scudder shook his head. "I've always said that they call common people *common* for a reason. I don't suppose you have any appreciation for the arts, do you Carlos?"

He did, particularly early 19th-century Latin American art, but Carlos didn't bother telling Scudder. He shrugged. "I guess you might say I'm a pretty ordinary guy."

Scudder put his hand on Carlos' shoulder and laughed. "With some extraordinary talents, according to Gerald! Listen, about what happened in there. I hope I didn't scare you?"

Carlos shook his head. "No problem, boss."

"Good," Scudder went on, "because I want to thank you for coming onboard. Jerry really came through for me when he found you. We may not need the extra muscle on this trip after all, but I've waited too long for a certain dream of mine to come true to let anything go wrong. Better safe than sorry, right? Plus, I'd been wondering how we were going to handle the whole language barrier thing down here. Then you came along––problem solved." He reached into his pocket for the keys. "Tell you what, why don't you let me show you what's in this baby." Scudder unlocked the door and both men climbed inside.

Ever since Sarah Coverdale had directed him to get close to Gerald Rudolph, Carlos had been reporting in whenever he could. He had managed to conceal a satellite phone, but hadn't had the freedom to call Sarah as often as she probably would have preferred.

It had been a stroke of pure luck that Gerald Rudolph had taken to him so quickly back in D.C. Some agents worked for months to infiltrate a group under investigation. It had been much easier with Rudolph... except for Carlos having to pretend that he was gay. *An agent has to do what an agent has to do*, was the mantra of any good spy. Sarah had taught him that.

As Scudder entered a series of commands onto the keyboard, the screen in front of them came to life. The view from 18,000 feet was spectacular, even at night. Carlos could see three highways, and several side roads cutting across rolling hills and the surrounding jungle. Lakes and ponds dotted the landscape, and when Scudder turned a dial they could see the hacienda, as well as the Jeep at the end of the driveway. They could even tell that the Jeep's top was down. Scudder turned the dial some more and the image zoomed in on Frack—sound asleep in the front seat!

Scudder turned red.

"Go down there and tell that slime-ball that if he doesn't want to start begging at the airport with a bucket around his own neck he'd better stay awake!"

"I'm on it," Carlos said as he exited the vehicle and obediently trotted off.

"And tell him I mean it!"

Carlos had no doubt that he did.

CHAPTER *TWENTY-FIVE*

El Marcositas had been named 70 years ago for a famous Honduran drummer nicknamed Little Marcos. He had traveled throughout Central America and the United States playing with all the big bands. Even Gene Krupa was said to have even been a fan. The hotel named in his honor had once been a showpiece—clearly, those days were long past.

Zack stepped over a man passed out in front of the hotel. The smell of mold permeated what passed for a lobby. Orange and white paint was peeling from every wall. A toilet with only a curtain for privacy sat in one corner; in the other, a woman fanned herself with one hand as she played lazily with her long, brown hair with the other. An emaciated old man, with few teeth and even less hair, eyed them suspiciously from across the counter. No doubt the two Americans smelled like the clientele this place was accustomed to, but, even as dirty as they were, it was still obvious that they were gringos, and white men were hardly, if ever, found here. Flenn handed the man a stack of Lempiras, without bothering to ask the price, and requested a room with a shower. The woman approached them but Zack waved her away as they climbed the stairs to their room.

The hotel room smelled old and overused. A can of

Lysol sat atop a pine bureau. Zack reached for it immediately. There was only one bed, which sagged from decades of use. A stained, yellow-and-green recliner sat in the corner with the foot-rest stuck halfway up. A faded picture of a sailboat hung above the headboard.

As Zack opened the bathroom door, a mouse dashed into a corner. Zack was about to stomp on it when Flenn stopped him. "We're in his house, not the other way around. Give him a minute and he'll go away and leave us alone." The mouse looked up at Flenn, then scurried through a hole in the baseboard. Flenn unbuttoned his shirt. "First thing I want, though, is to get clean."

Zack looked around. "That may be hard to do in this place. Besides, what are you going to change into?"

Flenn thought for a moment. "Why don't you go downstairs and see if that woman speaks English. If so, give her a twenty and tell her you want our clothes washed right away and that you'll double the money if she's back here in less than two hours. After we've slept, we can go out and buy some clothes of our own."

Flenn disrobed and made his way toward the bathroom. "Here," he said, handing Zack his black shirt, jeans, socks and underwear, along with two twenty-dollar bills. Zack was too tired to argue; the last few days had taken their toll. He did as Flenn suggested.

The woman did speak English and readily agreed, and Zack placed the clothes outside in the hallway. An hour and a half later she returned with the clean clothes. She entered their room without knocking—the lock hadn't worked in years—and found two naked men sound asleep, one in the bed, the other in the chair. The one on the bed had a large dirty bandage on his shoulder. "You need doctor?" she asked.

Flenn and Zack woke with a start and Flenn quickly covered himself with a pillow. Zack was less modest.

"Doctor?" she repeated, pointing to Flenn's shoulder.

"Yes, he does," answered Zack.

Zack fished in Flenn's wallet and handed the woman two more twenties. "Can you get a doctor to come here?"

"Here?" The woman looked around the room. "Maybe for a hundred."

Flenn jumped into the conversation. There will be fifty for the doctor and fifty for you if you don't tell anyone else we're here."

"Señor, I no tell anyone that *I* am here." She disappeared with the money as the two men got dressed; however, fatigue overcame them and they both fell back asleep minutes after she left. Neither one heard the woman return. She had with her a short, dumpy, bald man with an unshaven face and an unlit cigar hanging from his mouth. Zack woke first.

"This is doctor. I offer fifty, but he say he must have two hundred." She stood behind the pudgy, little man and shook her head as if to say, *don't give it to him.*

"I'll pay you seventy-five," Zack said as Flenn stirred. The doctor starred at the scruffy men and decided not to argue. His English was spotty, so the woman translated as he set about cleaning Flenn's wound. The doctor examined the stitches, before adding a few of his own. With nothing to numb the pain, Flenn clenched his teeth but didn't say a word. Neither the doctor nor the woman asked how Flenn had injured himself, for which he and Zack were silently glad. The doctor wrote down the name of a different antibiotic, saying that it should take care of this type of infection. He then told Zack that the closest pharmacia was a short walk away; the woman said she knew the place.

After she and the doctor left, Zack went to the pharmacy to buy the pills, some bottled water and several packages of cheese crackers. He also managed to find toothbrushes, clean towels, men's underwear, tee shirts and socks. As an afterthought, he picked up a bottle of Jack Daniel's as well.

Flenn was sound asleep when Zack returned. The mouse had come back; Zack tossed it half a cracker. Flenn awoke to eat and drink and take the first dose of the new antibiotic. "How much money have you got left?" Flenn asked.

"Not much," Zack said. "You?"

"About four hundred. I'd go to an ATM but your friend Schmitt's probably monitoring those."

"Don't call that weasel *my* friend." Zack said. "By the way, Sarah called while you were asleep. I asked her to send someone from the embassy with money and a few other things."

"Isn't that risky?"

"Risk used to be your middle name."

"That was a long time ago, Zack. Now I raise cats and preach stewardship sermons."

Zack watched as the mouse went back into its hole.

"Anyway, she agreed with you; said she didn't want to risk it." He glanced at Flenn. "Stewardship sermons, huh?"

"Yep. In fact, why don't you give ten percent of whatever you have left to that woman downstairs when we leave."

"Yeah, right. Ten percent? Don't tell me you give ten percent of your fortune to that little church of yours? I've seen the place. Don't get me wrong, but it certainly doesn't sport a million-dollar shine."

"I don't give any money to Saint Ann's, at least not that they know about. It's part of our deal. They don't pay me a salary, and, in exchange, they do the upkeep themselves and support various outreach ministries. Plus, they put aside some money each month for a new priest one day, should something happen to me." Flenn's voice trailed off. Zack knew Flenn was thinking of the missile attack and the children, so he continued to try and distract him.

"So, you want *me* to give my money, but you don't give *yours*?"

"Not that it's any of your business, but I support a ton of charities. In fact, I was talking with the villagers about building a school on the mountain when... " Flenn looked down at the floor.

"Flenn, you've got to quit torturing yourself. What Scudder did is on him, not you. It wasn't your fault. He is hellbent on killing you and doesn't care who he takes down doing it. I'm not a religious man, you know that, but this is pure evil. I think you know that, too."

Flenn looked up but didn't answer."

"Scudder got locked up for being a thief and a murderer, but frankly, he stayed locked up because he was an embarrassment to the CIA."

Flenn rubbed his shoulder. "Whatever deal Schmitt offered must have softened the blow." Flenn shook his head. "I would have given myself to them if it would have protected those kids."

Zack sighed. "I know you would have, but that choice wasn't on the table. We'll get our turn at Scudder, just as soon as you're able and we know exactly where he is. I just have to figure out how I'm going to get a weapon." Flenn reached for his wallet.

"Here's three-hundred. Go downstairs and ask our new friend to take you to get whatever you need."

"You sure we can trust her?"

"We got anyone else?"

Zack took the cash. "Okay, I'll be back. Get some rest." Zack closed the door behind him, but Flenn couldn't sleep. Instead he lay there thinking about the children, their parents, and mostly about Eric Scudder. As far as Flenn was concerned, Scudder had forfeited his right to live when he'd attacked innocent children. Scudder had crossed the line, and now Flenn was wondering if he would be able to do the same when the time came.

Flenn had killed before, several times, but not since his experience in Edinburgh, something he'd only told a handful of people about: Zack, his bishop, his father. No one else knew the reason for the sudden change years ago. *Who would have believed him anyway?*

If he killed Scudder out of revenge, he'd be trampling on everything he stood for now, everything he believed in. *Yet,"* he told himself, *had not the apostle Peter himself had something to do with the deaths of Ananias and Sapphira—the couple recorded in the Bible, who'd betrayed the disciples and ended up dead?* He remembered his New Testament professor talking about how this strange story from the fifth chapter of Acts seemed completely contrary to the message of Jesus. Flenn's eyes narrowed. He no longer felt that it was a strange story at all, since all he wanted right now was to watch Eric Scudder die.

CHAPTER *TWENTY-SIX*

The day after the drone attack...

Scudder had always enjoyed a good cigar, but this one was especially grand. *Scott Flenn was finally dead. Blown into a million pieces yesterday!*

He sat in a rocking chair on the back deck and blew smoke circles into the late afternoon sky, his hangover from the night before finally gone. Scudder thought back on yesterday and how he and Gerald had watched Flenn playing soccer with all those stupid kids. *Flenn had obviously been fond of the little punks.* Scudder wondered if even for a millisecond it had registered in Flenn's mind what was happening. Scudder sat back and blew smoke into the sky. It had felt good to push that button—twenty years of waiting for his dream to come true. He grinned from ear to ear. *Life is sweet!*

Gerald walked up the steps to the deck. "You been out for a walk?" Scudder asked. The skinny man didn't say anything in return, but sat down in the chair opposite Scudder. "You know, Jerry, life can be wonderful at times."

"It's done," was all Gerald had to say.

"Yup, it is done. And I feel... I feel great! I not only

got that bastard yesterday, but I took out whoever the hell it was that dragged him into the woods."

"Zack Matteson."

"Who?"

"Flenn's partner years ago. I just got word. It had to be him."

Scudder leaned forward, no longer looking as pleased with himself as he had been. "What was this Matteson guy doing there?"

"That's what's troubling Schmitt. He's not happy about this. Matteson and Flenn were friends. Could be he was just coming to help Flenn out at the village and was just horsing around. Let's hope so."

Scudder reclined back into his chair. "Well, doesn't matter anymore. They're both history!" He blew another smoke circle.

Gerald shook his head. "Schmitt is on edge about Mexico now, and I can't say as I blame him."

"Mexico is not for two more weeks. Nobody can possibly know about that. There's no way this Matteson character knew about the drone. Like you said, he was probably just down here with Flenn. All we gotta do is sit tight for the next couple of weeks."

"And our guests?" Gerald asked.

"I still haven't decided about Carlos. We may need to take him with us as an interpreter. As for the other two morons, well, we will be doing the world a favor."

"Schmitt hasn't authorized that yet!"

"Schmitt, Schmitt! Where the hell is he? In Washington, that's where. I run the show down here!" Scudder puffed the cigar as he leaned back into the chair. "I'll let you know, but I wasn't thinking of doing it until right before we leave for Mexico," Scudder said.

"Eric, there may not be a Mexico! Schmitt is afraid that… "

Scudder cut him off. "Schmitt again! There's no reason to be afraid of anything anymore. You know what, Jerry? Fear is the worst enemy of all. Tell your boss not to worry. I've got this. Schmitt told me himself that no one could possibly connect him with me, or figure out how he got me out of prison. The only person who knows any of that is you." Scudder smiled as he thought about his plans for Schmitt. Scott Flenn hadn't been the only one he had fantasized about during his time in prison. *Schmitt had left him there for 20 years—he was definitely going to pay for that, and soon.*

Scudder lifted his cigar. "Nope. Not going to worry about anything today. Scott Flenn is dead, and nothing is going to steal my happiness, not today." He looked Gerald straight in the eye. "Nothing."

CHAPTER *TWENTY-SEVEN*

It didn't take Zack long to find a weapon. He had told the woman from the lobby that he needed to buy a pistol. Without so much as raising an eyebrow, she simply instructed him to follow her.

The two of them walked from El Marcositas around the corner to a storefront a few blocks away. A young man, more like a teenager, was leaning against a rusty green Mazda 626. The kid sized Zack up before telling the woman his price. Zack insisted on seeing the weapon first. It was old, but clean and appeared to be in good shape. The dealer didn't ask any questions; he simply took the money and handed over the weapon along with an extra magazine. The deal was done in less than a minute, and the man drove away, $250 richer.

Zack returned to find Flenn tossing in bed. *Was it the infection, or nightmares?* Zack wondered. Either way, he hated seeing his friend like this. Flenn had always had a tender side, but back when they were chasing terrorists and assassins he had been able to put his emotions aside. Granted, the suffering of children had always been the hardest for either of them to handle, but then children were always the first casualties of war.

Zack climbed quietly into the worn-out recliner. *Who was it,* he asked himself, *who'd said that 'truth was the first casualty of war'?* Zack prided himself on being a bit of an American history buff, and it weighed on him that he couldn't remember. It was a reminder of just how exhausted he was. He hadn't had a good night's sleep since the call from Sarah telling him about Eric Scudder and the drone. That reminded him; he needed to recharge his phone.

Senator Hiram Johnson!

That was who'd said truth was the first casualty of war. Johnson had been an isolationist in 1918 and wanted America to retreat from the world stage after the carnage of the First World War. Plenty of naïve politicians seemed to agree these days. Zack knew first-hand the dangers faced by nations going it alone in the present world climate.

Politicians! Zack thought. *He had little use for any of them. His job was simply to serve his country along whatever path its leaders were taking on a given day.* Zack thought about the current state of things back home. The former president was in prison, even though it was not for the murder Zack had eventually discovered. He sighed. *That arrangement had, after all, been part of the deal.* The vice president had resigned six months later and the secretary of state had taken over, but now President Claxton was struggling with cancer and had announced that she would not run in the fall. Her own choice for V.P. had thrown his hat into the ring along with a slate of eight other men and three women from both sides of the aisle.

Fortunately, thanks to the man now moaning in his sleep, Zack had been able to stop yet another catastrophe and prevent the traitorous tycoon, Daniel Romero, from running as an independent in the upcoming election. Had Zack not uncovered Iran's plan to interfere in that election (in exchange for Romero's complicity in allowing the Iranians to attack Israel), the world would likely have been drawn into World War III.

Zack looked at Flenn, who was sleeping fitfully; probably dreaming about the children from the mountain. *The scene had reminded him of numerous war zones he and Flenn had been in years ago.*

No, he told himself, *Hiram Johnson was wrong. Truth was always a victim, even in peacetime, but children were the ones who suffered first and foremost in any war.*

CHAPTER *TWENTY-EIGHT*

Zack awoke to someone poking him. It was the woman from downstairs. "Thank you, but no," he said sleepily.

"Get up, señor! You and your friend must leave now!" She continued shaking him.

"What…why…?"

"El doctor. He is drunk and is down the street at a bar bragging about two rich gringos staying at el Marcositas. Get up! People will come here looking for you… muy bad people. Vamanos!"

Zack threw on his clothes on and woke Flenn.

"Time to leave, old chum."

"What… what time is it?" Flenn looked at his watch.

"Almost one in the morning. Come on! The lady here says some bad dudes may be on their way, and I can't handle them by myself. Not with just a one-armed bandit to help me." He tossed Flenn's clothes on the bed. "Hurry up."

Flenn looked at the woman. "Thank you," he said.

"Pray for me, Padre," she said to Flenn as they hurried out the door.

Flenn stopped short. "How did you… "

"Don't worry, I tell no one. The Asesinos are a street gang. They are, how you say, eh… 'small-time'. Most are

155

stupid punks, but word on the streets is someone hire them to look for a white man, a priest."

Flenn looked at Zack. "Just like Scudder to hire cheap hoods."

"Insurance," answered Zack. "Makes sense. He probably doesn't really think you're alive; just wants to cover his bases. Come on, hurry up, maybe we can find a taxi." They made their way outside where they saw three men running toward the hotel. None of them were holding a weapon, but Zack wasn't taking any chances. He stood in front of Flenn, spread his legs slightly apart, and pulled up the back of his shirt. He and Flenn had done this before.

Zack smiled at the men as they nearly toppled over one another in front of him. "Qué pasa, amigos... what's up?"

The gang members were shocked that the white men hadn't run. One of them had a shaved head, another had a nasty scar running from his right eye down to his chin, and the third was nothing more than a skinny teenager. "We are no your amigos! Where you think you go?"

Zack figured right, the bald one was the leader.

"To Starbucks, where else?" Zack smiled even bigger. "Now would you boys mind lying down on the sidewalk while I pat you down for guns, knives, and other nasty things?" The bald man translated for the other two, who began to laugh... until Zack took one step to the left and they saw Flenn holding the pistol he'd pulled from Zack's waistband.

Zack winked. "Guys, I've seen him hit an arms dealer at fifty yards, and you are only a couple feet away." The bald man glared angrily at Zack but signaled for the other two to get down on the broken concrete.

"Now what?" Flenn asked.

"I was hoping you had something," Zack said as he patted the men down and relieved each of a switchblade. "All we got here are three butter knives." He pocketed one and handed the other two over to Flenn.

"Sorry, but I got nothing," Flenn said as he looked around the empty street. "It's one o'clock in the morning, we've got three hoods on the sidewalk and possibly more on their way... oh, and no car."

"We've been in tougher situations;" said Zack.

Flenn looked at him. "Funny, I can't recall any at the moment." A horn honked as a late-model Toyota Tundra sped up to the curb. Flenn wheeled around and pointed the pistol at the driver's window. He lowered the weapon as soon as he saw the driver.

"Get in!" yelled the woman from the hotel, rolling up her window as Flenn and Zack jumped into the car. Flenn gave Zack the gun, and Zack kept it trained on their would-be assailants until the woman stepped on the gas. She sped around the corner as the three gangsters jumped to their feet and gave them the finger. "I guess I won't be working in this neighborhood for a while," the woman said.

"Wow! Thanks for saving our butts," Flenn said, "but I'm not sure where to suggest you take us right now."

"I know a place, Padre. It is much nicer than El

Marcositas, and out of the way. I think you will be safe there."

"Why did you do this for us?" he asked.

"Never mind that," said Zack, "where did you get this truck? It's a beauty."

Flenn shot him a look.

The woman laughed. "So, what else you think I do with my money?"

"We certainly owe you for saving us," Flenn said.

"Sí," she nodded. "So, why don't you start by telling me why someone wants you two so muchly."

"Long story," offered Zack.

"Long drive," she said. "Hotel is other side of town."

"Let's just say someone doesn't like us," Flenn explained, "and he's willing to pay for help to get rid of us."

"Some help," she said. "Those clowns could no help a cat chase its own tail." Flenn thought briefly about his own cats back home.

Zack turned toward Flenn. "You okay buddy?"

"Stop calling me buddy… okay? Do you know that you only call me that when you think I'm dying?"

"I do not."

"Caracas, Istanbul, Tehran, Beijing…"

"Okay, okay. How about I just call you asshole instead?"

The woman laughed. "So, who are you guys?"

"Missionaries from Utah," offered Zack.

"Funny, you no look Mormon."

Flenn asked, "You haven't told us your name yet."

"People call me many things... most are not so nice."

Flenn felt for her. "Well, right now I'd call you our guardian angel."

She peered into the night. "Mi madre used to call me her angel."

"Where is she?"

"In heaven. She die when I was little girl. My father go off to Tegucigalpa to find work, but never come back. I've lived on the streets since I was ten... that was fifteen years ago." Zack was surprised, she looked much older.

"She would sing to me at night. Sometimes, I feel I can still hear her voice."

Flenn nodded. "My mother's in heaven, too. I still miss her."

The woman glanced into the rearview mirror. "How about you, señor. Is your madre, your mother, still alive?"

"He never had a mother," Flenn said. "He crawled out from under a rock somewhere."

"You're funnier when you aren't on drugs," Zack sniped.

The pills! He'd forgotten to grab the bottle in the room in their hurry to get away. Damn! "My name is Escota," Flenn finally said.

Her forehead furrowed. "Your name is sheet?"

Zack chuckled. "Sort of, more like... "

"Shut up, Zack."

"I am Theresa," the woman said.

Theresa drove through the night, while Zack and Flenn watched for signs of a tail. Few cars were on the road. *The woman seemed as if she were on the up-and-up,*

Flenn told himself, *but she had known he was a priest and that the street gang had been hired to find him. Just what else did she know?*

"Hey, buddy," Zack said, "I mean Padre Sheet; did you get your bottle of pills back there?" Flenn shook his head then asked Theresa if there was a pharmacy near their destination.

"There is, but you should let me go get what it is you need in the morning, just in case those idiotas ask the doctor what he prescribed. They could get word out to the local pharmacias to be watching for any gringos asking for the same medicine."

"I thought you said they were stupid," said Zack.

"Their leader is not. His name is Juan."

"Is he your pimp?"

"Zack!"

Theresa looked over at Flenn. "Es okay, Padre. Your friend no trust me the way you do."

"Well?" Zack said.

She stared out the windshield. "I no work for nobody."

"So, why are you helping us?" Flenn asked.

"You are the priest who was in the village that was blown up, no?" Flenn's eyes grew wide. Zack slid his hand closer to the gun on the seat next to him.

"How do you know about that?"

"I heard that a white priest was killed with many children. When I see your black shirt, and how dirty you were... and smelled your friend back there... I knew you had been through *el tierra de la jaguar*."

"What is that?" Zack asked.

"Land of the jaguar," Flenn translated. That must be the name of the jungle we went through."

"Sí, land of the jaguar. I know you were in the village to help people, so I know you are a good man. Not like most men I see."

"What about those men back there, do they know who we are?" Zack asked.

She thought for a moment. "That was what they were coming to find out. All they knew for sure, is that you are white, which mean you have money. They were coming to rob you."

It's none of my business, Theresa, but why would a hooker care about the two of us?"

"Zack!"

"You are right, it is none of your business." She shrugged, apparently unoffended by Zack's callousness. "But I tell you anyway. A priest once helped me; I figure I owe him."

She turned onto a main stretch of highway. "After mi madre die, a priest take my brother and me into his home."

"Uh-oh," Zack said.

"Nothing like that," Theresa said. "He was a good man. He only mean to help us."

Zack wasn't buying it. "So, to thank him, you became a hooker?"

Flenn glared at him. "Come on, Zack."

"What?" Zack said.

She turned off at the next exit. "Your friend no like me," she said to Flenn. "I think maybe you do, no?" She glanced at him. "You have his eyes… the priest who save me."

"What happened to him?" Flenn asked.

She looked back out at the road. After a moment, she said, "He die." To Zack she said, "I get pregnant when I was thirteen, I try to give myself an abortion. As a result, God punish me and so I became a… what you call me? A hooker."

Zack looked at Flenn. "Well, you asked."

"Me?" Flenn said. He turned to Theresa. "I'm sorry, for what happened; but I don't believe God is punishing you."

"You are not Catholic?" she asked.

"No, Episcopal… Anglican… Church of England in America."

"I do not know of this Angry Can… "

"Doesn't matter," Flenn said. "You found yourself in an impossible situation, on the streets and pregnant at thirteen. I don't believe God punishes us for mistakes or for acting out of fear, but I do believe that he forgives anything we bring to him."

Zack rolled his eyes. "Really, Flenn, a sermon… *now*?"

"Padre, in case you have not noticed, I am a whore. I do not believe God forgives whores."

Flenn smiled. "You ever read the New Testament, Theresa? Some of Jesus' best friends were wh… prostitutes."

"Some of mine too," mumbled Zack.

Flenn turned toward the back seat. "I swear, if you don't shut up…"

"We are here!" Theresa pulled into a small hotel on the eastern edge of the city. It was far from grand, but it looked (*and certainly smelled*) much better than El Marcositas. "I will need money," she said. Flenn handed her what he had.

"What about you," Flenn asked. "Will you stay here as well?"

She thought a moment. "You would not mind? It would be safer for me right now. Juan will be very angry."

Flenn fished more money out of his pocket. "Will this be enough for a second room?" She took the money and was gone less than five minutes.

"They only have the one room," she said. Zack wondered if she'd simply asked for one room and pocketed the rest. As if reading his thoughts, Theresa handed Flenn the change.

"No," Flenn said. "Keep whatever's left over. You've certainly earned it." Zack shook his head.

The room was simply furnished, but was clean. There were two beds; Flenn and Zack gave Theresa one, and they shared the other. The three of them agreed that she would go to the pharmacia in the morning and purchase more of Flenn's antibiotics along with bottled water and something to eat.

Zack waited until he thought she was asleep, then whispered, "Are you sure we can trust her? She could turn us in, you know."

It was Theresa's voice that answered. "*She* is not yet asleep. But sí, you can trust me. I just hope I can trust you; please, stay in your own bed."

****

Carlos sat on the front stoop of the hacienda, cleaning his .45 with the expertise of a trained assassin. There wasn't much else to do. It had been days since Scudder had spent all that time in the Humvee with Gerald Rudolph.

An unopened beer sat on the concrete slab next to him for afterwards. He rarely drank anything stronger, and never when handling a weapon. The two porch lights and the full moon above provided more than enough light to do something he could have done blindfolded.

He heard someone coming toward him. Scudder had been out playing with his toy in the driveway again; he must have tired of it because he was heading his way. The big man had an odd look on his face, as if he were struggling with a dilemma. Carlos tensed. *A fine time to have his weapon disassembled!*

Scudder stopped directly in front of him. "Isn't that about the hundredth time you've cleaned that thing?"

Carlos feigned a smile. "Just trying to stay busy, boss. Anything I can do for you?"

Scudder looked around to see if anyone else was in earshot. "As a matter of fact, there may be. Let me ask you something;" He lowered his voice, "have you ever killed anyone before?"

Carlos' smile vanished. "Yes," was all he said.

Scudder grinned. "Good. You got any problems with doing it again?"

Carlos began reassembling his weapon. "Who you got in mind, boss?" He figured he already knew the answer.

"Two people, actually. I just need to know you've got the stomach for it."

Carlos assumed that if he said no, then he would be number three. He nodded his understanding. "Something that needs doing now?"

Scudder looked toward the house, as if he could see Frick or Frack through the walls. He didn't know which one was inside and which one was down at the guardhouse. Nor did he care. "No, not yet. We're going to be here for a couple more weeks, then we have another job to do. I'll tell you when."

"Right, boss."

Scudder nodded approvingly. He liked blind obedience. "So, you know the two I'm talking about?"

"Our local friends, I assume."

Brilliant man! One worth carrying along to Mexico, for sure, Scudder thought. "We may still need them for a while, so it will probably be right before we get ready to leave. Oh, and one more thing."

"Yeah, boss?"

"Don't breathe a word of this to Jerry. He has this mistaken idea that he runs this show now. Got it?"

Carlos nodded. "Got it, boss. Just between you and me."

Scudder smiled, pleased with how well everything was working out. He was starting to like this man; he might not kill him after all. Scudder stepped up to the porch and reached for the door handle. "You know," he said, as if to himself, "I killed a man once. I don't know why people get all worked up over it." He shrugged. "No big deal."

With that, he disappeared inside.

CHAPTER *TWENTY-NINE*

Flenn was still half asleep as he stumbled into the bathroom where Zack was taking a shower. He relieved himself then took a long look in the mirror, which was beginning to fog over. Flenn hardly recognized the person staring back at him. His beard was several days old, his hair matted and his eyes baggy. It looked as if he'd lost 10 pounds, which he probably had.

He heard the water turn off and Zack stepping out of the shower behind him. Flenn wiped the mirror to take a closer look at his beard, but what he saw behind him gave him a start.

"Theresa!"

She seemed amused at Flenn's embarrassment. Closing his eyes, he said, "I am so sorry, I thought he... I mean I thought you were, I mean... "

Theresa laughed. "Padre, you are the first man to ever see me naked! Now you will have to marry me!"

They could hear laughter coming from the bedroom. "It's not funny, Zack!"

"Oh yes, it is!" Zack said.

Flenn dressed quickly as Theresa came out of the bathroom to retrieve her clothes. He turned away. "It's okay," Zack said, "she's wearing a towel." Flenn opened his eyes and turned around to discover that Theresa was indeed wearing a towel—on top of her head.

"Damn it, Zack!"

Theresa laughed again as she picked up her bra and panties and headed back to the bathroom. "Que lastima," she teased. "Now I will have to marry you both!"

"I'm hungry," said Zack, waiting for his turn at the shower.

Theresa called from the bathroom: "I will bring us something to eat after I go to the pharmacia."

"Just so long as it's not protein bars or cheese crackers," Flenn grumbled.

"Or mangos," added Zack.

Theresa came out of the bathroom a different woman than the one they'd first met. It was as if her looks improved with her surroundings. *Maybe in her line of work,* thought Flenn, *one had to be a bit of a chameleon to appeal to the local clientele.* "How much money will you need?" he asked her, knowing that he and Zack only had a few dollars left.

"No worry. We can settle when I return." With that, she walked out the door, looking to Zack less like a 50-lempira hooker and more like a shopkeeper or librarian.

"That one has a story or two to tell, I bet," Zack said, flipping on a small television set sitting on top of a bureau.

"Probably; but then so do we," Flenn, reminded him. An episode of *The Love Boat* was the only English-speaking program on TV, so Flenn turned the sound off.

"What? You don't want to hear it?"

"Do you?"

Zack headed to the bathroom. "See if you can find a news channel; maybe you can figure out some of what they're saying. You were always better at languages."

"Unless a woman was involved," quipped Flenn.

Zack looked back over his shoulder. "Hey, the language of love needs no translation."

"Love! Yeah, right; what do you know about love?"

"Enough to know that I don't want to make it with that one, even if she is better looking now than she was yesterday. I hear HIV is a real problem down here."

"Go get your shower... and quit talking that way about her. She saved our bacon, you know."

"Don't say bacon," Zack called from the bathroom. "I'm starving!"

Flenn spent the hour watching a version of CNN in Spanish, which he was able to follow fairly well. A lot of the news was about Central American politics, local crime, and the police's so-called war against drug trafficking. Flenn knew that criminals often ran the show down here; bribery, graft, and corruption were as common as banana plantations. He also knew that San Pedro Sula was the murder capital of Honduras, if not all Central America. Ever since hurricanes had pounded the country more than 20 years ago, the fruit companies had moved out, leaving drug and sex trafficking the two most lucrative businesses in Honduras. Crime ran rampant, and police were too often in collusion with the criminals. Government officials and church leaders had, at times, tried to stand up to the drug lords but usually found themselves fighting an impossible battle, sometimes at the cost of their lives. Most of the drugs ended up in the United States, being passed around high school football stadiums or after-hour business parties. It grieved Flenn that people back home had no idea what their illegal habits cost others.

Zack finished his shower and came out of the bathroom clean-shaven. Flenn's eyes grew wide. "You didn't tell me you had a razor!"

"I like you better with a beard," Zack quipped. "Almost makes you look intelligent."

"Fork it over!"

Flenn felt almost human again after a shave, especially when he saw the bagful of sausage and egg burritos Theresa had brought. Zack was already on his second one. Theresa handed him a bottle of pills. "I am sorry, Padre," she said. "They only had three tablets. They say they have more this afternoon."

Showered and full, Zack offered to go get the medicine later. Theresa told them goodbye, but promised she'd come back to check on them later. Zack wasn't sure she needed to come back—especially considering the job that lay before them—but Flenn smiled and said he'd look forward to it.

Flenn and Zack spent the rest of the morning planning how to catch up with Scudder once Sarah found out where he was holed up. They agreed to stay out of sight as much as possible, except for when Zack would go out for food or to the pharmacia. As soon as Sarah called them, they would finalize their plans to take care of Eric Scudder once and for all.

Unless, of course, Zack thought, *Scudder manages to take care of us first!*

CHAPTER *THIRTY*

Zack crossed the busy street late in the afternoon, wondering if maybe he should have kept the beard. It probably didn't matter. If someone was looking for him, he'd be easy to spot down here, beard or no beard.

He purchased a candy bar at the pharmacia after being told that Flenn's medicine had still not arrived but would be available within an hour. Zack figured that probably meant two hours, and walked down the street to the McDonald's where Theresa had purchased breakfast. He bought a couple of hamburgers and asked for extra tomatoes and lettuce, which would have to suffice as salad. He took the meal back to the room, along with two large sodas. He and Flenn ate in relative silence, both thinking about their next move.

Flenn's shoulder ached, so he took his second antibiotic, even though it hadn't been 12 hours yet. With only one pill remaining, they would need to find another pharmacia if the one down the street didn't fulfill its promise. An hour and a half later, Zack went back to the drugstore. Sure enough, the druggist had filled the order. Like many Central American pharmacies, Zack didn't need a prescription, only cash. He looked at the shelves and saw bottles of painkillers mixed in with antibiotics, analgesics, and an abundance of Viagra and Cialis—all clearly priced and available for anyone with ready cash.

The druggist had a peculiar look on his face; Zack assumed the man didn't like Americans. He paid at the register and walked outside. Stepping onto the broken sidewalk, he felt something hard against his back. Baldy, from the night before, stepped out from around the corner and stood directly in front of Zack with a smirk on his face. "You left last night without saying goodbye, Gringo!" said Baldy as he patted Zack down. Fortunately, Zack had left the pistol with Flenn. Baldy found his switchblade in Zack's pocket and seemed pleased with the reunion.

Zack heard a car pull up behind him; he knew his chances of staying alive would decrease a hundred-fold if he let them push him inside. He raised his arms in submission, which immediately got the attention of people nearby. Several people began to point at the men. Baldy grew nervous, as did the thug pressing the gun into Zack's spine.

A lanky, heavily tattooed tough sitting across the street dropped whatever it was he'd been eating and began yelling obscenities at Zack's assailants. Baldy clearly recognized the man and yelled something back. Taking advantage of the moment, Zack wheeled around and hit the gunman hard in the gut, knocking the pistol out of his hand and kicked behind him, catching Baldy solidly in the left leg. He heard the bone snap as the gang leader fell, screaming in agony.

The tattooed man and three other toughs ran toward them. Before he could turn back around, Zack found himself falling to the ground, an enormous pain in his right temple. He hadn't noticed the driver getting out of the car with a blackjack. The last thing Zack remembered was being thrown into the car and hearing tires squeal on the pavement as the driver sped away.

****

What was taking so long? Flenn had waited hours, but still no Zack. Flenn kept staring at the pistol on the nightstand—much the same way his parishioner Doris Dilwicky often eyed the desert table at potluck dinners during Lent. He hadn't wanted Zack to leave the weapon, but Zack had insisted. Finally, Flenn picked up the gun and examined it. It was a Glock, the same type he'd once carried. He ran his left hand down the barrel. The weapon was a dull gray... not that much different from CIA issue. It felt comfortable in his hands. *Too comfortable!* He put it back on the nightstand and walked away.

Damn! Where are you Zack?

Someone knocked at the door, and Flenn glanced back at the weapon. Theresa's voice came from the other side. "I have surprise," she said. "Pizza!" Flenn let her in. She was carrying a six-pack of Salva Vida beer and a large, square cardboard box. "Lots of meat," she said, smiling. "I figure you guys need the protein."

Flenn closed the door behind her. "Zack's not here. He's been gone for hours!"

"Your friend? What happen to him?"

"He went to pick up my prescription. He tried to get it earlier, but they told him to come back in an hour." It was only just now dawning on Flenn that the pharmacist might have been setting Zack up.

"Perhaps he will come back soon, no?" Even as she said it, Theresa knew he wouldn't. She opened the pizza box and took out a slice. "I go check something."

"What? Where are you going?"

"I know some people in this barrio, I find out what happen to your friend."

Flenn eyed the pistol. "I'll come with you."

"You would get me killed, Padre. I blend in; you... not so much."

Damn! He knew she was right. Flenn picked up the gun and offered it to her. "At least take this."

Theresa smiled and lifted her dress. "I have my own." Flenn saw a tiny .42-caliber pistol strapped to her thigh.

"You need to eat, Padre. Drink a beer too," she said. "Honduran beer is good for you; make you strong like bull! I will be back soon." With that, she slipped out the door.

Flenn turned on the television to see if the local news mentioned anything about kidnappings... or murders... this afternoon. In fact, there had been several. The program showed graphic video of bleeding and broken bodies throughout the city. Thankfully, none were Zack. Flenn forced himself to eat, only because he knew that he needed to keep his strength up. The beer was surprisingly good, but he only allowed himself one; he needed his wits about him right now.

He stared at the empty can of Salva Vida, praying that Zack didn't need a lifesaver right now!

Perhaps there'd just been another delay with the antibiotic. Zack might simply be waiting for the medicine. Or, maybe he was scoping out some strip bar nearby. Flenn shook his head. *No, Zack was a lot of things, but he was forever loyal. He wouldn't have left him alone this long unless something had happened.*

Zack and Flenn had helped each other out of more scrapes than Flenn could remember. Flenn had several scars from their days together, and Zack had even more. One of Flenn's scars dated back to that time in Edinburgh. Flenn wondered what the visage he had encountered there would have to say to him now. Flenn was a priest now because of that man... and what had happened back then.

He looked at the pistol and felt ashamed. Violence was no longer his way of life. Yet, he couldn't escape the fact that Eric Scudder had killed those children without a moment's hesitation. Looking down at the pistol he asked himself... *What other choice is there?*

It seemed like forever before Theresa returned. She popped opened a warm beer and downed it, then grabbed a slice of cold pizza.

"There is good news, Padre, and bad. Your friend, Señor Zack, is alive."

Flenn breathed a sigh of relief. "What's the bad news?"

"That *is* the bad news."

"Theresa, please." Flenn said.

Theresa sighed. "The Asesinos have him. They come here today, but they are no allowed in this barrio without first getting permission from Manuel, the leader of the Jefes, which they did not have. So the local gang, the Jefes, they chase them away. Your friend broke one of the kidnapper's legs before the Jefes capture him along with another estupido."

"Where did the Asesinos take Zack?"

"The Jefes don't know. I no think they care either. The one with the broken leg—Juan—he is leader of the Asesinos. He was one of the men who tried to capture you and your friend the other night. I know him well. He is the king of ignorancia!"

"Will the Jefes let me talk to this Juan?"

"Are you loco?" Theresa sat down and finished the Salva Vida. She wasn't going back there anytime soon. "These men no care about you, and if Juan tells them there is a price on your head, they will kill you and collect it for themselves."

"He won't tell them."

"Why you so sure?" Theresa sipped her second beer more slowly.

"For the reason you just said—the Jefes would collect the money themselves."

Theresa nodded her head. "But maybe they agree to split it, no?"

"Would you?"

She thought about that for a moment. "You are right, Padre. Juan no tell them."

Flenn sat on the edge of the bed and tried to figure out what to do next. "Is there a bank nearby?"

"Sí, down the street. Why?"

"What time does it open?"

"The banks open early, around seven, I think."

"Good. I can have money transferred here overnight." Flenn stared quietly at the floor for a moment, trying to think through all the angles of the plan formulating in his head. After a moment, he looked up. "Listen, Theresa, you've done so much already, but can you do me one more favor?"

Theresa took a swallow of beer. "For you? Sure thing."

"Can you go back to the Jefes and arrange a meeting for ten o'clock tomorrow morning? Tell them I'll give them ten thousand dollars for Juan—five thousand now, and five thousand after we are all safely away. We can leave the money here in our room or something. Flenn rubbed his forehead. "Do you think they'd turn him over for ten-grand?"

Her jaw dropped. "The Jefes would sell their own madres for that much!"

"Good, now one last thing," Flenn said. "I assume that somewhere in this city is a good hospital?"

Theresa sat quietly and listened to the priest spell out his plan— one that she would never have come up with herself in a million years. "You are a good man, Padre," was all she said when he had finished.

Flenn looked at the gun on the nightstand and wondered.

CHAPTER *THIRTY-ONE*

Two uniformed guards brandishing M16s stood outside El Banco de Occidente. Four more were stationed inside, one in each corner, sizing up customers as they strode into the bank. All eyes fell on the tall white man with sandy brown hair as he walked through the front doors.

Miles away, two other men—looking nothing at all like security guards but more like kids who'd skipped school for the day—sat in a basement playing checkers. Zack Matteson watched from a chair where he'd been bound and gagged since arriving last night.

The bank was not much to look at on the outside, but inside, mahogany molding accentuated two-story high ceilings of white and gold. Three early 20th-century chandeliers, which would have dazzled the design team at the Waldorf Astoria, hung suspended high above. Tastefully displayed Honduran art stood atop black pedestals, each with an embossed acrylic plaque telling about the artist in both Spanish and English. Carved mahogany counters lined both sides of the lobby, with bulletproof glass in front of each teller.

In contrast, the damp, darkened cellar where Zack was being held had only a 40-watt bulb hanging from the ceiling and smelled strongly of mold. Directly across from Zack, two ancient barrels, containing God knows what, had been pushed in front of what appeared to Zack to be an old door casing, which had been painted over long ago to blend in with the rest of the room. Likely, Zack's two companions hadn't noticed the disguised door. Their only concern had been keeping their prisoner tied and silent.

Directly across from Flenn were several large doors, each presumably leading to an office or perhaps a conference room. A light-skinned man wearing a three-piece blue suit exited a door in the middle and greeted Flenn with a practiced smile. The man had been advised to be on the lookout for a tall Caucasian who would be arriving as soon as the bank opened. Flenn had used Zack's SAT phone last night to call his brother asking that $50,000 be waiting for him first thing in the morning. Flenn had asked David to be generous to the bank manager; he couldn't afford any delays. Flenn hadn't told his brother why he needed the money, nor had David asked.

Zack's head ached. He pulled against the tape around his wrists to no avail. At least his feet were free, which might come in handy once he could figure out how he was going to escape from these kids. The cellar had no windows and no visible exits other than rickety stairwell leading upstairs. Zack sat quietly, thinking about what to do next, wondering what might be on the other side of the door that had been painted to blend in with the rest of the room.

The man in the tailored suit escorted Flenn into an office where he offered coffee and pastries. Flenn ate, mostly to be polite. The coffee, however, was excellent. It had been days since he'd had caffeine... longer than he'd gone without in years. He'd finished three cups by the time the transaction was finished. Flenn placed the money in Zack's backpack, thanked the man, and returned to the hotel, where he stuffed five envelopes with $5,000 each. He placed another $5,000 in a separate envelope (which he stuffed under the hotel mattress), and $10,000 in the third and fourth envelopes, one of which he handed to Theresa.

"Que es esto?" She said, her jaw nearly touching the ground.

"You've earned it," was all Flenn said.

Their rendezvous was not far from the hotel. Theresa was to drop him off with the Jefes. If all went according to plan, she would pick up Flenn and the man Zack called 'Baldy' 15 minutes later. She'd hand the Jefes a note with the hotel name and room number, along with a key to the room, only after Juan and the priest were in the truck and she had her foot on the gas.

The teens guarding Zack could have been brothers. Both were small, had greasy hair, and wore wife-beater undershirts with torn blue jeans. A bottle of George Dickel sat on top of a barrel next to the checkerboard. Even in the dim light, Zack could see that neither boy had the butt of a gun sticking out of his waistband, affirming what Theresa had said about most of Baldy's gang only carrying knives.

Taking these boys out without the use of his hands was going to be tricky, but the hardest part would be getting past the thugs upstairs, where there might only be one or two hanging around... or the whole damn gang!

Zack watched his guards playing checkers as he planned his escape. The one thing he was glad of was that at least Flenn wasn't here. So far at least, it appeared Flenn had managed to keep himself in the shadows.

****

Flenn placed one of the envelopes with $5,000 into his pocket, and then stashed the pistol in Zack's backpack. He took the last of the antibiotics the doctor had prescribed—he'd have to go back to the ones Zack had brought in his first-aid kit and hope they'd be enough. The pills were definitely working; the pain was less and the angry red blotch was almost gone. More importantly, he was getting some motion back in his left arm.

He climbed into the Tundra next to Theresa and placed the backpack under the passenger seat. Ten minutes later, Theresa pulled up behind a dilapidated concrete building surrounded by teenagers and young men carrying machetes. Many were smoking, and some were passing around a bottle of Jim Beam. All of them eyed the tall white man as he climbed out of the truck before it sped away.

Flenn walked up to the meanest looking of the bunch. "Tu jefe me esperando." Indeed, their boss was expecting him. The muscular young tough, wearing a shirt two sizes too small, sneered at him as he gestured toward the door. A pungent odor of marijuana, beer, and sweat permeated the front room. What the building had once been, Flenn had no idea. The faded, green walls had huge chunks of plaster missing, and were stained here and there with God knows what. Old, worn-out mattresses were scattered across the floor—a rat ran for cover under one of them as Flenn entered the room.

The tough called out, "Manuel!" and a tall, thin, heavily tattooed man stepped into the room along with two other men, each carrying .22-caliber rifles. The tattooed man looked the American up and down. Something about the way the gringo stared at him gave Manuel the feeling that this man was dangerous.

Manuel spat on the ground in front of Flenn. "The bitch say you have ten-thousand American dollars for me."

Flenn stared straight into the gang leader's eyes. "The *lady* said you have someone for me first."

Manuel looked away. "What you want with that piece of *mierda*?"

Flenn's eyes narrowed. "What I want with him is none of your business. I was told we have a deal."

"I change my mind. I want all money now."

Flenn shook his head and reached into his pocket. Manuel stiffened as the other two raised their rifles. Flenn cocked his head and slowly removed an envelope. "Here is five thousand. I am prepared to walk out of here without this money and without Juan... if you are prepared to lose the other five thousand."

Manuel wiped his nose with the back of his hand. "What if I just take money and you no walk out of here at all?"

Flenn's eyes narrowed as he stared straight into the man's eyes. "Before your guards have time to pull their triggers I will have killed you." Manuel could sense when someone was bluffing; there was something about this man that said he could deliver. *Ten thousand American dollars was a lot of money. What did he care about what happened to Juan? After all, they were sworn enemies.*

Manuel backed up a step and grinned. "He no walk very good. You going to carry him?"

Flenn glared at him. "No, your boys are going to carry him. They will place him in my friend's truck when she returns. Then, and only then, will I tell you where you can find the rest of the money."

Manuel thought for a moment, and then smiled. "Your *friend*? You know who she is?" He turned to the man on his right and laughed. "Maybe we meet again, Gringo, eh?"

The corners of Flenn's mouth turned downward. "You should pray that we don't."

Manuel swallowed. "Sigueme. Follow." He turned

and led Flenn around a corner and down a hall toward what appeared to have once been a kitchen. Tied to a chair was the bald man who had accosted them in front of el Marcositas. The man looked up at Flenn and spat.

"Now is that any way for you to treat your amigo?" Manuel said. The bald man didn't respond.

Flenn looked around the room. "I was told you captured two men."

Manuel shrugged. "I only make deal for one."

"Where is the other?"

"Probably in hell. What do you care?"

Flenn tried hard not to react. *Damn it! He should have made the deal for both! It hadn't occurred to him; at the time he'd only been thinking of Zack.* Flenn bit his bottom lip. *How many more must die because of him?*

Manuel signaled to his bodyguards, who put their rifles down to untie the prisoner. The leader of the Jefes leaned within six inches of Juan's face, smiled, and, without saying a word, reached down and squeezed Juan's injured leg. Juan screamed in pain. Laughing, Manuel stood up and nodded to his men. They finished untying their prisoner and took him outside, just as Theresa pulled up. They dumped Juan into the back of her pickup, as Flenn jumped in next to him. The leader of the Jefes glared up at the two of them. "Aren't you forgetting something, Gringo?"

Theresa tossed the envelope and room key down on the ground as she hit the gas and sped away. "I'm a man of my word, Manuel," Flenn called out. "Remember that!"

CHAPTER *THIRTY-TWO*

Vida Vibrante Hospital truly did offer a vibrant life for its patients, but only those wealthy enough to afford it. Juan was shocked to find himself here, but inwardly relieved. He'd assumed that the priest had something different in mind when he'd taken him from the Jefes.

Juan hadn't contacted the fat man, the one who'd hired him to be on the lookout for a white priest. *He had waited after being bested by the two gringos the other night; plus, he hadn't been sure that this was the man Scudder had told him to watch for, not until Theresa had come to the man's rescue. Theresa had a soft spot in her heart for priests; had ever since she was a kid.* Juan and Theresa had their differences, but he didn't want her harmed. His plan had been to find her, capture the priest, and then call the fat man. Right now, however, the priest seemed to be holding all the cards.

Flenn had made all the arrangements with the hospital through Theresa, who'd once had a 'relationship' with someone in the laboratory. Five thousand dollars had gotten them a private room, a doctor, and two nurses.

The X-rays had shown that Juan's tibia was not shattered and could be repaired with surgery, which the doctor would perform that very afternoon—just as soon as the hospital verified payment from Flenn's bank. *Like so many things in Honduras,* Flenn realized, *even surgery on a gangster was available for the right price.*

Theresa had explained the situation to Juan what was going on while Flenn stepped outside the room. The gang leader had acted dismissively toward the priest's generosity, but Flenn had seen the man's relief when he realized his leg would be repaired. Theresa told Juan what Flenn was willing to do for his silence: triple the price Scudder had put on his head (a mere $1,000). Plus, he would give Juan an additional $2,000 if Zack was released unharmed.

Flenn waited outside the room, noting the contrast between Vida Vibrante and the hospital he'd seen last year when he'd first visited San Pedro Sula. That place had been more of a clinic really; little more than a gymnasium with bloodstained cots, an overworked doctor, and a few poorly trained nurses. The sick and dying had lain motionless while nurses had gone from bed to bed offering what comfort they could. Over in a corner, separated from the rest of the room by two yellow shower curtains was what had passed for the walls of the 'hospital's' only operating room.

Flenn shook his head at the contrast. This hospital was clean and orderly. Blue tile floors reflected the fluorescent light overhead, while colorful paintings adorned the pale, cream-colored walls. Here, at Vida Vibrante, the division between the *haves* and the *have-nots* was clearly defined.

He rubbed his temples. The coffee from the bank this morning had brought his need for caffeine back with a vengeance. A soda machine stood across the hall, and he was grateful that it took American dollars as well as lempira. It wasn't coffee, but it would have to do.

Flenn leaned against the wall and watched a handsome young orderly push a broom down the hallway.

At least Zack was alive. Juan had been captured and unable to issue orders otherwise. Theresa had assured him that the Asesinos didn't do anything without Juan's approval. What she had actually said was that the Asesinos couldn't wipe their own rear ends without Juan telling them how to do it. Obviously, this gang was nothing like the notorious one by the same name in Mexico. Theresa had said they'd stolen the name to make themselves look tough. Still, Flenn was anxious. *What if one of Juan's gang decided to take things into their own hands after all?*

At last, Theresa stepped out of the room. "He say he will accept your offer, but that he will no order your friend's release." Theresa rolled her eyes. "He plays the big shot, but he is afraid of this man Scudder."

Flenn slammed the wall behind him, startling the janitor, who turned to stare at them before returning to his broom. Theresa touched Flenn's sleeve. "Juan tell me where they are holding your friend. The rest is up to you and me, no?" She took a deep breath, then tried to smile. "Piece of pie."

"Cake," Flenn corrected. He scratched his head. "Juan told you all that without seeing the money first?"

"I give him some of the money you give me."

Flenn raised an eyebrow and smiled. "Theresa, you are a saint!"

"Padre, believe me, I am no saint."

"Maybe you weren't before, but you are now! We just have to keep him from getting to a phone and calling someone. Theresa found a nurse and had her call for the doctor. Flenn told the man that he wanted the patient sedated right away. No one saw him slip five $100 bills into the doctor's hands. The physician nodded and went off to sign the order. Flenn looked back at Theresa. "How do we know Juan gave you the right location?"

"It is the right place," Theresa said with a sigh. "I know it well."

A nurse with a syringe walked past them into Juan's room. "I don't know, Theresa," Flenn mused. "He could be lying."

She nodded. "Sí, Juan is a liar. In fact, he is many, many things," she hesitated, "but he will *no* lie to me."

"What makes you so sure?"

"Because, in all the years we have known each other, mi hermano has never lied to me."

Hermano?

Flenn stared incredulously at her. He reached out for the wall to brace himself.

"Your *brother*?!"

CHAPTER *THIRTY-THREE*

Asleep on the living room sofa with one leg hanging over the edge, the man Scudder called Frick was snoring loudly. Carlos kicked him. "Get up," he barked in Spanish. "The boss has a job for us. He said we should take the Nissan."

Frick stood, his breath and clothes smelled like beer. "I'll drive," Carlos said, leaning in. "And lay off the cerveza. You don't need to tick off the boss." The men walked behind the house to the old stable, a good 30 yards away, where Scudder kept the red pickup. The Humvee was parked next to the house, near the kitchen door for easy access, but they weren't allowed near it. Scudder was out there often, usually with a plate of something, just sitting inside staring at something in front of him. Frick had no idea what was inside the big truck, but he'd been told in no uncertain terms that it was none of his business.

The drive with Carlos to San Pedro Sula was long. The two men talked a little, but since Carlos was essentially the number-three guy, Frick was careful with what he said. He'd learned long ago not to offend people who paid him, especially when so little was required. Despite Scudder's unpredictability and moodiness, this was one of the easiest jobs he and his brother had ever had.

People stared when they pulled into the barrio. It was hard to miss a shiny new red truck in this section of town. A little boy watched as they parked in front of a dingy market and got out of the pickup. The boy's mother yanked him away and hurried down the street. Carlos handed Frick a wad of cash and sent him inside for bottled water and cigarettes. "Go inside and keep an eye on things, in case I need you. Don't draw attention to yourself."

Within minutes, three members of the Asesinos had shown up—exactly what Carlos was counting on. One kid slipped around the truck and tried to sneak up behind him. Carlos pretended not to notice and waited for the boy to get closer before whipping around with the barrel of his .45 pointing straight at the teenager's left eye.

The boy wet himself.

As quickly as he'd pulled the weapon, Carlos replaced it in his waistband and turned to the other two gang members. He addressed them in Spanish. "My boss sent me here to speak with your boss."

The bigger, and older, of the two toughs in front of him asked, "Who's your boss?"

A fat jerk who should have rotted in that Korean jail cell, Carlos thought. "The one who is paying Juan to keep an eye out for the white priest."

The big guy nodded, his muscles noticeably relaxing. "Juan is not here. He found the priest, but the Jefes got to him first."

Frick came out of the store and leaned against the wall behind Carlos.

"Who are the Jefes?" Carlos asked.

"A gang on the other side of town."

Carlos thought about that for a moment. Flenn was alive! That would certainly ruin Scudder's day. "Why haven't you called my boss?"

The teenager shrugged. "Juan's the only one who knows how to contact him."

"That's too bad," Carlos lied, secretly glad they had no way of reaching Scudder. "My boss wanted me to give Juan a message." In truth, the only message had been that he wanted Juan to go up the mountain and gather pictures from the blast site. Scudder wanted a souvenir. He had originally planned to send Carlos up to the village, but Gerald Rudolph had argued against it. Local police might be hanging around, Gerald had said.

The kid went on: "Tell your boss Juan is in the hospital now. Vida Vibrante. He called us, but was on too many drugs for us to understand him. They won't let any of us in that place, and whoever paid for him to be there seems to have placed him on some sort of no-call list."

Carlos reached into his pocket and pulled out a fifty. "Keep that to yourself. I'll see that my boss gets the message." The man pocketed the money even quicker than Carlos had drawn his weapon a moment ago. The three Asesinos walked away, the older two teasing the boy who'd peed himself. Carlos turned and was startled to see Frick behind him. "How much of that did you hear?"

Frick shrugged. "Only that their boss got caught by the Jefes. I know the Jefes; he's lucky to be alive. Can't imagine how he ended up in Vida Vibrante, though. Very exclusive." He shook his head. "I couldn't get in there, not if I was bleeding out of every hole in my body."

"Thanks for the image." Carlos climbed back into the truck. "Let *me* tell the boss. Not a word of this to anybody... understood?"

Frick nodded. "You got it. The less I say to Señor Scudder, the better." Frick wiped his brow. "I'm telling you, few people scare me, but there's something about that man."

Carlos started the engine. "You're smart. The boss is the kind of person who'd kill you in a heartbeat, and never think anything of it." *So was Frick, for that matter,* Carlos thought. This assignment was getting a bit like a three-ring circus, and Carlos was keenly aware of just who was on the tightrope.

CHAPTER *THIRTY-FOUR*

Father Scott Flenn had never taken a ride alone with a prostitute before. *Zack would've had some wise-ass thing to say if he were here,* Flenn thought, *but right now it didn't matter.*

He sat in silence as Theresa drove him out of the city and past long pastures of freshly mown hay. Finally, he looked at Theresa. "What else haven't you told me?"

"Qué?"

"Your brother...?"

"I am sorry, Padre,'" she said, "my life is, how you say, *complicated.*"

"I think the fact that you're Juan's sister might have been something you could have brought up—oh, I don't know—like when we first met you! Are you working with him?"

Theresa laughed. "Work for that idiota? Never."

Flenn shook his head. "I've got to tell you, it doesn't look good from where I'm sitting, Theresa."

She shifted in her seat as if trying to decide what, or how much, she should tell him. A moment later she slowed down and pulled the truck over to the side of the road. Off to the left were about a dozen cows grazing lazily by a small pond. In the distance Flenn saw a boy with a rifle—*probably guarding the cattle,* he thought.

Theresa looked at him, her eyes moist.

"Mi madre was a good woman. She work very, very hard for an American family, and make enough money to take care of Juan and me. She send us to school, feed us, buy clothes for us." She paused. "Then one day, the husband of the woman she worked for… he… " her voice trailed off.

Flenn lowered his eyes; understanding what she meant.

"Mama try telling his wife, but all the woman do is blame mi madre and tell her never come back. Without the job, things go from bad to worse. We leave our home, but some men came… Anglos. They took mama somewhere. I think maybe the woman's husband send them." Her voice trailed off. "Juan and me, we never see mama again."

Flenn felt a lump in his throat as Theresa stared out the window at the boy on the hill.

"My brother was trece… thirteen. I was only ten. He try to take care of me. He take me to a Catholic church; our mama had been a friend of the priest there. He was a good man. When he find out what had happened, he took us in his own home, feed us, send us to school for a few years; but, my brother…" She wiped her eyes. "My brother was very angry at what happen. After school, he hang out with a gang of boys that liked to pretend they were muy bad, like the big gangs up in Mexico. They even call themselves after one of them. When the padre find out Juan had joined the Asesinos, he was furioso! He went to their leader and told him leave Juan alone. The leader no like being challenged in front of his gang, so he pulled a gun on the padre. I do not think he mean to shoot him, but the gun go off."

Theresa paused, lost in that dark past. "Juan was not there that day, but when he find out, he was so very angry. I had never seen him like that." Theresa paused a moment. "He found the gang leader and beat him to death... all his rage just pour out of him. He then threaten to kill anyone else who challenged him." Theresa stopped to wipe the tears away. She glanced at the priest sitting next to her and saw in his face something she hadn't seen in years... *compassion.* "They were just dumb kids, Padre. Most of them were Juan's age. No one challenge Juan. That is how he became leader of the Asesinos."

"And you?"

Theresa gazed out the window. "To survive I become a whore."

"I'm sorry," was all Flenn knew to say.

She nodded. "So am I, Padre. My brother and I have no much to do with each other, but I know he blame himself for leaving me, and for what I become... became. I am sorry, my English used to be so much better than it is now. It comes and goes."

Flenn took a breath. "I guess you don't get much practice using it," he said. "So, you believed Juan back at the hospital when he told you where the Asesinos are keeping Zack?"

"Sí. It is in the old abandoned church where the padre used to hold services. No one go there after he die; the people, they were too super... super..."

"Superstitious?" he offered.

"Sí. The church has been abandoned for many years." She put her hand on the gear shift. "Juan tell me he had plans to take you there and then contact this man Scudder." She pulled back onto the road. "He also tell me that he has no called Scudder; he was waiting until he capture you."

"So, Scudder still thinks I'm dead." That was a relief. *He and Zack would have the element of surprise, but they'd need to find Scudder right away. Eventually, Theresa's brother would be alert enough to call him. Of course, Flenn thought, Juan might not contact Scudder at all, since he'd be endangering Theresa.* He rubbed his temples. The headache was returning. There was so much Flenn wanted to ask, so much he wanted to say; but only one thing that needed to be said right now: "Okay, so what is your plan?"

"There is a tunnel that leads to the basement of the church; that is where they will have your friend. Soldiers once use it during a time of revolution. It is no longer used by anyone, and I doubt they know the tunnel is even there. It is our best way into the church. Let us hope no one will be down by the river at the tunnel's entrance." She glanced at Flenn. "I'm afraid we will have to walk a long way to no be seen."

"I suspect your brother will only be out of commission for a day or so; we need to do this now," Flenn said.

"Sí," she agreed, "tonight."

"Have you been in this tunnel before?"

Theresa sighed. "I used to hide there at night after the priest die. I stay there many weeks until some boys..."

they saw me begging on the roadside; one day they follow me. I was twelve."

Flenn understood.

"I think they maybe feel bad and so they leave some money. It was then I learn how I will survive."

"You've been doing this since you were twelve?"

"It's not so bad, really. I decide when to work and where. I have a small apartment in a nice part of town where no one knows what I am. That is where I go when I left you and your friend. It is my peaceful place."

Flenn looked out the window. "Back home, working girls are usually forced to work for a pimp, which usually doesn't go so well."

"That is why I work for myself. Juan no let others hurt me, but that is all he do for me. I do less for him. I have nada to do with him since the padre died." Theresa wiped her eyes, but they were tears more of anger than of grief. "I am sorry. Sometimes when I am upset my English is not so goodly."

"Quit apologizing; your English is fine. So, where are we heading?"

She took a breath. "To a place where we can eat something and get what we need. I know a woman there; if you pay her fifty dollars she will help us. I will ask her to pick us up on a nearby road after we rescue Señor Zack."

"And we're not driving to this road ourselves because… "

"Es muy obvio." She shook her head. "Too obvious. We no risk seeing…" She was frustrated with herself, "…being seen."

Flenn leaned back into the seat, lost in thought for several miles. Eventually, he nodded. "Good," he said at last. "Looks like we have a plan."

CHAPTER *THIRTY-FIVE*

Theresa drove for another half-hour before pulling into a large roadside stand where a handful of people were eating and drinking beer under a canopy. They looked surprised to see a tall, good looking, white man getting out of a truck with a woman they all knew well.

Theresa told Flenn that she worked the stand at the end of each month, when the rancheros paid the laborers. She knew the woman who owned the place. Theresa had been bragging for the last ten minutes about the woman's baleada—a mixture of beans, cheese, sour cream, and avocado wrapped in a flour tortilla. A young girl who brought him a cup of coffee and a plate of three baleadas gave Theresa an approving smile. *Might as well be thought of as her date for the evening*, Flenn thought as he downed the coffee and signaled for another.

They sat at a table under the awning and ate while patrons drifted in and out. Flenn assumed that most of the people lived nearby and stopped here for a bite and a beer, or just to swap stories at the end of the day. They all eyed the tall stranger, but Flenn simply smiled and pretended to fawn over Theresa—something the people here neither judged nor scorned, just simply accepted. Theresa pointed out her friend, who was busily cooking on a wood stove under a canopy roof. Theresa told Flenn that the short, withered woman's name was Carmen. The old woman kept glancing across the tables at them until, at last, she handed her spatula to a younger woman and signaled to Theresa.

Carmen led Flenn and Theresa behind the stand where the three of them climbed into an ancient Chevrolet Vega. The faded yellow paint was almost completely replaced by rust. Most of the passenger-side floorboard had rotted away, forcing Flenn to spread his legs wide to keep them from falling through. Theresa and Carmen spoke quickly as Carmen guzzled a beer and tossed the empty can between Flenn's legs. He watched it disappear on the dirt road beneath him.

The women spoke too fast for Flenn to be able to follow the conversation. Carmen tossed him a flashlight and handed Theresa one as well. She muttered something unintelligible, and Theresa leaned forward to translate. "She said there is a machete underneath her seat and that you should reach between her legs and take it." Flenn scowled back at Theresa.

"Just do it."

Begrudgingly, he obliged.

"She likes you," Theresa teased. "She says you are muy handsome."

Flenn pulled out the machete. "Tell her thank you for the compliment, and for the machete, but I don't need this thing."

Theresa shook her head. "You'd better take it. She say it is her finest one… quite an honor."

"Finest one? How many does she have?" Flenn

thought it best not to insult their ticket out of this mess, so he gingerly removed the machete from its sheath. The steel had been polished to a mirror finish and was razor sharp. *This is not for coconuts,* he told himself.

Flenn peered out the windshield at the sky ahead. The afternoon sun promised maybe two more hours of daylight at the most. He sighed, glad that Zack was alive, but concerned about the kind of shape his friend might be in when they found him. Theresa's plan promised the advantage of surprise, but then what? Rescuing Zack and getting them all out alive were two different things. *Still,* he reminded himself, *Theresa seemed sure this would work… and what other options did they have? If she were planning to betray him and deliver him to the Asesinos, she could have found a much simpler way.*

Or would she?

This could be the perfect plan, he mused. *Take him to the old church with Zack and wait for Scudder to finish them both off. But then why arm him with a machete? Plus, she knew that he had Zack's pistol…* He shook his head and frowned. *No, he wouldn't let himself think like that.*

He pulled the pistol from Zack's backpack and checked that everything was in working order. A shiver ran down his spine; he hadn't carried a weapon in years, nor did he want to now, but what other choice was there? He had to save Zack and take out Scudder.

He took a deep breath.

Or die trying.

CHAPTER *THIRTY-SIX*

Carmen slowed down until she came to a stop by an abandoned grove of pineapple trees. As they climbed out of the car, Flenn prayed a silent prayer his mother used to recite long ago: *"Protect us from faithless fears and worldly anxieties, and grant that no clouds in this mortal life may hide from us thy light."*

Carmen and Theresa spoke briefly, presumably finalizing plans for their rendezvous later. At least that's what Flenn hoped they were doing. They were still speaking way too fast for him to follow, plus he was busy assessing the terrain for any signs of danger.

Carmen drove away as they walked into the grove. Flenn fell in behind Theresa, impressed not only by her knowledge of the terrain, but by her bravery. *They were about to walk into a gang-infested hideout facing God-knows-what, and she didn't seem the least bit nervous. Was it courage,* he wondered, *or something else?* He tried to chase the idea from his mind, but ever since he'd learned that Juan was her brother, he'd found himself watching Theresa's every move. It wasn't that he feared for his own safety, or, shamefully, even Zack's, as much as it was an over-whelming need to settle the score with Scudder. Flenn thought of the children from San Jose de la Montaña— children who'd still be alive if not for that psychopath.

Scudder deserved to die. He had been the one who'd killed the janitor's son 20 years ago, he had stolen the artifacts, and worst of all, he had murdered a dozen innocent children.

But he hadn't done it alone, Flenn reminded himself. Flenn didn't know who else was helping Scudder, but they would also have to pay, he told himself.

He took a deep breath.

And then it would be Schmitt's turn!

Jeremy Schmitt had been the driving force behind Scudder all along. First in Korea, and now this. Flenn brushed his hand over the gun in his waistband. *No, this wouldn't be over when Scudder was dead. Others would have to pay!* A wave of guilt swept over the priest as a voice in his head asked, *"Where does it all end?"*

They had been walking for over a mile when Theresa stopped to get her bearings. A few seconds later, she veered off to the right with Flenn close behind as they made their way down an overgrown footpath. Suddenly Theresa held up her hand—they both froze. She looked left, then right, her face taut as she quickly withdrew her pistol. Flenn followed suit with Zack's .45, although he didn't see or hear anything. Then it hit him. *He didn't hear anything at all!* The grove had grown eerily quiet.

"Jaguar," Theresa whispered.

A second later, they heard a low snarl just off to their left. "Get out your machete," she whispered. "They don't recognize a pistol but they know what a machete can do." Flenn obeyed and flashed the shiny blade in front of him, hoping that the invisible beast would see the blade and back off. Just then they heard a sound that would have almost been comical were the danger not so real.

"Did that thing just sneeze?"

"Padre, *shh!*"

Suddenly, they saw it. The jaguar was on the path in front of them, almost as if it had appeared out of thin air. It wasn't coming toward them or preparing to pounce, but was slowly walking away. Theresa checked to see if there were others, but the big cat was alone. A minute later, the birds began to chirp again. The cat stopped, then did something totally unexpected—it sat down and began to bathe!

"*Um*, is it washing up before a meal?"

"They only do that *after* they've eaten," Theresa said. She lowered her weapon. "He doesn't seem interested in us." The jaguar glanced up at her and cocked its head slightly. Then it looked over at Flenn holding a pistol in one hand and a machete in the other. Their eyes met, and something in the way the big cat looked at him made Flenn feel ashamed, as if the animal disapproved of what it was seeing. The jaguar sneezed again, stretched, and went back to grooming itself.

"Come on," Theresa said, heading off the path to the right, "let's go before he change his mind."

They made their way farther into the grove, checking behind them frequently. After a time, Flenn spoke up. "Assuming that thing doesn't chase after us, remind me just how we're getting out of here."

"Carmen will pick us up on the other side of the church. She's waiting for me to give her—how do you say it—a head's up. Then I will call a second time when we have your friend. She drives up, we jump in, off we go." She made a motion with her hand as if it was a speeding car. "Hopefully the Asesinos no chase us."

"Assuming we can do this quietly."

Theresa nodded. "I am assuming many things, Padre. Juan say they hold Señor Zack in the basement. I can sneak us in there… hopefully we get him out and no be noticed."

"What if they have a guard on him?"

She shook her head. "The door from the tunnel was painted over many years ago. It is not so easy to see. If we do this right, no one will know we have come and go, and there will be no reason for them to follow Carmen's car."

Flenn had to ask. "And if all does not go well?

She looked at him. "Then, Carmen, she drive like hell!"

CHAPTER *THIRTY-SEVEN*

Walking through the jungle reminded Flenn of his descent from the village. *When was that,* he asked himself, *just a couple of days ago?* It seemed like an eternity.

Flenn's shoulder ached but he forced himself to concentrate instead on the task at hand. Although he tried not to think of the children from the mountain, images of their faces looking up at him before the missiles struck kept flashing through his mind. *They were so trusting, so innocent.*

Flenn shuddered.

Damn Scudder to hell for all eternity for what he did!

Flenn took a deep breath; *he couldn't let his emotions have control over him, not with a jaguar behind them and the Asesinos in front!*

As they hiked through the forest, Flenn said a prayer for the parents of San Jose de la Montaña. Flenn's faith assured him that the children were safely tucked away in a land where there was no pain, only joy; but while he firmly believed the children were in heaven, he knew their parents were going through hell. He desperately wanted to ease their suffering but could think of only one way to do it... *well two,* but he hadn't worked out the second one quite yet.

The first was to take out Eric Scudder. Sarah

Coverdale, no doubt, had other plans, but it didn't matter. *He was going to kill Scudder, no matter what. Sarah would just have to accept it; and so would Zack.* Zack was a friend, but Flenn wondered just how far would that friendship take him. Zack was loyal to his work above all else. If Sarah ordered Zack to take Scudder alive, Flenn would somehow have to find a way to convince him otherwise.

As for the second way of easing the parents' suffering; Flenn would have to return to the village for that... alone.

He and Theresa were out of the pineapple grove now and walking through a large clearing. She explained that for centuries people had traveled out here to a large lake to hunt, fish, and trade with others living in villages along the shore. Over time, roads had been built and the people had been able to travel by buses or cars. Then, oddly enough, the roads that used to bring people *into* the villages became avenues which their descendants took *out* of them. Theresa told him that the old church had remained to serve the few who had stayed. She explained that the priest who'd rescued Theresa and Juan as children had tried to keep the tiny parish going, "But when he was murdered, the church die too," she said.

Flenn could just make out a collapsing fencerow ahead, and beyond it was the lake, much larger than he'd expected. Above, small, fluffy clouds were silhouetted by the late afternoon sun. Colorful birds flew gracefully overhead as the sweet smell of flowers drifted on the breeze. Flenn stopped for a moment to take it all in. The opening words of Psalm 19 came to mind as he gazed across the lake. *"The heavens declare the glory of God; the skies proclaim the work of his hands."*

The moment's peacefulness withered as Flenn remembered the children from the village, none of whom would ever again experience the beauty of their homeland.

Theresa led him along the shore as the last orange and yellow streaks of daylight were fading in the sky. She pointed up the hill. "La Iglesia!" Flenn looked at the old church sitting atop the precipice. Any other day, he might have found the scene picturesque, even charming. Now though, the dark stone edifice looming over them seemed more like a gruesome castle.

The pair wound their way around the lakeshore until they reached a small knoll. Underneath, Flenn could just make out what appeared to be a set of double doors covered by years of leaves and branches. A rusted chain and padlock bound the doors together. Flenn cleared the brush away and asked Theresa for one of the bobby pins in her hair. She didn't understand what he meant. He reached up and pulled one out, allowing a wisp of her brunette locks to fall lazily across her face. *She'd probably been an attractive woman once,* he thought, and *perhaps could still be if she had the opportunity to live a different life.*

He inserted the pin into the lock and tried to trick the mechanism into opening.

Theresa smiled. "Perhaps we should use the key, no?" She knelt, feeling under the leaves until she found what she was looking for, a large rock tucked near the door. She reached underneath and pulled out a small plastic bag. Inside was an ancient, rusty-bronze key. "This is where I used to keep it when I was a little girl," she said. "It is still here after all these years."

"Let's just hope it works," Flenn said as she pushed the key into the lock. The tumblers complained, but opened after some effort. Quietly, they removed the chain.

Theresa retrieved her phone to give Carmen a heads-up, telling her to be ready for the next call. Putting the phone in her back pocket, Theresa drew her pistol. "You stay here, Padre, I will be right back."

"What?" Flenn stiffened. "There's no way you're going in there alone. I'm going with you!"

"You cannot."

"I not only can, I will," he argued.

"Listen to me," she said, looking directly into his eyes. "I know my way around this tunnel. You do not. There are twists and turns and low-hanging beams. We can no use our flashlight because someone might see light coming through the other door. I can no get your friend out if I am trying to guide you too."

"But… "

She handed him her water bottle. His was already empty. "Look, do you want your friend or no? If so, then you stay out here and wait."

Flenn looked away; he knew she was right. He'd only slow her down. Before he could answer, Theresa took a deep breath and disappeared into the darkness.

Flenn had never been good at losing an argument, but he was even worse at standing around waiting. Still, the coolness of the dank tunnel felt good after their hike in the hot sun. Flenn wondered whether gasses might have built up inside the tunnel, especially since it had been closed off for years, but there was nothing he could do about it now except wait.

Outside, dusk was rapidly turning into twilight. A gibbous moon was rising on the horizon. The light reflecting off the lake made everything look surreal. He reached into his waistband and pulled out Zack's Glock... just in case. As he did, Flenn heard what sounded like a faint growl in the distance. Sure enough, there at the water's edge stood a jaguar. *It couldn't be the same one... could it?* The animal turned, looked straight at him, growled again, and then sauntered slowly toward the jungle.

Inside the tunnel Theresa was feeling her way along the cold and damp walls. She remembered most of the twists and turns from years ago, though she occasionally stopped to use the dim light from her cell phone to get her bearings. She recalled how she and her brother used to play in the tunnel. Later, after the priest was killed, she had hidden here from the rest of the world. It was also here where she had learned she could trade her body for money. Boys from the village would meet her here after school... She wiped her eyes as it all came back to her. It was as if the very walls were saturated with the pain of her past.

She had gotten pregnant just before her 14th birthday.

Frightened and alone, she had left the baby near the gate of an orphanage in San Pedro Sula. She had waited behind the bushes across the street, listening to her daughter's cries, while forcing herself to remain hidden. Eventually, one of the nuns had heard the baby and come to investigate. Theresa had never seen her daughter again. The tunnel was full of so many horrible memories; but then, so was most of her life.

Theresa wished now that she had allowed the priest to come with her. *Somehow, the padre made her feel better about… well, everything.* He had a kind soul, one that seemed to reach out and envelop her, making her feel safe. She had felt absolutely no judgment from the padre, nor pity either. She simply felt accepted, as if she was worth something in his eyes. She'd felt the same way with the priest who had rescued them after their mother was taken away. He had been the one to show them this tunnel as a shortcut to the lake. She and Juan had begged the kind man to let them paint over the entranceway, so that it could just be their little secret. The priest had obliged their childish whimsy, but only if they both promised to be better about saying their daily prayers.

She had buried so many of her memories of the man who had once rescued them, just as she had buried the memories of her mother. Now, back in the tunnel, they flowed over her like the tide of a massive sea. Theresa brushed away the tears and kept moving. She had a job to do. A man needed her, and not in the way most men needed her. This was a good man, a man worth saving. She had not known very many good men in her life, and she was determined to do all she could for the padre and his friend.

They were an odd pair, the padre and Señor Zack. She never asked how it was that they were together; she'd learned long ago that too much knowledge could be a dangerous thing.

What could be more dangerous than this? she asked herself.

She shook her head. *What on earth had compelled her to help these two white men? Just who were they, and why did someone want to kill them? Maybe when this was over she would ask the padre. Then again, maybe not. He was a holy man, she saw it in his face the moment they walked into el Marcositas. Had he always been a holy man? If so, how was it that he seemed so familiar with that pistol? And, what was his connection with the man she had come to rescue? Señor Zack was a good man, but he had a different soul... he had killed before, and would kill again.* She didn't know how she knew that, she just did. *What had brought these two very different men together; what bond was it they shared?*

Questions without answers... but then, she didn't really need answers right now. What she was doing felt right, and it had been a long time since something she'd felt this way. *Maybe she would never make it to heaven,* she thought, *but maybe someone up there would at least see that she was doing a good thing now in helping the padre.*

Theresa felt something smooth against her hand and knew that she had reached the slated walls of the tunnel. Only another 20 feet or so to the hidden entrance to the undercroft. That was where Juan had told her his men would be holding the padre's friend. *Almost there*, she told herself as she felt her way along. She had no idea what she would find on the other side of the door, but Juan assured her that none of the Asesinos knew about the tunnel—he'd kept it a secret in case he ever needed to use it himself.

At last she felt the door in front of her. Theresa retrieved her pistol and prepared to push. Hopefully Zack would be alone, and they'd be gone before anyone knew otherwise. If someone *was* with him, she'd just have to hold the guard at bay while Zack escaped. She would give Zack the phone and tell him how to call Carmen. The gang would be angry, but they wouldn't dare harm the sister of their leader.

Theresa had not prayed since she was a child, but maybe, she thought, a prayer wouldn't hurt right now—if not for herself, then for Señor Zack, and if not for Zack, then in honor of the two priests in her life who had treated her kindly. It was a simple prayer, a child's prayer, really, but it came from her heart. Theresa crossed herself, then braced her shoulder against the door, turned the handle, and pushed.

It didn't budge.

CHAPTER *THIRTY-EIGHT*

Even bound and gagged, Zack wasn't afraid. Truth be told, he was bored. The only time his two captors allowed him any freedom was when he ate or used the bucket over in the corner of the room. *God, when were they going to empty that thing?* They cut his hands loose for both activities, but only removed the duct tape from his mouth when he ate. Obviously, they weren't interested in anything he had to say.

A big man, with an ancient .38 strapped to his side, brought down food twice a day and stayed until after he ate, when they would tape Zack's mouth and hands back. Zack had nicknamed the big guy Louie. He'd already figured out how to disarm him the next time he came down the stairs; that is, if he had Huey and Dewey taken care of first. Armed with Louie's pistol, he figured he'd take one of the gang members hostage and hold the others off while he commandeered one of their vehicles and made his escape. It wasn't the perfect plan, but he'd pulled similar stunts before.

Zack looked across at his would-be guards. Huey and Dewey were playing checkers again—they were just as bored as he was.

"*Mmm, mmm...* " Zack shook his head at Huey who

was about to make the next move. The teen looked down at the checkerboard and saw that the move would have cost him the game. He smiled and moved his king to the left. Zack nodded in agreement.

Dewey countered by moving one of his own two kings. Huey placed his hand on a piece but Zack protested again. Huey put his finger on another piece and looked at Zack, who shook his head. He then touched his only other free piece and Zack nodded. In three more moves Huey had won the game.

Dewey threw down a couple of lempiras and they began the next match. Zack continued to signal Huey throughout the game, and Huey won again. In the middle of the third game and Zack's umpteenth *"Mmm, mmm,"* Dewey kicked the game board onto the floor and glared at Zack. The two teens had a heated exchange. Dewey pulled out his switchblade… Zack took a breath, pretending to be frightened. Dewey sneered as he cut him loose, but left the tape over Zack's mouth. The boy pointed to the checkerboard, which Huey had set back on the barrel, and then to the folding chair next to it.

Game on!

Zack beat the kid easily the first game, but let him win the next one. The bottle of Jack Daniel's sitting next to them was nearly empty, but Zack nodded toward it. Dewey shrugged, so Huey pulled the tape from his mouth. Zack took a small swig from the bottle.

The third game, the one that would decide the championship, went painfully slow. Zack dragged it out for as long as he could, until it came down to just seven pieces on the board. Dewey was concentrating heavily. It could be anyone's game at this point. Huey was watching off to the side as Zack put his finger on one piece, then another. Huey could see Zack's only obvious move, but apparently the gringo hadn't figured it out yet. The white man took another swig from the bottle and then put his finger on one of the red checkers. Unbelievable! The gringo was about to make the absolute worst move possible. Huey leaned in, dumbfounded that the man would make such a stupid move.

He never saw the bottle heading for his head.

As the kid crumpled unconscious to the floor, Zack shot out his left hand, grabbed Dewey by the throat, and yanked him across the table. The kid was small, but surprisingly strong, and managed to get in a few good punches before Zack placed him in a headlock. The spy pushed his training aside, refusing to twist the boy's head and waiting instead for him to simply pass out.

Zack went to work quickly, taping mouths, arms and legs, and pushing his unconscious guards to the furthest corner, away from the stairs. Louie, if he remained true to form, wouldn't be down for another half an hour. Zack unscrewed the lightbulb and sat in darkness, allowing his eyes to adjust to the sliver of light coming from underneath the door at the top of the stairs. As soon as he could see well enough, he'd climb the stairs and wait.

Thump!

Zack whirled around. Something—someone—was on the other side of the far wall, behind the painted door. He waited, but there was only silence.

A moment passed; another thump. The door flew open.

His jaw dropped.

No way!

CHAPTER *THIRTY-NINE*

Flenn didn't move until the jaguar was out of sight. After that, he checked to see if there were any other beasts that might be stalking him—four or two-legged ones—but saw only the small hillside to his right, the jungle to the left, and the lake directly in front of him. Behind him stood the door to the tunnel, and beyond that was the church where Zack was being held hostage.

To the right, from what Theresa had told him, was a seldom-traveled dirt road just over a little hill. Assuming that she and Zack each made it back, that's where they would rendezvous with Carmen. Unfortunately, the hillside could be seen all too easily from the church, which was why they hadn't come that way. Once Theresa returned with Zack, they'd have to risk it and move fast.

Theresa froze. If the door was blocked, there'd be no way to rescue Zack without risking her life. A shootout with her brother's gang would not end well. She took a breath then shoved with all her might. This time the door suddenly gave way, causing her to lose her balance and sprawl across the floor, sending her pistol sliding across the concrete.

The room was dark and silent. *No one was here!*

She risked using the flashlight Carmen had given her, but saw nothing other than a checkerboard and few blankets on the ground. About a dozen empty bottles were scattered across the floor. There was no furniture, no cabinets... just a couple of barrels. When she'd been a little girl, a Sunday school class used to meet down here––nothing from that time remained. The desks, chalkboard, pictures of Bible stories were all gone. She shone the light in the far corner and saw them: two unconscious Asesinos, face down on the floor!

Something touched her shoulder!

Theresa whirled around and shone the flashlight... directly into Zack's smiling face.

"Sorry hon, if I'd known you were coming I would have ordered pizza."

"Señor Zack!"

"In the flesh. Here, you dropped something." He handed the pistol to her.

She was elated to see him. "You are okay?"

"I'm fine, but those two in the corner will be waking up soon with a terrible headache." He grabbed her by the arm and ushered her toward the tunnel. "Since I don't seem to have any aspirin, I suggest we leave before that happens."

Inside the tunnel, Theresa turned to close the door behind them. She laughed. "They will think you vanished into thin air! What did you do to them?"

"Let's just say that they aren't very skilled at playing checkers." Zack nudged her forward. Now that they were heading away from the basement, it was safe to use the flashlight. Theresa handed the light to Zack and dialed Carmen's number.

Nothing.

Underground, her cell phone couldn't find a signal. She'd try again as soon as they were outside.

Flenn heard them before he could see them. Theresa had been quiet and light-footed entering the tunnel, but neither she nor Zack were moving cautiously now, and were hurriedly heading his way. "Is there anyone behind you?"

"Not yet," Theresa answered.

"Why?" Zack quipped. "Were you hoping for someone else?"

Flenn couldn't keep from smiling. "Always!"

Theresa tried her phone again; this time she got a signal. Carmen told her she'd be at the rendezvous in less than four minutes, about the time it would take for the three of them to make it over the hill to the road—without being spotted, Flenn hoped, by jaguars or Asesinos.

Theresa took the lead and the two men fell in behind her. No one spoke a word, but Flenn watched Zack for any sign of injuries. He seemed okay, better than Flenn was right now; his shoulder was aching fiercely. A large cloud crossed in front of the moon, making it easier for them to go unnoticed. Once over the embankment, they caught sight of two headlights approaching from the south. Zack and Flenn crouched down until Theresa gave them the all clear.

There was no place for Carmen to turn around, which meant that she had to keep driving straight ahead, in full view of the church. The three passengers ducked as Carmen passed the front entrance. Flenn was closest to the rear passenger window and risked taking a quick glance. Several young men were sitting on the front steps of the church, silhouetted by a small campfire. No one seemed interested in the car cruising past. Once they were well away from the church, everyone sat up. "You okay?" Flenn asked Zack.

Zack was sore and tired but grinned and said, "Never better. How about you?" Flenn's shoulder was bothering him, but not as much as the cold steel of the Glock pressed against his back. He pulled it out of his waistband, glad to hand it back over to Zack.

"I will be… once we find Eric Scudder."

CHAPTER *FORTY*

Making their way to Carmen's roadside stand, Flenn filled Zack in on how they'd managed to find him. At the stand, a large crowd had gathered; they were all drinking beer, laughing and talking. Theresa thought she recognized some of the Asesinos among the patrons and instructed Carmen to keep driving. She drove for another mile before dropping Flenn and Zack off on the side of the road. Theresa told them to wait while she went back to retrieve her truck.

"What if Juan's men follow you?" Flenn asked. "They probably know your truck when they see it."

She nodded. "Sí, that may be why they are there; they may be waiting for me," she said.

Zack thought for a moment. "Theresa, try to get to your truck without them noticing. I'm sure they will see your truck leaving, so when you come back here, pull over and Flenn will get in the truck with you. Drive ahead about fifty yards, then pull over again. If anyone's following you, they'll pull in behind you. I'll sneak up behind them." Zack looked at Flenn. "Do you remember what to do next?" Flenn nodded. He recalled doing the same maneuver with Zack once in Istanbul. *If anyone was following Theresa, they'd be concentrating on her truck and not looking behind them.*

Carmen and Theresa turned around and headed back to the stand. Minutes later, Flenn and Zack saw Theresa's headlights coming their way, fast. She pulled over and Flenn climbed quickly into the cab and crouched low. Zack hid in a thicket. He figured Flenn was explaining the details to Theresa as the cab lights dimmed and she drove away. Sure enough, another set of headlights came over the hill in their direction. As instructed, Theresa pulled over and waited as the car pulled in behind her. From his vantage point Zack could see it was a 1960-something Ford, in even worse shape than Carmen's wreck had been. Zack shook his head, wondering how the Ford was still on the road.

Theresa exited the cab and leaned against the rear of her truck. Zack couldn't see Flenn, but knew he'd be ready. Two young men got out of the Ford; neither appeared armed. As they approached Theresa, one of them pointed to the cab—the passenger door kept opening and closing, seemingly by itself. Just as one of the men reached into his pocket, Zack chambered a round. It was a sound they both knew well and they wheeled around to find his .45 pointed straight at them.

Theresa pulled her own weapon and instructed the men—boys—to lie face down on the side of the road. Zack patted them down and found a couple of switchblades, along with their cell phones. He kept one of the knives and tossed everything else into the brush.

Flenn jumped out of the truck the moment Zack appeared. He leaned into the gang's old Ford to turn off the ignition and retrieve the keys, which he also threw into the tall grass. Using some duct tape from the back of Theresa's truck, he tied their hands and feet together, covered their mouths, and rolled them into the underbrush. It would be a while before they'd be able to free themselves. As they drove away, Flenn prayed that the Asesinos wouldn't take out their frustration on Carmen's or her stand.

Theresa drove for hours before arriving in a little town where she said they'd be safe. Back home, it was customary to hand over a credit card when checking into a hotel. Fortunately, the clerk here hadn't asked for one. Cash, especially American cash, seemed to open doors just about everywhere. While Theresa paid for their room, Zack reached into his backpack for his satellite phone to call Sarah. "Damn!" he swore aloud. The battery was dead. At least he'd be able to charge it once they were in a room.

Theresa returned with a key and three bottles of water. Their room was on the second floor, and reasonably clean, with a television and plenty of hot water. Compared to where he'd just been, it seemed like a palace to Zack. Unfortunately, it only had one bed.

"I suggest we take turns watching out the window tonight just in case we have company," Zack said. "One of the *Ases-a-holes* might come looking for us."

"Asesinos," corrected Theresa. "It means assassins."

"Thank God they weren't, or Zack wouldn't be here," Flenn said on his way to the shower.

"Trust me, I spent two days with them," Zack said. "My name suits them much better."

Theresa laughed as she tossed him a bottle of water. "True, they are not very smart," she said, "except for Juan—do not underestimate him."

"You mean Baldy? The one you took to the fancy hospital?"

Flenn stuck his head out of the bathroom. "You wouldn't happen to know anything about his broken leg, would you?"

Zack smiled. "What can I say? He's a sucker for a roundhouse kick. Wouldn't last long in the ring. What's his story anyway?"

"Why don't you ask Theresa?" Flenn called from the bathroom. "She's his little sister."

Zack's eyes widened. "What?!"

Theresa shrugged.

"Your brother?"

"Sì. But not worry. The padre pay him very much money to keep him quiet."

"How much did you give him?" Zack called into the bathroom.

"A lot," Flenn called back.

"How do you know he won't double-cross you?"

"Because he is my brother," Theresa said, "and he has never let anyone hurt me. Also, because this job has cost him too much already. The padre paid for a good hospital with very fine doctors. Juan could have died from infection in a regular hospital, and he knows it. At the very least, he would have been crippled the rest of his life. The padre took good care of him. He will be fine."

Zack shook his head. "That sounds like Flenn these

days. Someone tries to sell him to a killer, and he ends up helping him."

"These days? The padre was not always this way?"

Zack crossed to the window and peered through the blinds. All was quiet outside. "Let's just say he had a come-to-Jesus moment when everything changed for him awhile back."

Theresa looked puzzled. "Come to Je-sus?"

Zack smiled. "You ever heard of a place called Edinburgh?"

She had not.

"Never mind. It's a long story." Zack watched a car pull into a parking space outside. A couple with three children got out and entered the office. The car was far too nice to belong to one of the Asesinos.

"Theresa, tell me about the cars in your country?"

"Qué?"

"The cars... they seem to be either very new or very old."

She came to the window and looked out at the parking lot which was filled with late-model vehicles. "For many centuries, we were either poor or rich in this country, no in-between. When the big pineapple companies come here, they create a... a..."

"A middle class?" Zack offered.

"Sí, a middle class. The first thing people want to do in Honduras when they have money is buy a car."

Zack nodded. "Same in America."

"Cars have," she was searching for a word... "muy estado..."

"Status?"

"Sí, status."

Zack looked outside at her Toyota. "You certainly have a nice truck."

"What else would I spend my money on? I do not drink, at least not much. I do not do drugs." She lowered her eyes. "I have no children."

Zack picked up on what she was not saying. "You mean with you."

"Qué?"

"You have no children *with* you, but you *have* children, am I right?"

She turned away. Zack decided not to press. He checked his phone; there wasn't enough charge to make a call. Flenn came out of the bathroom in his underwear. "I wonder if this place has a laundry."

"Sí, I saw one near the office." She looked at Zack. "Right now, I could use that pizza Señor Zack promise me back at the church."

"Me, too!" said Zack.

Flenn grinned. "You mean your hosts didn't feed you?"

"Beans," Zack said. "I don't want to talk about it."

Flenn groaned. "Knowing you and your relationship with beans, I don't blame you."

Theresa called downstairs and arranged for a meal to be brought up to the room along with a six-pack of Salva Vida. Flenn flipped on the television but the only program in English was *Hogan's Heroes*, a comedy from the 1960s depicting American prisoners in a Nazi prisoner of war camp. "Hey Zack, this remind you of anything?"

Zack pointed to the TV. "I bet they had better food," he quipped. "Why don't you take a turn at the window while I get a shower. I know I must stink to high heaven."

"Heaven's got nothing to do with the way you smell. Make it a long one!"

Flenn and Theresa waited for the food to arrive while Zack followed orders and took a long, hot shower. A lady brought up tortillas filled with meat and vegetables.

They watched back-to-back episodes of *Hogan's Heroes* as they ate. During the commercials, Theresa asked questions about World War II. She seemed to know very little about world history—only what she had gleaned from elementary school or from Spanish telecasts of CNN and the Travel Channel.

"I wish to go to Holland someday," she said in-between bites. "I have a book from there. I cannot read it, but it has many beautiful pictures of pretty flowers and big," she held her hands out, "how you say…"

"Windmills?" Flenn offered.

"Sí, yes, wind-tills. I want to see the land of the wind-tills."

"Mills," said Flenn. "*Windmills.*"

"Sí, wind…mills."

Theresa got up and made her way to the shower as Zack came out wearing a towel. Flenn called to her, "Take some extra towels with you this time!"

"Oh, leave her alone," Zack said following her with his eyes.

"I intend to. It's *you* I'm worried about."

Zack crossed to the window and peeked through the blinds. "I'll take first watch, but I'm warning you, Flenn, I'll be right here. So, no funny stuff, you two!"

Flenn hit him with a pillow. "Very funny; besides, I'm taking first watch. You need to sleep. Theresa can take over from me in a couple of hours." Ordinarily, Zack would have argued, but not tonight. He was too exhausted. The tortillas and beer had helped, but what his body needed most was a good night's rest. He dropped the towel and climbed into bed.

Flenn hit him in the face with a pair of underwear. "And put those back on."

CHAPTER *FORTY-ONE*

Flenn hadn't stood watch in years, although he had experienced many sleepless nights since leaving the CIA—offering last rites at 2 a.m., staying up all night with the parents of run-aways, and doing countless other things Zack probably would never be able to comprehend… or appreciate.

Zack, who was snoring loudly now, never had understood why Flenn had left the agency. Flenn had tried the best he could to explain what he'd experienced in Edinburgh, but Zack had been sure that his friend had lost his mind. Truthfully, Flenn wondered sometimes if it had all been a dream; but, in the end, it really didn't matter, Edinburgh had changed his life.

Flenn loved being a priest… at least he *had* loved it. Now, he mostly felt ashamed, as if he was turning his back on everything he had stood for since leaving the agency. He gazed out the window into the stillness of the night and tried to make sense of it all. *The priesthood had brought him peace and a deep sense of his place in the universe. But it had also had led him here to Honduras, and to the children of the mountain.*

Bzzzt!

Flenn jumped as Zack's satellite phone buzzed. Only one person had this number: Sarah Coverdale. He considered waking Zack, then thought better of it. *In for a penny, in for a pound.*

"Hello Sarah."

"Who is this?"

"Don't you remember your former partner?"

"Flenn?"

"In the flesh. Well, a bit more flesh than back when you knew me."

"God, Flenn, it's been ages!" Sarah sounded happy to hear his voice. "I would ask what you've been up to lately, but… "

Flenn finished the sentence for her, "But you already know."

"Jesus, Flenn… oops sorry; I still can't get used to it. You being a priest, a real priest this time, not like the one you pretended to be that time in Rome."

Flenn cocked his head. "How'd you know about Rome?"

"Haven't you heard? I made it to the big leagues; I know everything these days. My Lord, Scott Flenn, a real, bona-fide priest!"

"Yep," he answered. "Have holy water, will travel."

Sarah drew in a breath. "What's it like, I mean compared to being an agent?"

Flenn leaned back in his chair and looked through the blinds. "Let's see. I sleep and eat regularly, I don't keep a gun under my pillow anymore, I don't ever have to look over my shoulder, and my conscious is clear... at least it was."

"Flenn, this wasn't your fault. Scudder's had you on

his radar ever since Korea. I'm sorry I was two steps behind him, but, I'm close to figuring out why Schmitt got him out of prison. Once I can prove it, we'll take care of things on the Washington side." She paused. "I'm afraid it is still up to you and Zack to get Scudder. Whatever Schmitt's planning, Scudder is the key. Otherwise he wouldn't have gone to so much trouble to bust Scudder out of that South Korean jail."

"Bust him out?"

"Might as well have—Schmitt pulled all sorts of tricks to get the Koreans to let him go. You don't kill a local over there then try to sneak off with national treasures and expect to make many friends."

"Scudder never made friends anywhere," Flenn said. "It's hard to like an immature, narcissistic braggart like him."

"Well, I'm glad you guys finally answered the phone," Sarah said. "I was getting worried."

"We got sidetracked. Scudder hired a local gang of thugs for insurance. They proved to be a nuisance, that's all—not the brightest bulbs in the box. Oh, and we've made a friend down here." He glanced at Theresa, who was sound asleep. "She's been a great help."

"A woman?" Sarah seemed surprised.

Flenn laughed. "Why Sarah, you, of all people, are not being sexist, are you?"

"Of course not, but you know Zack's weaknesses better than I do."

"I think Donna cured him of that... ex-wives can have that effect, you know."

Sarah sighed into the phone. "Nobody can cure Zack Matteson!"

He looked at Zack and Theresa, both half naked and sound asleep in the same bed with their backs toward one another. "I wouldn't bet on that right now if I were you," Flenn said.

"I assume Zack's none the worse for wear?"

"He's okay. He's asleep, though, and I'm not going to wake him; so, whatever you needed to say to him you're just going to have to say to me."

Sarah hesitated, but only for a second. "Why not? Okay, I know where Scudder is. He's in a vacant hacienda about 25 miles outside Tegucigalpa. I'll give you the coordinates. And, there's more."

Flenn's eyes narrowed. "Tell me."

"I talked with the lieutenant at the base that set up his password for the drone. Zack will need it to disarm the thing once he takes the key from Scudder."

Flenn wrote down the coordinates Sarah gave to him. "Okay, what's the password?"

"You aren't going to believe this."

"Try me."

"It's you."

"What?"

"It is you. His password is Flenn."

Flenn simply shook his head. "Figures."

"You do remember how to spell it, right?"

Flenn didn't want to ask the next question, but he did anyway. "So, what are we supposed to do with Scudder once we find him?"

Sarah hesitated. "I may need him up here in order to hang all this on Schmitt."

"Scudder hasn't turned on Schmitt in twenty years, why would he betray him now?"

"I suspect he tried, especially when Schmitt didn't come to his rescue," Sarah said, "but the Koreans weren't listening."

Flenn thought about that for a moment. "So... the agency *did* abandon Scudder after his arrest?"

"Schmitt would have seen to it, lest Scudder start singing once he got home."

Flenn nodded. *Tucked away in a Korean prison, no one in Washington would ever know about Schmitt's involvement.* "So, why are they buddy-buddy all of a sudden?"

"Leave that to me. Right now, I need Scudder, so make sure you and Zack bring him in alive."

Flenn had never lied to Sarah, so he said, "I'll relay the message to Zack." And he would, just not until after Scudder was dead.

CHAPTER *FORTY-TWO*

Theresa took the second shift at the window but grew bored just watching the rain fall on the dark parking lot; so, with nothing better to do, she decided to go wash Zack's clothes downstairs instead. It was more for herself than for Zack; his clothes absolutely reeked.

Early on Theresa had pegged Zack as either a cop or a criminal, and since she couldn't see the padre befriending a criminal, she assumed that Zack was a cop. She had seen a movie once about the FBI; maybe he was a member of that. As she dropped coins into the hotel's washing machine, Theresa wondered about what had drawn her to these men. *So far, she'd infuriated her brother and faced down two different street gangs to help the priest and his friend. To top it all off, here she was washing their underwear at 3 o'clock in the morning!*

There was just something about these two. It felt right, helping them. It had been a long time since she'd felt good about something; and she definitely felt good about this.

Clean clothes and a hot breakfast were sitting on the bedside table when Flenn awoke.

"Please tell me there's coffee!" Zack stretched and

then reached for a sausage, still wearing nothing but a pair of briefs.

"There's a coffeemaker over there." Theresa pointed to the bureau. Zack got up, plugged it in, and poured water into the reservoir.

"Sorry, but I have dibs on the first cup," Flenn said. "Theresa was nice enough to wash our clothes last night. Show some respect and get dressed." Zack started to take off his briefs. Flenn pointed toward the bathroom. "In there!"

"You've become such a prude since you were ordained," Zack said. "I think Theresa might appreciate a perfect specimen of the male form."

Theresa shrugged. "Nah. You've seen one, you've seen them all."

Flenn tossed a pair of clean underwear and jeans, hitting Zack in the face. "Go!"

"Okay, okay. I suppose you're right; I wouldn't want to scare her."

"I've seen, remember. And believe me, I'm no frightened." Theresa and Flenn exchanged a grin as Zack slunk off to the bathroom.

Over breakfast, Flenn relayed what Sarah had told him last night. "We have two days before Scudder takes that vehicle back to the base, but at least we know where he is. Plus, she says that Scudder is sure we're dead, which is to our advantage."

"Yeah, but he still has his eye in the sky, remember?" Zack said, his mouth full of scrambled eggs. "That's to *his* advantage. He might see us coming." He pointed his fork toward Theresa. "And, what about her brother? He could have warned him."

"Juan no warn nobody," she said. "He just had surgery; he will no feel like talking to anyone. I know my brother; he is much more worry about himself than anyone else. Plus, he has the padre's money to keep him happy."

"Okay, but what about that other gang?" Zack asked.

Flenn had thought of that last night. "As far as I know, Scudder doesn't know anything about the Jefes; but you're right, we shouldn't take any chances. That's why I suggest we move tonight."

Zack took a breath. "Tonight? Without a plan? That would be suicidal!"

"I *have* a plan," Flenn said.

"Oh? What did Sarah say when you told her about it?"

Flenn looked down at his eggs. "Don't worry about that." Zack knew what that meant. Sarah must have told Flenn that she wanted Scudder alive.

Zack looked at his friend, a man who'd been through hell these past few days. Flenn didn't have children, but Zack did. He knew how he would feel if his two girls had been in the village that day. Finally, Zack answered: "So, what's this plan of yours?"

Flenn looked at him. "You don't have to do this, Zack. Just tell Sarah it was all on me."

Zack shook his head. "We're in this together."

"You sure?" Flenn asked.

Zack grinned. "Never been surer of anything in my life."

Theresa refilled the coffee pot and listened as Flenn explained his plan to take out Scudder and his crew. It was the first time she'd ever heard a priest talk of killing someone; and yet, with what had happened on the mountain, how could she blame him? She didn't know who this Scudder person was, but the moment he murdered those children, he gave up his right to live. The very thought that her brother could be involved with such a man sent a shiver down her spine.

Zack reached into his backpack for a map. Brushing aside the breakfast dishes, he unfolded it on the small table. "Theresa, according to the coordinates our friend gave Flenn last night, this is where Scudder is hiding." He placed his finger on a tiny section of the map near Tegucigalpa. "How long will it take us to get there?"

She leaned over to take a closer look at the map. "From here, about four hours, maybe five."

Zack checked his watch. "It's half past eight now. We'd best get going. We'll need some time to stop for supplies." He looked at Flenn. "Are you going to tell her, or am I?"

"Tell me what?"

Flenn sighed. "I'm sorry, Theresa, to have to keep involving you in this, but we really need you to take us to Tegucigalpa. After that, we won't bother you anymore."

She looked hurt. "Bother me? What means bother?"

"Inconvenience. Annoy."

"You no annoy me." She gestured toward Zack. "Maybe him a little bit, but no you."

Zack smiled. "You seem to have a fan."

"Look, Theresa," Flenn said, "we really appreciate all you've done for us, but this is about to get...," he glanced at Zack, "explosive."

Theresa brushed his comments aside. "I no care. El no me asusta. This Scudder—he no scareish me."

Flenn looked at her. "I can tell you don't mean that."

"How?"

"Your English is slipping."

Theresa looked away for a moment, then turned back to face Flenn and spoke slowly. "Okay, maybe I am a little nervous, but I can be muy..." she shook her head, frustrated... "I can be a lot of help."

Flenn shook his head. "People are likely to die." *One person in particular!* he thought. "After you drop us off, you will need to keep going. Enough people have been hurt already because of me."

"Because of Scudder," corrected Zack.

"Yes," Flenn seemed to be saying it mostly to himself, "because of Scudder. Please, Theresa, just get us there and then leave. I couldn't bear it if something happened to you because of us."

Theresa gazed at the priest's kind face. *Whatever he had done to incur the wrath of a madman, the padre did not deserve to come to any harm.* He was a good man. She placed her hands on his. "I want to help. Not just for you, but for the children. I do not believe my brother knew this man was a *monstruo*—a monster—at least not at first. But if Juan had a part in what happened in the village, then I owe it to the little ones to help."

Flenn tried to smile. "You've already helped us so

much. You've been an angel from God. We wouldn't be here without you; just promise me you will drive away once we get there."

A tear ran down Theresa's cheek. *No one had cared this much for her since she'd been a child, when the priest had rescued her. That priest had made her feel special, cared for, almost as much as her own mother had. Now, here was another man of God telling her that she was someone worth caring about. An 'angel' of all things!* She couldn't bring herself to worry him further. "How will you get away?"

Zack looked at Flenn, then at Theresa. "Don't worry about that."

Flenn squeezed her hand. "Promise me?"

She didn't want to, but finally she said the words he'd wanted to hear. "Sí, lo prometo... I promise."

Flenn leaned back and heaved a sigh of relief.

Zack looked up at the ceiling. *This woman had saved his bacon, and he was getting accustomed to having her along. Still, Flenn was right. This was going to be dangerous, and they had never involved civilians in their fights, not if they could help it.* He glanced at Flenn. *Scudder was not to be underestimated. If Flenn was right, and the truck was unguarded, or only lightly guarded, then Flenn's plan might work. If not, then it was on to Plan B.*

So far, Plan B was to simply go in with guns blazing.

CHAPTER *FORTY-THREE*

Tegucigalpa is to Honduras what Birmingham is to Alabama, Flenn thought as they entered the Honduran capital. *Both are hotter than hell, both have an overabundance of poverty, and both cities boast significantly high crime rates.*

Zack had slept most of the way, except when they'd stopped at noon for gasoline and sandwiches to go. Flenn hadn't eaten. He'd simply stared out the window as they drove into the central district.

Horns honked, people yelled, and playing children jumped out of the way as Theresa drove down the city's alleyways and backstreets until finally stopping in front of what looked like a broken-down garage with a portion of the front wall missing. "This is where you find what you need."

She accompanied Flenn and Zack inside, where a skinny, bedraggled man with a dirty shirt, buttoned only in the middle, looked her up and down. Accustomed to such ogling, Theresa quickly rattled off a list of supplies that Zack had said they'd need. Oddly enough, the man had everything in stock, including a used .45 that he brought out from a back room. Flenn recognized it as a Taurus 24/7 series. He took the gun and two magazines without saying a word or trying to bargain the man down from his exorbitant price. Zack stepped up to the counter as Flenn paid for the gun, a crowbar, a roll of duct tape, mosquito-repellant wipes, and an extra backpack to hold it all.

Outside, Flenn surveyed the neighborhood. Short, squat buildings, painted in bright greens, yellows, and blues, lined both sides of the street. People sat in the shade of the doorways or under rusted awnings as the late afternoon sun beat down upon the brown-bricked street, baking anything that dared step out of the shadows. Flenn glanced down at his own arms. They were darker than when he had left Alabama. The shade of the jungle had kept his skin from burning, but if he stayed out very long he'd need sunscreen. *Maybe he'd get some tomorrow,* he thought, *if there was a tomorrow.*

They headed out of the city, with Zack going over the details of Flenn's plan in his mind. It was poetic justice, Zack had to admit, but he just wasn't sure how he was going to be able to explain it to Sarah Coverdale afterwards. Zack took out his SAT phone and tried calling her but got no answer. He needed to know if there was a numeric passcode to the Humvee in case Scudder had locked it. *If not, well, that was why they had bought the crowbar.*

Zack looked up at Flenn from the backseat. *This could well be their last mission together, but then how many times had he thought that before?* Technically, their last mission had been in Edinburgh about 10 years ago, although they'd worked together on a couple of projects since then. Just a few months ago, for example, Flenn had helped him manage to stop two megalomaniacs from taking over the White House. Zack recalled how the deputy director of the CIA had gone ballistic when he'd heard how Iran was planning to interfere with the upcoming election. Fortunately, Iran's plans had been thwarted, and the head of Iran's intelligence was now in custody in London. Zack imagined that there were consequences being implemented even now by the U.S. government that no one other than key Iranian officials would ever know about.

"I gotta take a whiz."

Flenn glared back at his friend. "Always the gentlemen, aren't you, Zack?"

"Oh, excuse me, Reverend," Zack quipped. "I have to go to the powder room."

Theresa pulled over and pointed to the forest surrounding them on both sides. "Take your pick," she said.

"Gentlemen to the right, ladies to the left," Zack said as he hopped out of the truck.

Zack hadn't been out of the vehicle but a few seconds when Flenn opened his own door, "Well, maybe that's not such a bad idea."

Theresa got out, as well. "Sí. Not such a bad idea at all."

The trees were so thick that Flenn couldn't see which way Zack had gone. Flenn took several steps into the jungle and felt a cool breeze blowing through the trees. *Amazing how much the temperature drops when you get out of the sun,* he thought. He finished his business and turned back toward the truck, then nearly jumped out of his skin. Not 20 feet away stood a jaguar!

"What's taking him so long?" Zack checked his watch. It had been several minutes since he and Theresa had returned to the vehicle. "Maybe I should go have a look." He pulled out his pistol.

"That won't do you much good in there; here take this." Theresa handed him the machete. "Wild animals may be in there. They know what *this* does." Zack pulled it from its sheath and walked back toward the jungle, pistol in one hand, machete in the other.

Flenn didn't move a muscle. The only weapon he had was the switchblade; the .45 they'd bought was still in the truck. The jaguar didn't move; it just stood there and stared at this tall, white man with sandy brown hair. The cat was about the same size and had similar markings to the one that they'd encountered the day before.

"Flenn?" Zack called. "You in there? Flenn?"

The big cat turned its head in the direction of Zack's voice. Flenn took the opportunity to reach into his pocket and pull out the switchblade. He flicked it open, the jaguar turned and...*No, it did NOT just do that! The jaguar looked like it had rolled its eyes!*

"Flenn!"

The cat sauntered off slowly with a grunt, much the same way Flenn's grandfather used to when Flenn had played his music too loud as a teenager. Gramps never ranted and raved, never yelled or cursed. He just grunted... the same way the jag just did.

"Wait there," Flenn called out. "I'm on my way. Don't come any closer, there's a jaguar in here!"

A second of silence, then Zack answered, "Don't worry, I won't. In fact, I'll be in the truck if you need me!" Instead of retreating, however, Zack tightened his grip on both weapons and moved through the jungle toward the sound of Flenn's voice.

"Put those away, I promise I won't hurt you," Flenn said when he saw his friend coming to the rescue.

"Yeah, yeah," Zack said, relaxing his grip on the machete. "I bet you say that to all the girls. Where's the jaguar?"

"Gone. Funny thing though, I swear that cat rolled its eyes at me!"

"You mean like this?" Zack rolled his eyes. "Let's hurry up, we've got a date tonight, remember?" They both froze at the sound of a roar not far behind them. Zack aimed toward the sound as the two of them slowly backed out of the jungle. "Here, take the machete!" Zack tried to hand the weapon to Flenn, as the creature bellowed again.

"*Umm*, no thanks. I don't think it likes me being armed."

Zack shot a glance in Flenn's direction. "You're kidding me, right?"

Flenn didn't take his eyes of the jungle. "Well…"

Zack forced the blade into Flenn's grip. "I don't care what *he* likes… *I* don't like you being unarmed."

Theresa heard the next roar and jumped into the driver's seat. "Vamonos! she yelled as Flenn and Zack backed their way hurriedly to the truck.

As Theresa sped away, Flenn looked over his shoulder but saw no sign of the jaguar. "Just how many of those things are out there?" he asked.

"Not as many as before," she said. "Many people kill them now." Flenn remembered reading about the poachers and drug lords who'd virtually eradicated the species in some parts of Central America. He shook his head. "If I didn't know better, I'd swear that's the same cat that I saw before."

Zack, in the front seat now, turned and looked at him. "Not to sound racist, but you do know that they all look alike, right?"

"Not really," Theresa offered. "Jaguars are very different from one another. Each one is unico."

"What's unico?" Zack asked, relieved to be on their way. "Does that mean a union? Don't tell me there's an organized jaguar guild out there?"

Flenn glared at him. "How is it you speak Russian, Chinese, and some Farsi but have no knowledge of Spanish?"

Zack shrugged. "I've never worked down here. And when did *you* start learning Spanish, buddy boy?"

"A lot of Latinos live in Birmingham. I've picked some up along the way."

"Ok, smarty, so what's unico?"

"Unique."

Theresa slammed the steering wheel, "Unique! Yes, unique!" They both looked at her. "Jaguars are unique!" She glanced at Zack and grinned. "And so are you two. I have never met anyone else like you!"

"Gringos?" Flenn asked.

"No."

"Good looking?" Zack offered a cheesy grin.

She shook her head. "No, that's not it." His smile disappeared.

"Odd?" Flenn asked again.

"Sí, that's it; odd!" Theresa laughed.

"I still think she meant good-looking," Zack muttered as he watched the green and yellow landscape of the countryside go by. They traveled for several minutes when Theresa announced that they were getting close.

Zack looked around but saw only trees and brush. "There's nothing out here." Theresa shook her head and told them to watch for a road off to their right. The GPS in her truck indicated they were less than a mile away from the turnoff.

"Drive slowly so we can get a good look at the terrain," Zack said.

He had no more than gotten the words out of his mouth when they saw a Jeep and a small guardhouse blocking a turnoff about a quarter-mile up the road. Flenn and Zack ducked down and told Theresa to keep driving, but to take note of everything she saw. Once safely past, she gave the all clear.

"There was a man with a rifle standing next to the Jeep," she said. "A narrow road behind him goes up and over a little hill. I couldn't see anything beyond the hill."

"What about fences;" Zack asked, "did you see any fences?"

"Sí. There was a wooden one next to the road, but it was in bad shape."

Flenn leaned forward. "Any trees leading up the fence line?"

"Sí, very many trees," she pointed out Zack's window, "like it is here."

Zack and Flenn looked to their right. The forest was thick; impossible for a drone's camera to penetrate. Zack looked at Flenn. "Your call."

Flenn stuffed a water bottle into each backpack and handed a third to Zack from the backseat. "Let's do it."

"Theresa," Zack said, "pull over up there, next to those trees."

Theresa raised an eyebrow. "What, you are no getting out *here* are you?"

Zack smiled. "Afraid so. He picked up the machete she'd offered earlier. "Can I pay you for this?"

"Take it; but why here?"

Flenn explained: "Those trees will offer us enough cover to remain unnoticed. We'll work our way through the woods while it's still daylight, get the lay of the land, find out where Scudder is and then…"

"Yes? Then what?"

Flenn looked away. "Then we will do what we came here to do," Zack said. "I'm afraid this is goodbye."

"But how you get away?"

Zack spoke up. "There is a vehicle here, one that belongs to our government. We'll be fine."

"I still say I should come with you!"

"Like we explained back at the hotel, Zack and I have

to do this on our own. We can't thank you enough for all you've done," Flenn reached up to squeeze her shoulder. "Please, pray for us."

"I do not think God hears my prayers, Padre…"

"He most certainly does," Flenn said emphatically. And with that, he slipped out the door and walked into the woods carrying the pistol they'd purchased in Tegucigalpa. Zack hesitated for a second by the open car door.

"He means it, you know."

She nodded. "You will need more than my prayers. Please, let me help you."

Zack smiled. "There is one thing you can do for me."

"Qué?"

He pulled a piece of paper out of his pocket on which he had written the name *Donna* along with a telephone number. "Call my ex-wife and tell her to tell the kids… " Zack hesitated, and then slowly put the piece of paper back in his pocket. "On second thought, just take care of yourself."

He turned and followed Flenn into the woods. Theresa put the car in gear. A single tear rolled down her cheek as she pulled away and headed back toward the city.

CHAPTER *FORTY-FOUR*

"Sure wish I had managed to find some jellybeans down here somewhere," Zack said as he leaned against a tree halfway to the house where Scudder and his gang were hiding.

Flenn took a drink from the water bottle. "Yeah, I wouldn't mind a cup of coffee about now either. What about the guard at the gate?"

"I'm guessing when we take out the house, he's likely to get in that Jeep and take off."

Flenn nodded. "Okay. It's not the guard I want anyway."

Zack retrieved the SAT phone; this time, he was able to get through, though there was considerable static on the line.

"Hi Sarah; guess who."

"Zack, where the hell are you? Tell me what's happening."

"We're down to two now," Zack said. "Sent our lady friend home. I have to admit, she was pretty amazing, saved our bacon more than once." He looked at Flenn. "We're almost in place, waiting for nighttime so the party can begin. One thing, though."

"What's that?"

"Does Scudder's big toy have a key code to unlock it?

We don't have transportation anymore, and I assume you'd like us to return that thing to its rightful owner."

Sarah saw right through him. "Son of a... You're going to blow him up, aren't you?"

"I didn't say that."

There was a long silence before Sarah finally spoke. "You do know what's at stake here, right?"

"Yeah," Zack said.

"Damn it, Zack! Do you realize what you're asking me?"

"We're not asking."

"Zack!"

"There were children, Sarah, lots of them. We owe this to them... and to Flenn. We're going to do it one way or another, but a key code would sure make it easier." Sarah Coverdale didn't answer.

"Ma'am? The code?"

Finally, she sighed over the phone. "Call me when you get in place. I'll see if I can send a signal from here that'll unlock it. I'll call right now and get the code from Soto Cano. This sure as hell better not trigger anything with Schmitt. If he gets wind of what I'm trying to put together against him..."

"Got it," Zack said. "I'll call in a couple of hours."

"Zack, listen to me. I've got a man in there with Scudder. I need to get him out first. I'll warn him, but you will need to give me time once you are ready."

"Sure. We'll give you five minutes."

"You'll give me fifteen, or I won't give you the code."

Zack relented, but only a bit, and told Sarah he'd give

the informant 10 minutes but no more, then replaced the phone in the backpack. He looked at Flenn, who was sitting on a log drawing on the ground with a stick, lost in thought.

"You sure this is how you want to do it?"

Flenn nodded. "It has to be done."

"But you don't have to be the one to do it. You've already told me the password once we're inside. I don't think I'll forget your name."

Flenn rubbed his shoulder. "No, I have to be the one." Flenn stared off into the jungle. "I'm not doing this because Scudder wanted to kill me. And I'm not really doing it just for those kids, although that's a big chunk of it." Flenn took a deep breath. "A man like Scudder will keep killing. There's no stopping him. I don't know what he and Schmitt have planned, but I'm sure it will just be more of the same."

Zack nodded. "You and I used to call these things 'righteous kills.'"

Flenn shook his head; doubtful now that killing someone could ever be called *righteous*. "Is Sarah going to be able to get her informant out?"

"Yes."

"Good… because, once we're in the vehicle, we'll have to be quick."

"Let's just hope the drone is still hovering overhead on autopilot."

"We've been over this," Flenn reminded him. "Scudder is going to have kept it close by."

Zack nodded. "Right, piece of cake, unless…"

Flenn read his mind.

"Theresa won't talk."

Zack was thinking of Juan. It had worried him ever since he'd learned that Theresa was Baldy's sister. "Let's hope not," Zack said. *If he had learned anything from his time in the CIA, it was that almost anyone can be turned. That was why he and Flenn had become such good friends—they both knew that they had each other's backs... and always would.*

"Let's go over it one more time," Flenn said.

Zack took a swing of water. "Once we find the Humvee, I'll call Sarah. She should be able to unlock it. If no one's guarding it, great. If someone is, then... "

Flenn looked at him. "You will take care of him."

"Right. We'll wait a few minutes for the informant to get out, then you'll set the coordinates for the drone to fire on the house. I'll take care of the guard by the road if he's stupid enough to come see why his boss just blew up."

"Flenn looked at his watch. So... when do we want to do this?"

Zack smiled. "You got somewhere you need to be?"

"I just want a few minutes to pray first."

Zack didn't share his friend's beliefs, but he honored them. "Let's find the house first. Looks like we've got another hour or so of daylight left. We need to be in position before dark." He handed Flenn the water. "Anything else?"

"Just remember what we talked about. When it comes time, I will be the one to push the button."

Zack looked away. *Sure, Flenn had killed before; they both had; but, he saw his friend in a different light these days.* Flenn was a priest, and from what Zack could tell, a damn good one. Zack had brought him in on cases from time to time, but he had never asked his friend to harm anyone since Flenn had left the agency. Flenn had taken a vow in Edinburgh never to kill again.

Edinburgh! Zack would never forget what had happened there. If any part of what Flenn said had also happened, then Zack knew Flenn was walking a tightrope. *Unless, of course, there was such a thing as divine retribution, and Flenn was its agent. If so, then Scudder was about to receive a double dose!*

Zack had never met Eric Scudder, although he'd heard Flenn talk about him during the early years. Zack and Flenn had gone through training together at Langley, but hadn't become partners until they were assigned a particularly nasty bit of undercover work in Ireland. The two of them had hit it off pretty much from that assignment on. It was at least six months later before Zack learned of Flenn's background—that he came from billionaire stock and had served in an elite unit in the Air Force with military intelligence.

Zack had thought about enlisting in the military himself, but had opted to train for the FBI instead. Someone in Homeland Security had made a deal with both agencies and exchanged a man from Langley to Quantico, and then offered Zack to Langley in return. Zack always referred to the deal as a 'prisoner swap,' although he was glad he'd landed in the CIA. He had considerably more freedom of movement as a spy—and less accountability. *It's difficult to follow a chain of command when you are ankle deep in mud pursuing a Chinese bomb maker. No,* he thought for the thousandth time, *the CIA was the perfect place for him, just not for Flenn, not anymore.*

Flenn pulled out his pistol and went over it carefully. "Not the cleanest weapon, I've ever seen. Wish I had time to check it out first."

"Be careful," Zack cautioned. "You accidentally fire that thing and they'll be on us like white on rice."

"Can't you ever come up with any new clichés?"

Zack studied Flenn. He knew Flenn's shoulder was hurting; that was clear from the way he was favoring it. But there was more pain in Flenn's mind right now than there was in his body.

They made their way through the trees until they finally saw the guard at the end of the drive. He was sitting in the Jeep, a rifle propped in the seat next to him. The man looked to be a local. Guards with guns were commonplace in Honduras. Zack and Flenn had seen several in front of buildings in Tegucigalpa earlier— banks, markets, even around some houses. Zack had noted that in Honduras, the poor survived underneath corrugated plastic propped up on sticks, while the rich lived in homes with razor wire and armed guards.

The duo made their way up the hillside, parallel to the long driveway, sticking to the cover of the forest. It was nearly dusk when the orange slate roof came into view. The house was about the size of a three-bedroom colonial in D.C. *The first missile should take the entire structure down,*

Zack figured, *the second would simply make sure that nothing survived.*

Zack and Flenn crouched low and watched as a man carrying a rifle came out of a side door. Maybe a .30-caliber, Zack thought, though he couldn't get a good look. The man was heading down the drive, presumably to relieve the guard in the Jeep. He and Flenn would remain here in the brush and watch. Zack was thankful for the bug wipes he'd stuffed in his backpack; so was Flenn, right now. Otherwise, stretched out for an hour or more on a forested floor at the edge of the rainforest would have made them a feast to any hungry insect.

Flenn tapped Zack on the shoulder and pointed. Behind the house stood what appeared to be an old barn. Beyond that was an overgrown pasture where horses had likely grazed years ago. Parked beside the house was a green-camouflaged Humvee. Zack and Flenn watched for half an hour, but saw no one else come or go. They waited a few more minutes until darkness began to fall, then Zack reached into the backpack and sent the signal to Sarah.

CHAPTER *FORTY-FIVE*

Dusk turned into night. The ensuing darkness enveloped Flenn and Zack as rainclouds blocked the starlight. The moon had not yet risen.

Had it not been for his cigarette, Flenn and Zack wouldn't have seen the guard from the Jeep saunter up the drive and enter the house through what appeared to be the kitchen door.

"Now's our best chance," whispered Zack. He and Flenn crawled out of the woods toward the Humvee behind the house. Flenn could hear music coming from inside the house. He recognized the song, *Owner of a Lonely Heart*, by the rock band, *Yes*. Without saying a word, they rose as one and darted behind the vehicle.

Zack tried the passenger door. *Damn!* It was locked.

Just then, someone opened the same door they'd seen the guard go in; Flenn and Zack dropped and rolled underneath the Humvee. All they could see was someone's pants legs heading their way. Both men slowly drew their weapons. Two feet stopped next to the vehicle.

"Hello?... Yeah, it's me." Flenn felt every muscle in his body tighten. *Was the man talking to them?* "I'm sorry... No, I couldn't answer before; I just now managed to get out of the house." They both realized the man was talking on a phone. "What? Right now?... You sure don't give a guy much warning... Okay, okay, Sarah, I got it. I'm out-ta here."

The informant!

The man flicked his cigarette onto the ground just a couple of feet from Flenn, then ground it out with his foot until the ember was extinguished. They heard the informant speak again, this time in a whisper: "If you can hear me, wherever you are, I'm on your side. Just give me a couple of minutes to get to the end of the drive. I'll take care of the guard, then I'm outta here."

Zack and Flenn never saw the man's face, but heard his voice as the informant added softly: "Good luck." They watched as the feet turned and headed toward the road. Zack glanced at his watch. Less than a minute later, he heard a soft click above him. He and Flenn crawled out the opposite side then carefully made their way to the driver's door. Zack reached for the handle. *Sure enough, it was unlocked.*

"Good 'ol Sarah," Zack whispered.

"At least she got her man out," Flenn mumbled. They scrambled into the vehicle and locked the doors. "Now what?" Flenn asked, never having operated a drone before. Zack, however, had been trained in the operation of armed drones shortly after Flenn had left the CIA.

"Give me a minute. This is a different model, but the principle's the same." Zack slid back a panel where a large screen showed a dimly lit scene of the house and surrounding area. Flenn had been right; Scudder had kept the drone flying in a circular-holding pattern overhead. No doubt he was simply using the drone as a toy until he had to turn it back in to the airbase. Judging from the volume of music inside, no one was concerned about being discovered. Zack manned the controls, and both men watched as the drone's camera zoomed in on their location. Flenn saw the altimeter on the corner of the screen. It was currently flying 17,337 feet above them. Although the picture was dark and grainy, they could make out the informant as he approached the Jeep. The guard on duty stepped out of the vehicle to greet him, and the informant lifted his right hand. There was a flash and the guard collapsed to the ground. The informant stood over the man, and there was another flash.

"Whoever he is, he knows what he's doing," Zack said. "He's obviously one of us."

Flenn's stomach tightened at the word "us." He took a breath. "Okay, show me what to do," Flenn said, trying to shut out the image he'd just witnessed.

"Patience is a virtue," Zack said quietly, not taking his eyes off the controls. He pressed some keys on a computer keyboard and the image changed as the house next to them filled the screen. Zack tapped in a few commands and nodded his head. "*Umm, hmm,*" was all he said. Flenn crouched quietly behind him. He knew that he was close to finishing what they'd come for, but it seemed surreal. Soon, Zack would have the coordinates locked into the drone and, as agreed, would turn the controls over to him.

Revenge had never been a game Flenn was good at. Killing had been completed one job at one time, and only when necessary. He'd justified it back then by telling himself that taking one life was saving many more. This time it was different; this time, it was personal.

A familiar darkness began to overshadow him. He had learned to ignore that darkness as he and Zack had travelled the world fighting terrorism at their country's bidding, but it had become increasingly difficult by the time they were assigned to Scotland. Flenn had been rescued from that darkness and had been given a new start. He'd resisted at first, but once he'd finally given himself over to the light he'd never gone back... that is, until now.

"Okay, she's armed with both missiles," Zack said, habitually reaching into his pocket for a jellybean that wasn't there.

Flenn didn't say a word; he simply motioned for Zack to trade places with him. Zack got up, checking outside to make sure all was quiet. He thought he could make out Foghat's "*Slow Ride*" playing from inside the house. Once he was sure no one had spotted them, Zack pointed to a single red button on the bottom right of the panel. "All you have to do is push that one. Push it twice in quick succession."

"Why twice?"

"Double the impact—hit that scumbag with his last two missiles, a one-two punch!" He placed his hand on Flenn's good shoulder. "Just to be sure."

Zack stood behind Flenn and watched as Flenn place his finger over the button. "This vehicle has been reinforced," Zack said. "It was built to withstand blasts from IEDs—improvised explosive devices.

"I know what an IED is." Flenn snapped. "It doesn't matter; I never expected to come out of this alive."

"Gee thanks, pal."

Flenn felt a rush of shame. He hadn't meant it that way. "Sorry," he murmured. Flenn swallowed. The image of the informant killing the guard flashed through his mind, as did scores of other killings he'd either seen or been a part of years ago. He now found himself in the world he thought he'd left behind. *Once he pushed this red button, there was no going back... maybe there never had been. Maybe he had left the priesthood the day Zack shoved him into the jungle; the day the children died.*

"Why don't you get out now and head to the road, just to be sure."

Zack grinned. "What, and miss the fireworks? No way!"

Flenn knew it was useless to argue, so he paused, took a deep breath, and...

Zack knocked Flenn's hand aside and quickly pressed the button twice. Seconds later; a bright light flared and the Humvee was rocked by the ensuing explosions! The Humvee was lifted a meter into the air and came down... hard. Flenn and Zack were thrown violently onto the floorboard. Amazingly, neither one was hurt beyond a few bumps and bruises. The bulletproof glass, tempered with heavy deposits of nickel sulfide, had not blown out, although every window was creased from one side to the other. They rolled out of the vehicle and stumbled toward the trees as the house collapsed beside them. Red-hot flames shot 30 feet up into the night sky.

Rivulets of sweat poured down their faces from the intense heat as Zack and Flenn ran toward the edge of the jungle. When they turned they saw that nothing remained of what had stood only seconds before. The house had collapsed in on itself. Smaller, secondary explosions of water heaters, electrical devices, and whatever else had been inside continued to light up the darkness around them.

"Nothing survived that," Zack whispered in awe, his face aglow in the light of the flames. *The missiles were aptly named—Hellfire!*

Flenn recognized the danger before Zack did. He grabbed his friend by the arm, the way Zack had grabbed him in the village days ago, and yanked him further away from the Humvee. "The flames, they're heading our way!" Indeed, the fire was swiftly making its way toward the vehicle which was about to become another bomb. "Run for it!" Flenn yelled.

They scrambled toward the driveway and were halfway up the small hill when another huge blast propelled them to the ground. Flenn and Zack both drew themselves up into a ball and covered their heads as debris fell around them. Zack looked up. "Damn! There goes our ride!" Flenn saw the shell of the Humvee completely engulfed in flames. They both stood up and watched the fire as it began to spread into the jungle. Trees burst into flame as the underbrush ignited around them. Flenn watched in horror, as everything to the left of the Humvee became an inferno.

"No!" he screamed. "Don't let this happen!"

Without warning, the clouds which had hovered over them for the past hour suddenly opened and a torrent of rain washed over them. In just minutes the flames were completely extinguished. Zack looked over at Flenn, dumbfounded. Neither said a word. Not that they could; the stench of burning oil and wood filled their nostrils and they were beginning to choke.

Soaked to the skin, they turned and headed toward the road. "I've got to hand it to you," Zack said hoarsely, when he could finally speak.

"What?" Flenn didn't bother to look at him, his heart and thoughts still a world away.

"Making it rain like that… nice touch."

Flenn shrugged. "Wasn't *me*."

"Maybe the guy you work for?"

Flenn sighed. There was an ache in his heart tonight… one that he hadn't known in years. "Maybe…but..."

"But what?"

"I'm not sure… but I don't think I work for him anymore. I think he just fired me."

CHAPTER *FORTY-SIX*

Boredom had weighed heavily upon Eric Scudder the last few days. With Scott Flenn finally blown to dust, he'd had little to do except wait for Jeremy Schmitt to make the final arrangements for Mexico.

The details of the heist Scudder had already worked out in his head. The incense bowls were going to be on exhibit in four cities: Tijuana, Mexico City, Monterrey, and San Louis Potosì. Schmitt had already discovered that the museum in San Louis Potosì was the most vulnerable. It would take some doing, but the alarm system there was ancient. There were only two guards on Sunday nights, both older men. They'd never see it coming. Scudder figured he'd have Carlos take care of one guard while he and Jerry eliminated the other. Getting out of the city wouldn't be difficult, although leaving the country might me more problematic. Schmitt was supposed to be working on that. The plan was to pass Scudder and Gerald off as part of a drug enforcement team working in Honduras. Schmitt was planning to secure a private plane to get them from Mexico City into Brownsville, Texas. From there, Scudder and Rudolph would simply drive with the treasure to D.C.

Scudder wasn't worried about Mexico. The heist was

simply payment for getting rid of Scott Flenn. *If everything went south, and he ended up back in prison... well, Flenn would still be dead.*

With Flenn gone and Mexico not for another two weeks, Scudder had nothing else to occupy his time and so he had gotten into the custom of sleeping in the afternoons.

Today he had slept late; it was already dark outside. He awoke and wandered into the living room where Gerald was eating a sandwich and watching TV. "Whose turn is it on guard?" Scudder asked.

"Frack," Gerald answered, reaching for a soda to wash down the ham and cheese. "Frick just got back a few minutes ago."

"And Carlos?" Scudder liked knowing where everyone was. It gave him a sense of control.

Gerald shrugged. "Not sure. He was just here; try the kitchen." Scudder found Frick listening to music on an 80's-style boom box they had found upstairs. He was also eating the last of the ham from the fridge. "I don't guess you thought of leaving any of that for me?"

Frick looked up, a string of ham hanging from his mouth. "Sorry, boss."

"You seen Carlos? I still haven't heard from that gangbanger I sent you two to find."

"Carlos was just here. I think he go outside for a smoke. No worry about Juan, boss. He is in very good hands."

Scudder headed for the door. "I'm not *worried* about the slime-ball, I just need to know why I haven't heard from him. I want those pictures!" He turned and stared at Frick. "What did you mean 'Juan is in good hands?'"

"Juan is in a very good hospital recovering from his injuries. Top notch."

Scudder's mouth fell open. "What? What injuries?"

Frick's heart skipped a beat. "I am sorry, boss. Carlos say he tell you when the time was right, that I should stay out of it."

"Well, Carlos isn't here, and he hasn't told me a damn thing, so why don't you tell me what you know before I lose my temper!"

Frick stammered apologetically: "I… I… mean no… no disrespect, boss. Carlos, he tell me…"

"I don't give a damn what Carlos told you; tell me what you know about Juan!"

"He's in Vida Vibrante Hospital in Tegucigalpa… a hospital for the rich. One of his gang, he tell Carlos that Juan call him from the hospital. The man say Juan was, how you say, not good in his thinking. The medicine they give him is very strong. Carlos say he tell you and for me to no worry about it."

"How did Juan end up in a hospital?"

"A fight with another gang," Frick said. "He was where he no should be."

"How did he get into a hospital that's only for the rich?"

"They no say," Frick answered nervously. "Someone with a lot of money must have put him there." Scudder didn't like what he was hearing. He needed to find Carlos, and right now!

Scudder stormed into his bedroom to retrieve his pistol and then rushed out the door onto the small deck. It was too dark to make out much of anything, so he made his way around to the front of the house. He had almost reached the front porch when he suddenly felt himself flying through the air on a wave of heat and light! The sound that came next was deafening; a horrible cacophony beyond description; like nothing Scudder had ever heard before. It was as if the yawning gates of hell itself had just opened and were swallowing him alive!

CHAPTER *FORTY-SEVEN*

The downpour had long since ceased, but drizzling rain continued to fall intermittently as Flenn and Zack walked into the night. Neither said a word as they trudged down the deserted road.

The plan had originally been to drive the Humvee back to Tegucigalpa, assuming Sarah could get it running with a second automated code. The keys would likely have been blown into oblivion along with that dirt bag, Eric Scudder. As luck would have it, the Humvee was permanently out of commission, leaving them no other option but to walk and hope to hitch a ride after daylight. Zack had tried making conversation but Flenn was unresponsive. Eventually, Zack gave up. Somewhere off in the distance they could hear the chatter of monkeys—the blast and subsequent fire having awakened the jungle.

One by one, the stars began to peek through the dissipating clouds. At last, moonlight broke through and they could see the road ahead. Only the ghostly silhouette of trees and empty highway lay before them.

Zack pulled a water bottle from the backpack and drank deeply. He offered it to Flenn, who refused. "Drink! I don't want to have to carry your dehydrated carcass back to the airport with me." Flenn took the bottle and drank, then handed it back.

"I'm not going to the airport."

"What do you mean you're not going to the airport?"

"Just what I said," Flenn quipped.

Zack stopped. "Of course you're going to the airport. Don't be an idiot."

Flenn kept walking. "You need to go and help Sarah stop Schmitt. I've got somewhere else to be."

"Where? Getting your nails done?" Zack trotted to catch up.

"I'm going back to the village."

"What on earth for? You can't help those people, and I seriously doubt they want to see you."

Flenn didn't answer.

"Damn it, Flenn, it wasn't your fault! This is all on Scudder. *You* and I both know that."

Flenn sighed. "The parents of those children don't know it."

"Exactly! So, who do you think they're going to blame? You, that's who. You can't go back there!"

Flenn lowered his voice. "I'm going back, Zack; I have to." Zack decided to drop the argument—for now. They were both too exhausted to think. He'd convince Flenn to go home with him later, one way or the other.

They walked in silence for another half an hour, passing the water bottle back and forth, before Flenn asked him, "Why did you knock my hand away? *I* was supposed to push that button."

Zack didn't answer.

Flenn insisted, "I would have done it."

"I know you would have; that's why I did it."

Flenn thought about that for a moment. "You were trying to save me from killing again?"

"I think I did more than just try."

Flenn was silent for several minutes. At last he said, "Don't you need to contact Sarah?"

Zack stopped short. "Oh, my God! I can't believe I forgot." He swung his backpack off his shoulder and pulled out the phone. He looked at the display; it would need charging soon. "I'm surprised she hasn't called us. She must be sitting on pins and needles!"

Flenn shook his head. "Is there a tired cliché you don't use?"

Zack just smiled. He let the phone ring for some time. "That's odd... no answer. She said she'd be waiting for my call."

"Can't you leave a message, just to say mission accomplished and that you're okay?"

"Nope. This is a secure line. No voicemails; she didn't want Schmitt to have access."

"Is that even possible these days? I thought secure conversations were a thing of the past." Flenn was convinced that the digital age had just about wiped out the concept of privacy. He looked up at the night sky. *Here they were, in the middle of a deserted road in Honduras, but somewhere there was a satellite overhead that could probably find them—if someone wanted to, that is.*

Zack dropped the phone into the backpack. "It is a different world, and a different agency than the one you left, Flenn." He picked up a stone and threw it off into the jungle where he heard it hit a tree. "In some ways it's better, but in others, not so much."

"Absolute power corrupts absolutely," Flenn said, quoting the phrase that had been printed on a large banner at Langley, where he and Zack had first met decades ago. It had been meant as a running commentary on much of what was happening in the world back then... Korea, the Middle East, Bosnia. Now, it seemed to apply back home as well, especially after the mess left by the last guy in the Oval Office. Not that corruption had started with President Ripley; the CIA had faced plenty of charges of malfeasance itself in the past—all secretly, of course. The American people had little idea of what really went on in the CIA, or how the tug and pull of competing forces at Langley often went from the sublime to the ridiculous.

Zack and Flenn walked on, the light from the moon spilling across the lush yet seemingly lifeless landscape. Drizzling rain fell intermittently, preventing their clothes from drying, finally prompting Zack to take off his shirt. "You don't want to do that," Flenn cautioned. "You'll be covered in mosquitoes." Zack was just reaching into his bag for the bug wipes when headlights appeared off in the distance.

Zack dropped the wipes back into the bag. "Wanna chance it?"

"A ride? Sure. Beats walking in wet shoes."

Zack waved the shirt to try and flag the vehicle down. "You do the talking," he said to Flenn. "People like you better. Plus, I can cover you if there's trouble."

"And you also don't speak Spanish," Flenn added.

"Well, there is that."

Judging from the distance between the headlights, the vehicle ahead was a truck or an SUV. Zack's eyes grew big as the vehicle slowed down. "You don't think...?"

"Looks like her truck," Flenn said. A large Toyota pulled up beside them, and the passenger window rolled down. A familiar voice asked, "You boys need a ride?"

"You were supposed to go home!" exclaimed Flenn testily.

Zack smiled from ear to ear as he rushed to open the front passenger door and climbed inside. "Never look a gift truck in the mouth," he said as Flenn got into the back. "You'll have to overlook the padre this evening, he's in a grumpy mood."

"Shut up, Zack. Theresa, we told you to leave, why didn't you?"

Theresa put the truck in gear. "I did. I drove all the way back to Tegucigalpa and checked into a hotel for the evening. I sat there for a long time, but the thought of you two out here on your own make me worry, so here I am."

"You were heading the wrong direction to have come from Tegucigalpa," said Flenn, frowning.

"Okay, so I drive up and down the road a few times. I see a man in a Jeep leave and I follow him for many miles until I was sure you were no with him."

"The informant," Zack said to Flenn. "Wonder where he's heading?"

"Who knows? Probably just trying to get the hell out of Dodge."

"What is this *Dodge*?" Theresa questioned.

Flenn shook his head. "Just an expression. So, you stopped following him, then what?"

"Then, I turn around and see you walking down the road looking like two wet fishes out of the pond."

"A long way from *my* pond," said Zack, "but, we're at least heading back there. Can you take us to the airport?"

"No flights at night from Tegucigalpa," she said. "I will take you to the hotel and we will get you into dry clothes. I still have them; you left them in the truck."

"Sounds good to me," said Zack.

"Sí, you sleep tonight, then you can fly in the morning."

Zack agreed, but Flenn didn't say anything; instead he just sat in the back of the truck, thinking about what he had to do next.

CHAPTER *FORTY-EIGHT*

Sarah Coverdale couldn't take her eyes off the phone. She couldn't risk making the call herself; it might go off and expose Zack and Flenn to God knows what. *Come on, Zack, call me!* She nearly jumped out of her skin when her office door suddenly burst open.

"How sure are you about this?" Deputy Director Carl Moore held up the dossier in his hand as he closed the door to Sarah Coverdale's office. She had left the file with him only this morning. Moore was not smiling.

"As sure as you were about President Ripley." Her boss had been one of the first predictors of the collapse in the Oval Office. He'd also privately forecast that the vice president would step down and that the Republican Speaker of the House Diane Claxton would end up serving the remainder of the term, which was exactly what had happened. Claxton had announced that she would not run for election after finding out she had cancer, which had brought on a surge of candidates from both parties for the upcoming primaries. It had also brought about an Iranian plot to control the election, but Sarah didn't know anything about that, or the role Zack Matteson and Scott Flenn had played in stopping the plot dead in its tracks. Deputy Director Moore knew, of course, and was still poring over the intelligence reports being shared from London after the top Iranian spymaster defected to the Brits back in December.

Moore looked out Sarah's office window. "Your report says Zack Matteson is in on this, is that right?"

"Yes, sir. He and a former associate of his."

The deputy director nodded. "You mean Scott Flenn. Isn't he a priest now?"

"Yes, but Matteson is still a close friend. Zack went down there to try and save him."

Moore glanced at the file and was silent for a moment, as if making a decision. He looked up. "I need you to come with me."

"Sir, I'm expecting a call any moment; I really can't leave right now."

"Yes, you can. Let's go to my office."

"Carl, this call is vital..."

"My office—now."

Sarah looked at the phone on her desk, and then slowly followed the deputy director down the hall and through his secretary's office. "Heather," Moore told the woman, "hold my calls until we come out. I don't want to be disturbed."

"Yes sir," replied the 30-something blonde with shoulder length hair. Moore opened his door and Sarah walked into the office to see Jeremy Schmitt sitting on a small leather sofa on one side of the room, holding a glass half-full of dark liquid. Schmitt stood as they entered the room. Sarah's training kept her from running for cover; although, right now, Sarah was wishing for the Smith & Wesson she kept in the top drawer of her desk.

"Sit down, Sarah." Moore pointed her to a chair opposite Schmitt. "What's your poison? White wine? Something stronger?"

"Nothing for me, sir; thank you." Sarah sat as instructed and tried not to stare at Jeremy Schmitt, as he sat back down and sipped at his drink. Schmitt, dressed in his usual charcoal gray suit, white shirt and red tie, seemed relaxed and amicable enough.

"Jeremy, do you know what this is?" Sarah's heart jumped into her throat as the DD held up the file she had given him.

"Haven't a clue, Carl."

"Sarah put it together for me," Moore said. Pulse racing, Sarah managed to sit motionless, looking as composed as if she were sitting at her daughter's piano recital, which she had missed to be here this evening. "It is a dossier on the mental health of several our agents."

Sarah stared at him. *What?*

"I asked her to look into a few particular agents, some of our cowboys out there. A few of them stay out of reach too long, which I think can be detrimental to their mental stability. I'd like to ask you, just off the top of your head to give me a list of people you think we ought to add. I don't want you to think about it, I just want your gut reaction. Who would you say are our most dangerous cowboys?"

Schmitt raised his glass to his lips. "Sir, I really can't; I mean if you gave me a day or two to think about it..."

"No, I'm looking for a spontaneous reaction. I've found those are often the best. Who do you think should be on this list?"

"Well, there is one name." Schmitt finished off his drink.

Moore placed the dossier folder on his cherry desk and leaned against it. "Who's that?"

"Zack Matteson."

Sarah wasn't sure what the deputy director was up to, but she was willing to play along, relieved that this hadn't been a larger conspiracy after all. Carl Moore was a good man, and she felt a bit ashamed for having momentarily doubted him. The DD opened the file as if searching for something. "Matteson? That wasn't one of the names you gave me, Sarah. What are *your* thoughts? You used to work with his former partner, didn't you?"

Sarah nodded. "A few months in Korea. That's when we tagged that piece of crap, Eric Scudder." She glanced at Schmitt, who was impassively studying the bottom of his now empty glass.

"So, what are your thoughts about Matteson, Sarah?" the director prompted.

"Zack's quite capable," she said, "loyal, gets the job done. I won't say we haven't had complaints, but nothing worth listing him with those others I gave you." She pointed to the dossier, going along with the ruse.

"Come on, Sarah," Schmitt leaned back into the sofa. "Matteson is a loose cannon. He's out there on his own, always playing at whatever scheme or conspiracy he thinks is afoot, seldom reporting to anyone."

"Maybe." Sarah didn't want to arouse Schmitt's suspicion by defending Zack any further. "I'm just saying that I've never had a problem with him."

The director jumped into the conversation. "Okay, I'll put Matteson's name on the list; wouldn't hurt to take a look. Anyone else, Jeremy?"

"Nobody that jumps to mind. Can I get back to you in a day or so?"

"I suppose." Moore turned. "Sarah, can you stay a minute? We need to talk about that situation in Poland."

Schmitt stood, leaving his glass on the coffee table. He pointed to the dossier in Moore's hand. "Carl, why don't I take that with me so I can look it over?"

"Sure thing…" Schmitt didn't see Sarah's eyebrows rise, "…just as soon as I'm finished with it. Thanks, Jeremy." The two men shook hands, and Schmitt nodded to Sarah before closing the door behind him. The Deputy Director sat down on the sofa and pushed Schmitt's glass aside.

"So, what do you think?"

"I think that you just scared the hell out of me! Maybe I *will* have that drink, now."

"Sure, wine?" He walked over to his fully stocked liquor cabinet.

"Scotch. Neat."

Moore smiled to himself as he poured.

"Just to be clear, sir, *nothing* is going on in Poland."

"I know." He handed her the glass. "I thought it was interesting that Jeremy wanted us to include Matteson on our make-believe bad agent list here, didn't you?"

"Insurance," she answered. "He probably thinks Zack's dead, but wants to double down, just in case.

"Dead?"

Sarah had acted alone in sending Zack in the first place. She was out on a limb now with Zack and Flenn using a drone strike against Scudder. None of this had been pre-approved.

"What haven't you told me?" he asked her.

Sarah blinked. *The moment of truth. Lie to her boss or not?* Sarah wasn't afraid of the repercussions. She had served the agency well over the years, and if it all came to an end now, so be it. She just didn't know if she should tell her boss *everything*.

"Well, sir…"

Moore held up his hand. "Hang on, is this something I *need* to know?"

"At some point, yes sir."

"Anything that can incriminate you?"

She thought about that for a moment. *Could a Senate investigative committee find fault with the killing of an American citizen, much less a former spy? Sure they could.*

"Possibly."

This time it was Moore who was lost in thought. He walked to the other side his massive desk, sat down, and pulled out a notepad. He motioned for Sarah to sit in the chair opposite—definitely a boss–employee moment. "I didn't get this job by avoiding the truth. I'm not a politician. I think it is best that you tell me everything."

"Yes sir, but can I do it in the morning? That call I was expecting…"

"Will have to wait. Right now, I want to know everything you know. Start by telling me just how you found out Scudder was released."

Sarah spent the next hour explaining what had happened in South Korea, how she and Flenn had figured out that Scudder had stolen the artifacts and killed the original thief. She told Moore how she had never been able to credit Scudder with having enough connections to be able to fence stolen Korean artifacts. It had taken her until now to put all the pieces together, all of which had led straight to Jeremy Schmitt's door. "Schmitt and Scudder have been in this together from the beginning," she said.

The deputy director listened as Sarah explained how she had developed a New Year's Day ritual of ensuring that Scudder was still safely tucked away behind bars. "Frankly, sir, when you brought me into your office and I saw Jeremy sitting here, I…"

"You thought that I was in on it, too?"

"Just for a second, sir."

"Quit with the 'sir' crap. It's just you and me, Sarah."

"Yes sir, I mean Carl." She looked at the notepad.

He leaned back in his chair. "I haven't written anything down yet… go on."

Sarah told him about Flenn; how she had surmised he was in danger with Scudder on the loose. "When I found out that Flenn was going to Honduras, I knew that was the most likely place Scudder would strike." She also told Moore that she had managed to get an informant into Scudder's inner circle.

"How'd you do that?"

"I have a lot of loyal former students. It was easier

than I thought it would be. I knew Schmitt would put someone alongside Scudder to keep an eye on him, so..."

"So... you made him *your* spy?"

Sarah's eyes narrowed, and her lips pursed. "Not hardly. It was Gerald Rudolph."

Moore nodded. "The same Gerald Rudolph who's been working for Jeremy for the past twenty years?"

"The same. I did some checking. There's a bar he frequents. I sent one of my old students to..."

Moore nodded. "You don't need to go into the particulars. I get it. Who did you send?"

"Ernesto Padilla."

He leaned forward. "Padilla? Can't say I recognize the name."

"Neither would Schmitt, that's why I chose him — that and also the obvious."

"That he's gay?"

"Actually, he's not; but he is a Latino with knowledge of the people and the landscape. Under the identity I gave him, he also had quite a checkered past. Just the sort of guy Scudder and Schmitt would want down there."

"Why were you certain it would happen in Honduras?"

"It was on March 3 that Scudder was arrested, the same date Flenn would be out of the country... call it a... *hunch*, I guess." She couldn't help but smile at the irony. She'd always taught her students to follow facts, not feelings.

"Sounds more like good detective work to me," Moore said.

"I knew Scudder was in a hurry to put a team together. They needed my guy to translate for them. Scudder also had my guy find a couple of local thugs once they arrived."

The deputy director nodded, waiting for her to continue. Sarah was anxious to get back to her phone, but it would just have to wait. If this was some sort of setup to get her to spill everything, which she doubted—and even if Schmitt burst through the door right now guns in hand—it was too late. Scudder was dead by now, as was Rudolph. Sarah filled Moore in on how she had discovered Schmitt had procured a military drone from the airbase near Tegucigalpa, and that Scudder and his men were holed up in an out of the way location. Finally, she came to the events of the past few hours.

The director sat motionless, lost in thought. Once or twice he picked up a pen to write something on the pad, but each time he put it back down again, until finally he returned both pen and pad to their drawer. *Some things were better left without a paper trail.* At last he sighed, then stood. "Sounds like you've got all the bases covered. Let me know how this ends. Good work."

Sarah heaved a pent-up sigh of relief. She now had approval, as unofficial and deniable as it might be, for everything that had transpired. "I want you in my office at eight tomorrow morning. We'll need to talk about how best to take care of Jeremy Schmitt at an appropriate time." He checked his watch. "Just not right now. I have a dinner engagement. If I leave now, I'll just make it."

Moore walked her to the door. "One more thing. I

want both Zack and Flenn to report to me as soon as they land at Dulles."

Sarah turned. "Sir, Flenn no longer works for us."

"As soon as they land." He opened the door. "Understood?"

She did.

CHAPTER *FORTY-NINE*

Escaping the bowels of hell wasn't going to be easy. Thick smoke made it nearly impossible to breathe, flames roared, and immense pain was shooting through his arm. Scudder knew he would either suffocate or burn to death if he didn't get out of here right now!

The blast had thrown him onto something sharp, but it took him a moment before he could see the rebar sticking through his left arm. He'd been propelled through the air onto the remains of a capped well. The small rod protruding through his arm was less than half-inch in diameter but it felt the size of a girder. As flames lapped at his feet, he realized there was only one thing to do if he was going to survive whatever the hell had just happened. Summoning all his strength, Scudder pushed himself off the ground; and, with a piercing scream befitting the carnage around him, he managed to slide his arm off the iron rod. Anyone would have been hard pressed to hear his screams over the sound of falling timbers and exploding propane tanks.

Scudder staggered to his feet where he limped, fell, and crawled his way to safety. He put his right hand on the wound, finding surprisingly little blood. The rod had been searing hot, cauterizing the wound on both sides. He collapsed onto the ground and stared back at the flames. The night sky itself seemed as if it were on fire! Nothing could have survived that, he told himself, absolutely nothing. *Gerald, Frick, Carlos… gone.*

Where the hell was Frack? Scudder searched for him but what he saw was the very last thing he expected to see: two men making their way down the drive and toward the road. The flames illuminated their faces as if it were daylight. While he did not recognize the one, he would never forget the face of the other.

Scott Flenn was alive!

Whether it was pain or rage that caused him to pass out didn't matter. The only thing that would ever matter to Eric Scudder from this point on was finding a way to find and kill Scott Flenn.

CHAPTER *FIFTY*

Flenn awoke before Zack and Theresa. With Scudder and his men dead, there'd been no reason to post a guard at the window last night. He leisurely showered, dressed, and went downstairs to the café for coffee.

The hotel was the nicest Flenn had seen in Honduras, with a beautiful courtyard and gated access. Theresa, no doubt, had spent most of her life in seedier places, so she had treated herself—and them—to a little luxury last night. Flenn ventured outside to the courtyard. It continued to amaze him how Honduras was a country of such stark contrasts, the very rich and the very poor, living closely together but worlds apart.

He sat at a small café table just outside the hotel restaurant *El Morazán,* named for the martyred hero of the battle of Trinidad, Francisco Morazán. Large kapok trees shaded much of the garden, including the lanai where he quietly sipped an Americano. A waiter brought out a platter of sausages, Eggs Benedict and croissants. "I'm sorry, I didn't order these," Flenn said, politely.

"But I did!" He turned to see Zack Matteson standing behind him. "I thought you'd be as hungry as I am. Neither one of us had anything to eat last night."

"Nor did I!" they heard a woman say. Zack pulled a chair out for Theresa who was dressed this morning in black jeans and a satiny white camisole. Zack asked the waiter to reset the table for three.

"I'd order us champagne, or at least mimosas," Zack said to Theresa, "but I'm not sure the padre is in much of a celebratory mood this morning."

"Too bad," said Theresa. "I have never tasted champagne." Zack looked at Flenn who nodded, then went off to find the waiter. Soon four glasses appeared, three with orange juice and champagne, and one with just champagne.

"Try the one without orange juice first. See if you like it." Theresa did, then made a face and put a finger to her lips as the bubbles rose.

"Not what I expected," she said.

"Now try the mimosa." She liked the second drink much better. Zack lifted his glass. "I'd like to propose a toast: to our lady friend here, may she know health and prosperity from this day onward." Flenn couldn't refuse such a note of goodwill and picked up his glass, only to put it right back down again. *He was in no mood for a drink, especially with what lay ahead of him.*

"Theresa," Zack asked, "after breakfast, would you mind taking us to the airport? Flenn and I need to get to Washington." Zack had finally reached Sarah and was told that Deputy Director Moore wanted the two of them in his office ASAP. Sarah expected that Jeremy Schmitt would soon be headed to jail based on what he and Flenn would tell Moore. (Zack had met Carl Moore on only one occasion—a few months ago when he had presented him the dossier on Daniel Romero and Benjamin Rye.)

Zack and Theresa chatted happily over breakfast. Flenn just picked at the food on his plate. Zack sat back and surveyed the gardens around the courtyard. He commented on a large, red flower that he said reminded him of the famous Rolling Stones logo. "Those flowers are called *Hot Lips*," Theresa said. " I'm sure there is a fancier name, but that is what we call them." She pointed out the common names of several of the beautiful flowers around them. Zack was not usually impressed with such things, but he was fascinated with the fact that Theresa knew so much about them. "I wanted to be a gardener when I was a little girl," she explained. "The woman mi madre work for, she knew a lot about flowers, and taught me muchly."

Zack smiled. "About flowers, not adjectives, I take it."

Flenn kicked Zack under the table. "Leave her alone; I think her English is great."

"*Ouch!* Theresa knows that I'm kidding."

Theresa laughed. "No, I am *muchly* hurt and if you do not buy me another one of these..." she held up her glass "...mimosas right away I will cry my heart out *muchly* in this very chair."

"Ha, ha; well, we can't have that. Flenn, go order the lady another drink."

"Why me? You're the one who insulted her."

Zack raised his eyebrows, as if he wanted some alone time with Theresa.

Surely not! thought Flenn.

"Yeah," Zack said, "but you seem to be finished with your breakfast and we're not."

Flenn shook his head, but went inside, found the waiter, and ordered two more mimosas. He gazed out the window at Zack and Theresa as they sat, talking and laughing. *Maybe… in another time and place,* Flenn thought. He walked into the lobby and asked for a pen, some paper and an envelope. He was handed a pad of linen paper infused with a slight scent of jasmine. He wrote a quick note, stuffed it in his pocket, then returned to the table.

"So, Señor Zack, when is your boss expecting you?" Theresa asked. "Right away, or can we sit here… maybe have one more drink?"

"We just got these," Zack pointed out, but Theresa seemed hopeful for a third. "Okay, but I'm not so sure about you driving us to the airport."

Theresa laughed out loud. "You are kidding me, no? I can out-drink my brother and his gang any day."

Zack lifted his glass. "Here's to the Ases-a-holes!"

She laughed even louder as she clinked her glass to his. "To the Ases-a-holes," she repeated.

Flenn sat for a while as they drank and chatted, then excused himself to the restroom. He leaned over and whispered in Zack's ear, "I may be in there awhile. Enjoy yourself." Flenn walked into the café, found the waiter and handed him the note, which he'd placed in the envelope. "Please, take this letter to my friends out there, but only after they've finished their drinks." The waiter nodded and took the envelope along with the $20 bill Flenn pressed into his palm.

Flenn hesitated, looking once more out the café

window at Zack and Theresa laughing as they finished their breakfast. Flenn drew a deep breath. This would be the last time he would ever see either one of them.

CHAPTER *FIFTY-ONE*

Drenched with rain and sweat, Scudder had managed to make it to the stables where he'd parked the Nissan. Miraculously, it was unscathed by the fire. He was glad Flenn hadn't known about the truck. *The Jeep was gone, and so was Frack… fled for his miserable life, no doubt!* In the dark, Scudder hadn't noticed Frack's lifeless body lying in the tall grass by the side of the road.

Scudder had stashed $20,000 in the truck's glove compartment last week, and was glad now that he had. He would use part of it to repair his wounded shoulder, the rest to *destroy* Scott Flenn!

He stopped to ask directions to Vida Vibrante. The clerk at the all-night gas station had stared at his wounded arm as he told him how to find the hospital. With Jerry dead and all the phones destroyed as well, Scudder had no way to contact Schmitt. However, that was the least of his worries. Somehow, he'd failed to kill the priest, and in his self-congratulatory mood had allowed Flenn to find him. He slammed the steering wheel several times as he shouted: "Stupid, stupid, stupid!"

He managed to find the hospital easily enough. Ten hours later Scudder's wounds had been cleaned; he'd been re-hydrated, and had been given IV-antibiotics and painkillers. The latter had helped him sleep for at least six of those hours. When he awoke, his first thought was to check his trousers for the cash he'd stuffed in them. Amazingly, it was still there. He shouted for an aide to pull out the IV line. The woman called for the doctor, who tried to argue that Scudder needed to stay overnight, but Scudder would have none of that. Instead, he settled his bill; nearly two-grand, and then demanded to see Juan. The doctor claimed he had no idea who Scudder meant, but a description and $500 encouraged the man to go and locate him. It wasn't difficult: Juan was the only gangbanger in the hospital with a broken leg paid for by a tall American. Speculation about the relationship between the rich American and the young thug had circulated throughout the hospital.

When Scudder was taken to Juan's room, he took a cursory look at Juan's leg and then barked, "Wake him up!"

The doctor protested. "He needs more rest, señor. He…"

Scudder handed the man another hundred. "Wake him up and get him ready to leave! He's going with me."

The doctor pocketed the cash, then ordered a nurse to rouse the patient. He glared at Scudder. "We will wake him, señor, but whether he wishes to leave is entirely up to him. His bill has been paid, his leg is far from healed, and I will not force a patient out of the hospital before he is ready."

Scudder raised an eyebrow. "What if he says that he wants to leave with me?"

"This is not a prison, señor," the doctor said stiffly, heading for the door. "He may leave whenever he chooses."

Scudder watched as a nurse disconnected the IV fluids and gave the patient a shot of something. Juan was alert within minutes and was startled to see the fat man who'd hired him to watch for the priest standing over his bed. Scudder didn't seem angry, though; instead, he was smiling.

"Remember me?"

Juan nodded.

"Can you understand what I'm saying?" Again, the younger man nodded. "Good. I need your help, and I'm willing to pay you twice whatever the priest gave you." Scudder patted Juan on the arm. "Trust me, he only put you here to get you out of the way. Don't give him a second thought; he's not your friend." The fat man smiled. "But *I* am."

Scudder noticed Juan staring at his sling. "Yeah, this is what that so-called priest did to me," he sneered. "He was trying to kill me, but I was too smart for him. And so are you. You don't owe him a thing."

The fat man tried to look sincere. "You don't owe *him*, but you do owe *me*. You didn't call me when you found him." Scudder frowned as if talking to a naughty child. "I'm very disappointed in you." Juan sat up, attempting to explain. Scudder held up his hands. "None of that matters; all is forgiven. You do still want to work for me, don't you?"

Juan nodded, not at all sure that he did.

"Good," Scudder said. He fished in his pocket and pulled out a large roll of American dollars. "There will be more, lots more, if you will help me find that priest." Scudder smiled. "I need you, Juan." That was the first true statement Scudder had made. *The fact was, he would kill Juan as soon as this business was over, if for no other reason than to get the money back.*

Eventually, he'd return to the United States, find a way to contact Schmitt, and get back on track for the Mexico job. Right now, however, the only thing that mattered was finding Flenn... and killing him. He wouldn't just shoot him; no, that would be too quick. He wanted to see fear in Flenn's eyes and hear him beg for his life.

"What do you say, Juan, will you help me?"

Juan looked at the money. *Theresa had told him that the priest was a good man, and that many children had died... but what was that to him?*

He looked at the man who had just given him a small fortune and nodded.

"Nurse!" Scudder barked. "Bring this man some crutches!"

****

Zack was angry... and worried. He'd had no choice but to fly to D.C. on the first afternoon flight, direct orders from Deputy Director Moore. He and Theresa had searched the hotel grounds for any sign of Flenn but none of the staff had seen him slip away. Flenn could be anywhere by now. Sure, Zack knew where Flenn was heading but he was too smart to go there right away. He might wait a day or two, just to be sure that Zack had left, and then make his way to San Jose de la Montaña. *God knows what the parents of those murdered children might do to him!*

Flenn's note had told them both goodbye. He had left instructions for Zack to contact his brother, David, and see to it that Flenn Industries built a school in the village in memory of the slain children. Theresa had agreed to go to the village and try and stop Flenn. Maybe she could get there first and at least explain to the villagers what had really happened to their children. Zack had to give her more details than he wanted so that Theresa would understand just what was at stake.

"So, you and the padre work for the CIA?" she had asked.

"No, only I do. Flenn used to work with me, but he left a long time ago to become a priest. Scudder was sent to prison decades ago, and has held a grudge against Flenn all this time." His eyes narrowed. "Unfortunately, Scudder's been getting help. Someone in the agency.

"I have to go back now to stop him, so it is important that you let those people on the mountain know that Padre Flenn had nothing to do with their children's deaths. Tell them how it's been destroying his soul, that he's thought of nothing except their children since all this happened. Tell them that he's been helping me find the man that did this terrible thing." He searched her dark eyes. "Theresa, if you don't make those parents understand, they may hurt Flenn." He didn't need to say anything else after that.

CHAPTER *FIFTY-TWO*

Flenn checked himself into el Marcositas for the night. It didn't feel right to stay anywhere else. He only had a couple hundred dollars, which had been enough for a bus ride to San Pedro Sula, a taxi, a room and then another taxi tomorrow morning. He had stuffed the rest in an envelope and left it in the room for Theresa.

He wouldn't eat anything from this point on. His fasting was not for himself, but for his parish back home... and for the parents of the slain children.

The same grizzled old hotel clerk gave him a key to a room upstairs. The man was wearing the clothes he'd had on last week. Flenn turned for the stairs, but stopped when he felt a light tapping on his shoulder. He turned and the frail man searched Flenn's face with anxious eyes. "Theresa?" he asked. Flenn put his hand on the old man's shoulder.

"Theresa es bien," he assured him. "Muy bien." The man nodded and gave Flenn a toothless smile, then went back to his desk where he pulled out a bottle of something and offered Flenn a glass. "No, gracias," Flenn said as kindly as he could. The old man lifted his glass in a salute and waved Flenn up the stairs.

The next morning Flenn woke early, said his prayers, and made his way downstairs to find the old man smiling from ear to ear. "Qué esta posando?" Flenn asked.

"I will tell you what's going on," he heard a familiar voice say. Flenn turned and saw Theresa leaning against the same wall where she'd been standing when he had first seen her. "Señor Zack has gone to Washington," she said with a smile. "He has asked me to be your bodyguard."

Flenn couldn't help but be glad to see her, yet he said, "Thank you, Theresa, but I have to do this by myself."

"He tell me you say that."

"I need to do this alone."

"He say you say that too."

Flenn shook his head. "I'm sorry, but no; and, that's that!" Flenn was seldom forceful, but when he was, few had been courageous enough to argue with him. Theresa was one of those few.

"You listen to me, Padre. I have fought with men all my life, and I will fight with you right here and now if that is what it takes, but you are no leaving here without me!"

"Theresa!" Flenn cautioned.

"Padre!" Theresa warned in return.

Flenn shook his head and stormed out the door with Theresa close behind. Apparently, he'd just met his match.

Out on the sidewalk he stopped and turned around. "All right, but only to the top of the mountain. I go into the village by myself. Understood?"

She smiled victoriously. "We will see."

They climbed into her truck and headed across the city and up the mountain. Theresa assured Flenn that Zack had indeed boarded a jet and flown back to D.C. yesterday. She also told him that there had been no mention on the radio of an explosion or house fire outside of Tegucigalpa. The brief rainstorm had put out the flames long before anyone had seen them. Flenn couldn't help feeling sorry for whoever it was that owned the hacienda.

They made their way up the winding dirt road toward the village. Theresa didn't recognize the skinny, shirtless member of the Asesinos sitting on a fallen branch reaching for his cell phone.

"So," Theresa asked, "what is it you are going to do once we get there? Are you going to tell these people what happened... about this man, Scudder?"

"I'm going to tell them why their children died," Flenn said softly. "That a madman wanted to kill me, but a friend found out and managed to save me." He sighed. "Just not their children."

Theresa shook her head as they passed an abandoned truck on the side of the road. "You are either very brave or very foolish, Padre."

"I'm neither. This is just what must be done. They deserve to know the truth."

They rounded a long curve, when suddenly Flenn lurched forward as Theresa slammed on her brakes to avoid hitting a large, red truck parked sideways across the road. Seconds later two men leapt out of the jungle;

they were pointing rifles directly at Theresa and Flenn.

She recognized one of them as a member of her brother's gang. "Enrique, what is the meaning of this?" she snapped in Spanish.

"Get out of the truck!" the boy shouted back. "For your own good."

"Hell no! You aren't going to shoot me; Juan would tear your throat out!" Then in English she yelled to Flenn: "Stay in your seat, Padre, I'm backing us out of here! They won't dare shoot me."

Flenn felt the splatter of blood a millisecond before he heard the gunshot. A fat man with his left arm in a sling stepped out from behind a tree holding a derringer. "But... *I* will!"

CHAPTER *FIFTY-THREE*

Flenn's hands and mouth were bound tightly with duct tape. Scudder had ordered the men to find something to wipe the blood off the priest before throwing him in the back of the Nissan. Flenn struggled against the restraints until Scudder walked over and drove his fist, with all the rage and strength he could muster, straight into Flenn's groin. Flenn fell hard, but somehow refused to utter a sound. *He wouldn't allow Scudder the satisfaction, not after what he'd done to the children... to Theresa.*

The big man rubbed his knuckles. "Damn, that felt good!" He wanted to hit Flenn a second time, but there was no need. He'd soon finish what he came to do, and this time it would be up close and personal... *Oh, so personal! He knew just where to do it, too. The cliffs overlooking the ocean, where he had spent the day while Jerry and Carlos had been at the beach.* Scudder had scoped out the terrain looking for a place to dispose of Frick and Frack once they had outlived their usefulness. *It was a solitary place where he could take his time. No doubt it would be messy... but, oh, so much fun!*

The Asesinos carried Theresa's body into the jungle, while one of them drove off in her vehicle somewhere up the mountain. The others climbed in the back of the Nissan beside Flenn. Scudder ordered them to keep Flenn down so no one would see him when they drove through town. "Shoot him in the kneecap if he tries to get up," Scudder shouted.

The guards assumed Flenn didn't speak Spanish after they had hurled vile insults at him and got no reaction, so they began to talk freely. Flenn discovered that they were planning to switch vehicles outside San Pedro Sula. He overheard something about Rio Coto, which Flenn knew only as a resort area with beautiful beaches and a few steep cliffs.

After what seemed like an hour, Flenn felt the truck slow down and pull over onto the side of the road. The Asesinos got out of the back and Flenn sat up but saw nothing but brush and trees on either side of the road. Flenn heard Scudder talking to someone. There were two other men standing in front of a rusted-out Dodge Neon. One man Flenn had never seen before; the other—*Juan!*

Theresa's brother was on crutches and his face was pale. Someone must have helped him change into jeans and a white tee. An ancient, cumbersome Smith & Wesson revolver was tucked into his waistband. Juan and Scudder spoke for less than a minute, after which Juan motioned to the others. They returned to the truck and ordered Flenn into the back of the Nissan's cab. The Asesinos then climbed into the old Dodge and drove away.

Juan crawled into the front passenger seat and stared back at Flenn. "Do not try anything, amigo. I may be crippled, but I am a very good shot."

Scudder laughed. "Don't kill the good Father here; just keep him from escaping."

"Why is he covered in blood, Señor Scudder?"

"Because your boys can't do what they are told. I ordered them to clean him up!"

"That is not his blood?"

"Someone got in my way. Don't ask questions. Just see to it that he doesn't try anything until we get there." Nothing more was said for next hour. Flenn watched the scenery change from brush to forest, and back to brush again.

"Would you look at that?" Scudder pointed to the opposite side of the road. A jaguar stood next to the highway, watching them approach. "Wonder if I could hit that thing from here?" Scudder slowed down, pulled out his pistol, and rolled down the window just as a large flatbed truck loaded with watermelons came over a hill and passed them on its way to San Pedro Sula. By the time it was gone, the jaguar had vanished.

Scudder drove for several more miles before turning down a side road. "You doing okay back there, Flenn? Wouldn't want you to be uncomfortable." He laughed. "Interesting place, Honduras. Some of the poorest slobs in the world live here, but it has some really beautiful scenery."

Juan stared out the front window, still wondering why Flenn was covered in blood. *Had one of his men gotten in the way?*

"We came to this miserable place a couple of weeks before you did," Scudder prattled. "By the way, thanks for posting your plans on your website; that was really helpful." Flenn just stared out the window.

"We had some time on our hands, so one of the locals—you know, one of those guys you and your friend blew up—well, he told us about this place that is truly amazing. Sandy beaches, beautiful cliffs... there's this one place that's breathtaking; far away from everything, and this bumpy old road leads right to it. You'll love it. Well, *I will!*

"At the top of the hill the road just stops. I guess someone once had a house up there. Anyway, there's this little green pasture at the end. Very secluded... no one around for miles. The pasture leads straight to a sheer cliff, which hangs a couple hundred feet over some huge, sharp, nasty looking boulders. The tide covers them a couple of times a day; anything that fell from that cliff would be washed out to sea without a trace." Scudder laughed. "We'll be there in just a minute; then you can see for yourself."

The trees broke as the truck crested the hill. Scudder stopped the truck. "See! What'd I tell you? Isn't it spectacular? You can see nothing but ocean for miles. One hell of a view—so much better than anything I've seen for the past twenty years rotting in a Korean jail cell!"

Juan had never been here before. From the way he was taking it all in, Flenn wondered if Juan had ever even seen the ocean, or had been out of the slums since he joined the Asesinos. *Doubtful. Just as it was equally doubtful that he knew Scudder had murdered Theresa. The Asesinos hadn't told him. Probably too afraid.*

Suddenly, Scudder pressed hard on the accelerator and the truck leaped toward the edge of the cliff. Juan grabbed for the dashboard to steady himself with one hand, grasping for the door handle with the other. Flenn didn't react. Scudder was all about the show; always had been. He wasn't about to kill himself now, not when he had the upper hand. Sure enough, the maniac slammed on the brakes and stopped about five feet from the edge.

Scudder glanced over at Juan, who had wet himself. "Oh, grow up," Scudder said disgustedly. He gestured toward Flenn. "Get him out of the truck."

It took Juan a moment to climb out of the truck using his crutch. He opened the cab door and cut the tape from around Flenn's ankles and legs. Juan never said a word, just hobbled backwards and motioned for Flenn to get out.

Scudder stood on the edge of the cliff gazing at the sea. Flenn thought of charging him and sending them both sailing over the edge, but he assumed that either Scudder or Juan would drop him first. Plus, for some reason, Flenn no longer wanted to kill Scudder. It was odd; all he felt now was contempt... mixed, strangely enough, with pity.

How Scudder had found Juan, he didn't know, nor did it matter anymore. Flenn knew that he was about to die and was preparing himself to meet his creator. The how of it all was unimportant, whether from a gunshot, knife blade, or a beating. He assumed Scudder had brought Flenn here to throw him off the cliff; but he wouldn't simply push him over the side. *No, he was too consumed with hatred; Scudder would want to make this as painful as possible.*

Scudder looked at Juan. "Take that tape off his mouth."

Juan obeyed.

Flenn glared at Scudder. "You've gone mad, Eric, completely mad." Juan remained quiet even though he felt the same way about the fat gringo.

Scudder smiled. "Just thought I'd get your blood rushing a bit, old friend."

"We were never friends, Eric." Flenn strained again against the tape around his hands; intense pain shot up his wounded shoulder.

Scudder glanced at Juan, then back at Flenn. "The priesthood has made you soft. You should know never to trust anyone." He cocked his head to one side and smirked. "Did you really think that helping this lowlife was going to change him?"

"Maybe," Flenn answered. "Along with ten thousand dollars."

"Ten grand to save your life?"

"No, to save his."

Scudder just shook his head, then barked at Juan to wait by the truck. Scudder turned Flenn around and pushed him toward the middle of the pasture. "His life's not worth saving." Scudder hadn't even attempted to lower his voice.

"Not according to my book," Flenn said.

Scudder laughed. "Your book? What, the Bible? You ever read that thing, Flenn? Nothing but a bunch of superstitious nonsense! I'm surprised at you; never saw you as the gullible type. Oh, you could be too trusting at times, I'll grant you that. You were also fast on your feet, and smart—almost as smart as me."

"I'm not the one who spent the past twenty years in jail."

Scudder poked Flenn's wounded shoulder with the pistol. "And yet look where we are now. Your hands tied behind your back and me holding the gun." Scudder looked around. "As you know, this wasn't my first option. Blowing you into little bits along with anyone you cared about—that's been my favorite fantasy over the years. Thought I had done it, too. Oh well, I guess this will have to suffice. Want to venture a guess as to what comes next?"

"I don't have to guess," Flenn quipped. "Eternal life for me, misery for you."

Scudder jabbed him again. "Give me a break, Flenn. You can't really believe all that crap!"

"Believe it, practice it, live by it, and will die with it comforting me. No matter what you do to me, Scudder, I'm not afraid to die."

"Yeah, not now maybe, but you will be. When I'm done with you, I'm going to throw you over that cliff and listen to you scream all the way down."

Flenn shook his head. "That's where you screwed up again, Eric. Sure, you can hurt me, you might even make me wish for death, but you can never make me afraid of it."

Scudder scowled. "You really think I believe that you're not afraid of me; not afraid of what I'm going to do to you?"

Juan could hear the white men talking but they were

speaking too quickly for him to understand it all. Theresa had been the one who'd learned English best when they were kids. Juan had given up early on—their mother had said that he always gave up when things got difficult.

Flenn turned around to face Scudder. "I'm not afraid, not in the least," Flenn said. "When you learn from your mistakes, and when your heart truly does find faith, there is no room for fear." Raising his voice slightly he added, "I suppose I am afraid of one thing, though."

"Yeah? What's that?"

"What Juan's going to do to you when he finds out that you killed his sister!"

Scudder stiffened and looked over his shoulder to see if Juan had heard. If he had, the leader of the Asesinos showed no signs of it. Scudder turned back around. "Nice try Flenn, but he either didn't hear... or doesn't care. Funny thing, if I had known that woman was his sister I could just as easily have told him that you had killed her, but what would have been the point? It's not like these are really *people*, you know, not like you and me."

The truth was, Juan *had* heard, but had learned long ago not to react—*Never give someone the advantage of seeing more than you want them to see.* Juan simply stared blankly at Scudder and the priest, as if he hadn't understood a thing.

But he had!

Could it be? Was Theresa dead? Had the American pig really killed her?

"She didn't have to die you know," said Flenn slowly. "You could've let her go."

"Just shut up and kneel down," Scudder ordered.

"Hell no! I won't kneel before you or anyone other than my maker!"

With his injured arm, Scudder didn't have the strength to force Flenn to kneel, nor did he relish the thought of having Flenn's blood splattered all over him, so he backed up and pointed the pistol at Flenn's knee. "Fine, have it your way."

Flenn didn't respond. He hadn't been lying to Scudder: He felt no fear. He had hoped to bring Scudder down, but now that the tables were turned, Flenn simply accepted his fate.

Scudder's eyes narrowed. He lowered the gun slightly. "One thing: I never did understand why you turned on me in Korea. You could have waited until we got home to file a report, yet you called the Korean police. Why? Do you have any idea what prison is like over there? *Do you?!*"

"My God, man! Forget about the Koreans. You murdered children, Eric, innocent children!"

Scudder shrugged "Poor kids with no future. I did them a favor."

Every agent usually found reasons to justify their actions. The term *collateral damage* had been invented for that very reason. *But did Scudder really believe what he'd said?* Something in the man's eyes told Flenn he did.

"Those children had a future, Eric! They had their whole lives ahead of them. You took that away. Just like in Korea, you set your mind on what you wanted, and didn't care who got hurt! There were ten or twelve kids with me in that village! They had mothers and fathers. They had futures, meager as they might have been, friends to meet, people to fall in love with, babies to make…"

"Shut up!"

Flenn ignored him. "You took that all away!"

Scudder raised the pistol. "I said shut up!"

"No, Scudder, I won't shut up. You're going to kill me anyway. I'm not afraid of you, whether you believe me or not, because I know there is more to life than these few years on earth."

"You're about to find out!"

"And all because you chose to set this in motion by stealing some stupid incense bowls twenty years ago!"

Scudder bristled at Flenn's smugness. "No, damn it, because you turned me in!"

Flenn shook his head. "You stupid son of a… you still don't get it, do you? I wasn't the one who turned you in, I never had to. Someone else beat me to it."

"You're not really trying to save your skin with a lie, are you? God, Flenn, even I'll say it … that's beneath you."

"Believe what you want, but I want you to hear one more thing."

"One last word, huh? Go ahead, but make it quick."

"Sure, actually three words… I forgive you."

Scudder's face turned as red as the button Zack had pushed inside the Humvee. "You sanctimonious piece of… ! *You* forgive *me*! I spent twenty years in prison, and you have the audacity to look me in the eye…"

Flenn didn't let him finish. "I have the audacity to look you in the eye and say I forgive you for what you are about to do to me. That's my right, and that is what I choose to do! But I can't vouch for those children you murdered, or for their parents and families." He spoke slowly and clearly. "And I can't vouch for Theresa. Nor can I vouch for the U.S. government, which is about to name you an enemy of the state now that Zack Matteson and Sarah Coverdale are onto your friend Jeremy Schmitt!"

Scudder was shaking with fury. "You lie!"

"I'm not lying, Eric."

Scudder went ballistic. He lunged for Flenn, striking him hard across the temple with his pistol. Flenn couldn't deflect the blow, but did the next best thing by managing to roll with it. He fell to the ground, bleeding from a deep cut on his forehead. Scudder towered over him, shaking in fury. He aimed the pistol straight at Flenn's face.

Flenn heard the gunshot, but strangely, didn't feel a thing. Scudder was still standing over him, but was teetering, trying to steady himself. Juan had managed to shoot Scudder through the same arm which had been injured in the blast.

"That is for my sister!" Juan yelled angrily, pulling the trigger again.

Nothing. The ancient gun had jammed!

Before Juan could squeeze the trigger a third time, Scudder turned and emptied the entire magazine into him, sending Juan over the edge of the cliff.

Scudder stumbled to where Juan had dropped the gun, picked it up and turned back toward Flenn. "Enough of this!"

Flenn braced himself as he got back to his feet, but something rushed by him in a blur of yellow and black. Flenn watched, incredulously, as a jaguar headed straight for Scudder!

Even from this distance, Flenn could see the terror in Scudder's eyes. The fat man tried to fire, but again, nothing. Scudder turned and ran in the only direction possible—straight toward the cliff!

The animal never slowed, but lunged for Scudder with a roar, sending them both hurtling over the edge. Flenn heard Scudder's terrified screams as he plummeted to the rocks below, and then... silence.

He approached the edge and peered down to the surf below. Two mangled bodies were splattered across the rocks as waves lapped nearby. Flenn looked all around. There was no sign of the jaguar. None whatsoever.

CHAPTER *FIFTY-FOUR*

Flenn managed to find his way back to San Pedro Sula by stopping at a gas station and asking directions. He spent the last of his money putting gas into Scudder's truck… or was it the CIA's truck? What did it matter?

He had only one thing left to do now, and as difficult as it would be, he was ready. Once in the city, he managed to eventually find the road that led up the mountain. He passed the spot where Theresa had been shot and crossed himself as he said a prayer for her soul. He thought of getting out to find her, but she was with God now, as he assumed he soon would be.

The tiny village of San Jose de la Montaña was a half mile farther up. He stopped the truck, turned off the ignition, and left the keys inside for anyone who happened along. He stepped out of the truck and looked around. The jungle was thick on both sides of the road. The sweet smell of exotic flowers wafted through the air. Somewhere off to his left was where he and Zack had made their way down from the mountain a week ago. Above him, the sky was blue and cloudless. Flenn heard running water nearby and wondered if the stream led to where he and Zack had seen the three jaguars that night. A slight smile flashed across his face as he recalled how one of them had relieved himself next to Zack as they slept.

He thought of the jaguar that had dashed out of the jungle yesterday and sent Scudder to his death. Flenn had searched for a long time along the rocks and out to sea, but had never found a trace of the animal. He wondered if it had been deranged... rabid even? Or, could something, *or someone*, have been driving it? If his life were a C.S. Lewis novel, he would have half expected to see the big cat mysteriously appear before him now and walk with him these last steps toward what was to be his final destination.

Flenn's life hadn't been Scudder's to take, which only convinced him that it had belonged to the parents of the slain children all along. With each step toward the village he recalled the faces of the little ones that day. *Happy, trusting, smiling... all looking up at him, the gringo priest who'd promised their parents that he would build them a school.*

Flenn felt his gut tighten. *How he wished that Scudder had come after him at his home in Birmingham; anywhere else but here.* There had been no purpose in the death of these children, none whatsoever. *An evil act by an evil man.*

Flenn walked on until he could make out the small cross on top of the church. Rounding a bend, he came upon two little boys playing in a puddle. They had fashioned a boat out of a mango skin and had stuck a stick through a leaf for a sail. Flenn tried to speak to them, but his throat was so tight that he couldn't, so he just kept walking.

Ahead, he saw the familiar houses of twigs and tin. Several people were sitting under the rusted awning of the market across from the church. Nearby, a middle-aged man with a machete was cutting bananas off a tree. As the villagers saw the tall priest they began to point and murmur. Flenn didn't try to hear what they were saying; he didn't think that he could bear it.

The man with the machete stopped and stared at him. Flenn walked past the store until he saw it—the spot where the children had died, a small crater, still stained here and there with what Flenn knew to be the children's blood. He hesitated, then stepped down into the hole.

Here was where they had stood, he told himself.

Here was where they had played together.

Here was where he would die.

A crowd had gathered around the priest but he didn't dare look into their faces. Instead he turned and gazed up at the cross on the top of the church. Out of the corner of his eye, he saw the man wielding the machete come up behind him. He turned and recognized him as one of the parents of the children who had died that day. Their eyes locked only for a moment, but it was long enough for Flenn to see the man's overwhelming grief. Flenn crossed himself—then knelt before him.

The crowd grew thicker as Flenn waited for the blow. Whether it would come from this man, or from someone else, didn't matter. He prayed for forgiveness for whoever it would be.

Flenn closed his eyes.

Nothing happened.

He waited a full minute before opening them again. The man had replaced the blade in its sheath. Flenn searched his eyes for a reason. Where he had seen grief before, he now saw only compassion.

"He's not going to hurt you."

Flenn recognized the voice.

"None of them are."

He looked toward the top of the church steps and saw Bishop Juan Hernandez. "They do not blame you for their children's deaths."

"It would be a shame," another voice said, "if they deprived me of one of the best priests in my diocese." Unbelievably, standing next to Hernandez was Flenn's own bishop, Tom Morrison!

The crowd parted to let the two clerics pass. Flenn remained on his knees. "No, Tom, no! I deserve this. Their children..."

It was Bishop Hernandez who spoke. "Their children loved you, and so do these people. Your friend came here and explained to them what happened."

Flenn didn't understand. "My friend? Zack Matteson was here?"

"No, this was a woman. She came here yesterday to tell the people what had happened to their children and why."

What?

The Honduran bishop went on: "They know that a very bad man was trying to kill you. The villagers contacted me to ask how they could help you."

"Help *me*?" Flenn searched the faces of the people crowded around him. No one appeared angry. In fact, just the opposite. Each face seemed to reflect the compassion of the first man.

Tom Morrison stepped down into the crater and put his hand on Flenn's shoulder. "Isn't this what you and I always preach about? Mercy, forgiveness... caring?"

A storm of uncontrollable grief, and yet unimaginable release, welled up within Flenn. For the first time in decades he did something he had trained himself never to do... he began to weep openly in front of others. It was as if a dam had finally burst, and a torrent of tears had come to cleanse his soul.

The villagers entered the crater one by one, gathering around the priest to put their hands on him as he shed tears of grief and release—such sweet release. No one, not even Flenn, noticed three jaguars quietly watching from the edge of the jungle.

CHAPTER *FIFTY-FIVE*

Puchica's Guatemalan Bar and Grill wasn't the kind of place Jeremy Schmitt was accustomed to frequenting after work, but it was where he'd been directed by the cryptic email.

The place was dark and smelled of fried beans and cigar smoke. Only a few patrons were here tonight. A long bar ran halfway down the small restaurant; behind it, a woman was washing glasses. A soccer game was playing on the television at one end of the bar. Schmitt sat at the opposite end and ordered a gin and tonic. He looked around the restaurant but didn't spot anyone who seemed to be waiting for him.

A few minutes later the door opened and a stocky brown-skinned man walked inside, glanced around, then walked straight over to Schmitt. The muscular man sat next to him and ordered a beer. Schmitt looked straight ahead without turning to acknowledge the stranger. "You Hernandez?"

"Yep," was all the man said as the woman gave him his beer.

Schmitt took a sip from his glass. "I just have one question," he said, staring at several large bottles of tequila on the shelf behind the bar. "What the hell happened?"

"I don't really know." Carlos said. "I was on guard duty and everyone else was inside when the house suddenly blew up."

"No survivors?"

Carlos shrugged. "Just me, boss."

Schmitt didn't say anything for the longest time. Finally, he finished his drink, ordered another, and stood up. "Let's go sit in the corner." Carlos reached for his beer and followed him to a corner table away from prying ears.

"So, you're saying that the place just blew up?"

"That's what happened, boss. I swear it."

Schmitt stared into the man's eyes. "Scudder and Rudolph?"

Carlos shook his head. "Dead. Along with Frick and Frack."

"Who?"

"Two local guys Scudder hired as extra muscle."

Schmitt lifted his glass. "Did Scudder or Rudolph happen to say anything to you about Mexico and what we had planned there?"

"Quite a bit," Carlos lied. "That was how I knew to contact you."

Schmitt thought for a moment. "Gerald told me you are a man with numerous talents. Are you up to finishing the job?"

Carlos grinned. "If the price is right."

"I'll give you half a million."

Carlos shook his head. "Double it and you have a deal."

The bartender brought over another gin and tonic along with a fresh beer for Carlos. Schmitt waited for the woman to leave. "Double? You seem to think highly of yourself. You any good getting around security? The place I have in mind is not going to be all that tight."

"It's my specialty," Carlos answered. "How do you know about their security?"

Schmitt's eyes flashed. "Because I've spent an entire year researching this thing!" He took a breath. "If Scudder hadn't blown himself up playing with those damn drones, I wouldn't have to be asking you this, but okay, I will pay you a million in cash but I need to know you are as good as Gerald said you are."

"I know how to get a job done, boss," was Carlos' only reply.

Schmitt didn't like this arrangement but he had been waiting for 20 years and there wasn't going to be another chance. He reached into his jacket and pulled out a detailed map of the museum where the exhibit was on display. "These are ancient Korean incense bowls. I tried to get my hands on them years ago, but Scudder blew that one, too. Everything is marked on here," he said, handing Carlos the map. "Times, type of alarm they're using, the guards' schedule—you'll find it is all here. Just get in there and get out. And don't get caught." His eyes narrowed. "If you do, I'll see that you're dead within the hour."

"And if I change my mind?"

Schmitt glared at him. "Same; it just might take longer. Believe me, there's no place on God's green earth where you'll be able to hide from me."

Something struck Schmitt on the shoulder. He looked up, thinking that a small piece of plaster had fallen from the ceiling. *Plink!* This time the object bounced off his chest and onto the table. It was small and black. He picked it up. "Who the hell is throwing jellybeans in here?" Schmitt turned to see the last person he expected. "Matteson, what the hell are you doing here?"

Zack popped a jellybean in his mouth and smiled. "Just came to catch a rat," he said. Carlos pulled back the collar of his shirt to reveal a wire attached to a small microphone.

Schmitt's hand darted inside his jacket but before he could pull his weapon a familiar voice came from around the corner. "I wouldn't do that if I were you, Jeremy." Carl Moore and Sarah Coverdale stepped out of the kitchen where they had just heard everything. All the patrons in the bar stood and turned toward Schmitt—all agents. The bartender smiled as she pulled out a sawed-off shotgun and laid it on top of the bar.

Carlos nodded to Sarah, then stepped away. Zack reached into Schmitt's pocket and relieved him a Colt .45. Carl and Sarah both smiled as they sat across from Schmitt, where Carlos had been sitting only a moment ago. "Looks like we have some catching up to do, Jeremy," Carl Moore said. "About 20 years' worth, I'd say."

EPILOGUE

"We give thanks to you, O God, for the goodness and love which you have made known to us in creation; in the calling of Israel to be your people; in your word spoken through the prophets; and above all in the Word made flesh."

Father Scott Flenn looked out at his congregation, the people he cherished most in this world, and continued with the communion prayer. "For in these last days you sent him to be incarnate from the Virgin Mary, to be the savior and redeemer of the world."

Flenn knew the words from the prayer book by heart, and it felt good to be standing behind the altar of Saint Ann's saying them once again.

"In him, you have delivered us from evil, and made us worthy to stand before you." He looked up... his heart skipping a beat. For a moment he thought he saw Theresa standing in the very last pew, the one closest to the door. He blinked, but then saw only Delores Dilwicky, who was always anxious to be the first out after Sunday services. Still, he could have sworn it had been Theresa standing there, dressed in white and smiling up at him.

His congregation waited patiently, thinking he had lost his place in the liturgy. They, of course, knew nothing about the past few weeks or why their vicar had stayed in

Honduras longer than expected. He'd only told them that the needs had been greater than he'd anticipated. Father Flenn had already let his congregation know that he would be returning to San Jose de la Montaña in the fall to oversee the building of a new school for the children of the mountain. The community was even now meeting with a team of architects Flenn had flown down to Honduras. Their only instructions had been to design whatever it was that the people said they wanted. Flenn would be financing the entire project, including paying for teachers and a resident schoolmaster. His only condition was that the villagers allow him to name the school. They had agreed wholeheartedly, especially upon learning that he intended to name the school *Holy Innocents'*.

Tomorrow, Flenn would fly to Dulles and take a cab to Langley for the first time in years. He'd resisted making the trip, even when the Deputy Director of the CIA had called him personally. In the end, Flenn had agreed, but only because Director Moore had threatened to come to Birmingham and attend services at Saint Ann's with Sarah and Zack and an entire entourage of field agents.

Whether Carl Moore would have really come, Flenn didn't know, nor was he willing to take the chance. No, Flenn's past would remain just that, in the past—a gift that had been given back to him as he knelt in a crater on a Honduran mountaintop.

Flenn's priesthood was intact, and, while he had teetered on the precipice in his desire to seek revenge on

Eric Scudder, he had maintained both his sense of calling and his life's purpose.

Tomorrow, he would no doubt see Zack Matteson. He already knew that Jeremy Schmitt had been confronted and arrested. Sarah had called him with the news. Flenn also knew from Sarah that Schmitt's scheme was never going to be revealed to the public... too big of a black eye for the CIA. Instead, Schmitt's overseas bank accounts had been seized and investigators were looking into each piece of Schmitt's sizeable art collection. If anything had been acquired illegally, and no doubt much of it had, he would spend the rest of his days in a federal prison.

The Honduran military, for its part, was furious about the loss of their drone. Without the Humvee's master computer or an operator, it had run out of fuel and crashed harmlessly into a lake. Soto Cano Airbase was demanding answers that the CIA wasn't about to give.

Tomorrow Flenn would simply report—no, *tell*—Director Moore about what he had witnessed, along with the details about his time with Scudder 20 years ago. Flenn had been asking himself how a trained investigator such as Scudder had fallen under the thumb of Jeremy Schmitt in the first place. Had it simply been the money, or was it something else? Maybe it had been the chance to grab onto the coattails of an advancing bureaucrat. Instead, Gerald Rudolph had become Schmitt's number two while Scudder had sat in prison plotting his ritual of revenge. Flenn could only guess at what Scudder's eventual plans were for Schmitt and Rudolph. No doubt he'd worked out something equally diabolical to repay

Schmitt for having abandoned him in Korea all those years.

Scudder had assumed that Flenn had reported him to the police that day in Seoul. He hadn't, and neither had Sarah. Flenn thought back on that morning 20 years ago. He couldn't recall if he had actually witnessed Lee Qwon get on that bus or not. Maybe Sarah had been right about Lee working for Korean Intelligence after all.

In the end, what did it matter?

Whatever it was that drove people like Scudder and Schmitt was not something Flenn wanted anything to do with... now or ever for that matter. He had been called to a new life, one that had started ten years ago in Edinburgh.

Of course, Zack Matteson would continue to chase down those drawn to the darkness; and, truth be told, maybe that was Zack's calling in life. Once upon a time, it had also been Flenn's, but he served a different master these days. Not greed, not the agency, not even that of home and hearth, but one which claimed his deepest senses of loyalty and had graced him with the greatest sense of belonging he had ever known.

As Flenn continued with the service, he glanced up at a large rendition of Noah's Ark hanging over the entrance to the nave. Flenn had never noticed it before, but all of the animals were depicted looking toward Noah and the gigantic boat. Only one was looking behind him, its face pointed not toward the ark, but directly at the altar... directly at Flenn.

It was a jaguar.

*Don't miss Father Flenn's
Next Adventure...*

The Poisoned
Chalice

Join the Father Flenn Mailing List:
www.fatherflenn.com

FARNE
PRESS

Acknowledgments

I have nothing but the greatest respect for the many mission-minded people who unselfishly offer care and assistance to people in impoverished places throughout the world. Thank you to everyone who is willing to see beyond borders and race to help the poorest of the poor.

Thank you to Margaret Shaw, my editor; and to my wife, Diane, whose careful attention to detail has proven invaluable. Thank you also to Larry Vinson and Jim Brown for their wonderful assistance. My deepest gratitude goes to my family—for their love and support, and for enduring my endless obsession with the *Father Flenn* series. Thank you also to Win Schepps, Paul and Sandy Ash and to my parish family of Saint Mark's. I greatly appreciate their encouragement and inspiration over the years.

Lastly, a special thank you to the rapidly growing number of fans of Father Flenn! I hear that Zack Matteson may be on his way to join Father Flenn soon in England. *Of course, it could be just a rumor…*

Follow Father Flenn at:
www.fatherflenn.com

About the Author...

Scott Arnold is author of **Uncommon Prayer: A Father Flenn Adventure**. He is past vice-president of Homewood Counseling Associates and formerly the editor of two Tennessee newspapers. Arnold resides in Alabama with his wife, Diane, and grandson, Dominic, where he is rector of Saint Mark's Episcopal Church.

Manufactured by Amazon.ca
Bolton, ON

13374500R00196